oh my
stars

Also by Sally Kilpatrick

The Happy Hour Choir

Bittersweet Creek

Better Get to Livin'

Orange Blossom Special

Bless Her Heart

Published by Kensington Publishing Corporation

oh my stars

Sally Kilpatrick

KENSINGTON BOOKS
www.kensingtonbooks.com

KENSINGTON BOOKS are published by

Kensington Publishing Corp.
119 West 40th Street
New York, NY 10018

All Kensington titles, imprints, and distributed lines are available at special quantity discounts for bulk purchases for sales promotion, premiums, fund-raising, educational, or institutional use.

Special book excerpts or customized printings can also be created to fit specific needs. For details, write or phone the office of the Kensington Sales Manager: Kensington Publishing Corp., 119 West 40th Street, New York, NY 10018. Attn. Sales Department. Phone: 1-800-221-2647.

Kensington and the K logo Reg. U.S. Pat. & TM Off.

eISBN-13: 978-1-4967-1076-5
eISBN-10: 1-4967-1076-2
First Kensington Electronic Edition: October 2018

ISBN-13: 978-1-4967-1075-8
ISBN-10: 1-4967-1075-4
First Kensington Trade Paperback Printing: October 2018

10 9 8 7 6 5 4 3 2 1

Printed in the United States of America

To Ryan, my expert on all things Christmas
And my model for all things heroic

ACKNOWLEDGMENTS

Book five, y'all! Let me start by thanking each and every one of you who has read one of my books or bought it as a gift or suggested it to a friend. Thank you. You help me do what I love.

Thanks to Kensington—especially Wendy, Lulu, Paula, and Michelle. Special thanks to my agent, Sarah Younger, for insight on this book and life and goats and for generally being awesome.

Speaking of goats, thanks to Mary at Decimal Place Farm for giving me the grand tour and teaching me all about goats, udders, and cheese. She even gave me a snack, and it was tasty! If you're in Atlanta, you should look up her cheeses—one of her haunts is the Freedom Farmers Market. Thanks also to Kaitlyn at Shoo Fly Soap Company for helping me learn about making soap from goat's milk; I had a character fictionally use her delightful honeysuckle and vanilla recipe. Thanks to Sweet Olive Rescue Farm for giving me another reason to tromp around pastures and for teaching me about llamas and alpacas and sheep, oh my!

To Patti Callahan Henry and Kim Wright, thank you, thank you for your lovely blurbs. To Anna, Tanya, Mom, and Ryan—thanks for reading and offering helpful suggestions. Cassie Register has accepted texts at odd hours as I worked on how an abandoned baby would navigate its way through the foster care system. Cliff Wu has answered long and involved emails about pediatric situations, and former student Ashlie Dumas has double-checked my medicine. Heather Leonard has once again offered expert legal advice to the fictional.

This is the point where I tell you any mistakes you find are mine and mine alone, probably a literary liberty I took to bend the story to my will. (mwa ha ha) That said, I did my best to be as accurate as I could. Any mistakes you find are mine, and mine alone.

A special shout-out to my 2017 Barbara Vey Readers Luncheon tablemates; they generously donated their names to various animals in the Nativity menagerie: C.J., Leonard, Elizabeth, Kathy, Dawn, Donna, and Teresa. Deanna Raybourn also graciously allowed me to name an animal after her, and I think that gave the llama a little *je ne sais quoi*.

One day on Twitter, Elantrice Hugh helped me figure out what to do with my abandoned baby, when I was in a pinch. Jennifer Meyering helped me find Elantrice. Liana Brooks also chimed in on the subject. Speaking of Twitter shenanigans, Sasha Devlin did her best to distract me from writing with her #BrownEyedBabes, but I persevered.

Oh, and a special thanks to Anne Golden for giving me an awesome title. Oh my stars, indeed.

To Antoinette, you know how you help. *Mwah* to the Hobbit and Her Majesty, I love you and you are growing up too quickly, but I am proud of the fine people you are becoming. Thank you for getting yourself to school some mornings and for always understanding when I'm writing or traveling or both. Thanks to my parents (Jim and Jane) and my bonus parents (Bill and Terri) for their never-ending support and for taking care of the kiddos. Finally, thanks to Ryan for, well, everything. Not only do I love you, but you have a most impressive recall of Christmas movies.

Chapter 1
Ivy

And it came to pass in those days, that a decree went out from my mother that I would be playing the Virgin Mary in the Dollar General drive-through Nativity whether I liked it or not. Never mind the fact that my name was not Mary, that I was not a teen, and, most importantly, not a virgin. Still, decrees from my mother were similar to those from Caesar Augustus: both had to be obeyed. Thus I found myself in flowing robes with a demure head covering as I knelt by a manger while the yellow and black of the Dollar General sign illumined my face like a commercialized Star of the East.

"How much longer?" asked my faux husband through gritted teeth. He, like Joseph, sported a beard but his had been meticulously clipped and he smelled faintly of an expensive woodsy aftershave. Those tasseled loafers peeking out from under his robes definitely weren't Bethlehem issue.

"An hour or two. Maybe?"

We held our pose as cars drove slowly by, sometimes pausing to take a picture. I didn't know about him, but my legs were starting to cramp, and I had an itch on the back of my neck that I would've paid someone to scratch. Heck, the llama a couple of feet behind me could've scratched it and left behind llama slobber for all I cared.

"Miss Idabell tell you to take off your watch?" I asked.

He chuckled, and the corners of his eyes crinkled because we were both far too old to be bossed around yet, here we were. "She told me it would 'distract from the miracle of Christmas.' Told me to leave my 'fancy phone' in the car, too."

"And did you?"

He snorted, and I knew that fancy phone was still in his pocket. It might be worth calling him just to watch him try to get to it underneath his robes. Unfortunately, I didn't know his name much less his phone number, and, no matter what my sister Holly said, I had no intention of asking for phone numbers.

Phone numbers led to sweaty palms and wondering why people didn't call. Then those sweaty palms and paranoia gave way to a date. That date would lead to acid reflux–inducing anxiety about a first kiss. Then something more. Then a relationship. Possibly marriage. Nope. Been there, done that, got the airbrushed T-shirt from a Gatlinburg souvenir shop to prove it. Once upon a time, I had believed in not only happily-ever-afters but also being open to the signs of the universe, something my first husband used to tease me about. Then he'd inadvertently taught me all about richer, poorer, sickness, health, and the parting powers of death.

I hadn't seen a single "sign" since, and, if I had women's intuition, she wasn't telling me a blasted thing. At least Mary had an angel visit her and tell her what was what.

Canned Christmas carols danced on my last nerve. Our Nativity scene organizer claimed good instrumental hymns, like good men, were hard to find. If I hadn't already been working full time in addition to my ill-advised stint as Mary, I might've made it my personal mission to prove her wrong. Maybe next week I would look up instrumental songs for the sake of the next Mary and Joseph.

Thank the Lord my stint would only be one week.

Finally, just as I thought the cramp in my leg would be listed on my death certificate, Brother Leon from Grace Baptist Church gave a benediction and sent us all on our merry way.

"I'm Gabe, by the way," my Joseph said as he extended his

hand. I'd heard the name, but I couldn't place it. I would've re-membered him, too, with those warm brown eyes that crinkled at the edges.

"Ivy."

HIs hand enveloped mine and was softer than I was used to but large and reassuring nonetheless.

We'd skipped the introductions at the beginning because I'd been running late. I'd been running late because my mother and I were arguing. My mother and I had been arguing because she didn't tell me about my evening stint as Mary until ten minutes before I walked out the door.

"So," he said awkwardly.

"So."

"You back tomorrow, too?"

I laughed. "Oh, yeah. I'll be here all week. Try the veal. Don't forget to tip the waitstaff."

He chuckled at my lounge singer imitation, and I had to give him some credit for laughing at my very bad joke. He jabbed a thumb in the direction behind him. "Better not tell her that."

I looked behind me to see Star, Romy and Julian's black cow with the white face. Everyone knew Star because she didn't really think she was a cow and so didn't think fences applied to her. She'd calmed down some now that she wasn't a spry little calf, but she still got out every now and again just to keep us all on our toes. At least she was gentle enough that whoever found her could put a halter on her and lead her back to the Satterfield place where she belonged.

And to think I thought I wouldn't get anything useful out of completing the 4-H Heifer Project with my uncle Edgar.

"This old girl? I would never!" I said as I scratched the little black star on her forehead. "Besides, she's too old to be veal. Aren't you, girl?"

The cow snuffed and butted my hand off her head.

"I deserved that," I admitted.

"Hey, now. Don't mess with my wife's cow," Julian McElroy yelled. He'd been one of the shepherds and was ushering a swaybacked palomino into a trailer. "You gonna pull your weight, City Boy, or are you going to make goo-goo eyes at Ivy Long?"

Gabe rolled his eyes but grabbed Star's halter.

The cow didn't move.

Since she weighed over a thousand pounds, Gabe didn't budge, either.

"Don't let her step on your toes," Romy said, rushing in with her black curly hair bouncing everywhere. "I'll take her."

Star followed her eagerly, and Gabe looked at me dumbfounded.

"Cows," I said with a shrug.

Julian, meanwhile, spoke to one of two donkeys. "Look here, not a one of us wants to be here all night."

The creature dug in her feet and protested with a hee-haw that reminded me of that television show my grandparents used to like so much.

"Yo, get those goats, will ya?" Julian asked Gabe before whispering something to his recalcitrant jenny. She finally walked forward. Julian McElroy had always attracted asses. And women. But mainly asses.

"Mister Gabe, see my rabbit?" asked Portia, Julian and Romy's adorable little girl, who'd showed up for the last fifteen minutes of the night. So my Joseph was now on one knee talking to the little girl.

Oh. *That* Gabe.

He was Lester Ledbetter's son. According to all of the local authorities on such things, Gabe *said* he'd left his job as a pediatrician to come home and learn about goat farming. Also according to those authorities, someone had sued him in Memphis and he'd come home to lick his wounds.

Portia had skipped off, but the goats crowded around Gabe, nosing into the pockets of his jacket. He could handle children, but he didn't seem particularly well suited to kids. They danced around him, almost tripping him. Then one of the goats, the one with the yellow plastic chain around her neck, jumped up on the back of the remaining donkey, putting her front feet on the donkey's rump. The donkey looked over her shoulder in disgust.

"Elizabeth, get down from there! That poor donkey doesn't want any of your mess tonight," Julian said, as he took control of the goat situation.

"Elizabeth?" I couldn't help but ask.

Gabe shrugged. "Dad says he names the animals after his favorite people."

"More likely he named them after old girlfriends."

Before he could respond to that, the goat ran past us with Julian hot on her hooves. "Come back here!"

"Maybe I'd better help," Gabe said with a grin.

"Maybe." A figurative butterfly fluttered around in my stomach. I told my stomach acids to eat it and headed to the back of the building.

About that time Gabe cussed, and I looked over my shoulder just in time to see him checking the soles of his tasseled loafers. I giggled at the thought that he had a bit of farm animal souvenir on his shoes. Served him right for wearing something so fancy where livestock would tread.

The goat ran around the side of the stable as the llama ambled past me. Gabe looked at one animal, then another, but Julian headed after the goat so he finally darted after the llama. We could've charged extra for this show, maybe play that Benny Hill saxophone song instead of carols.

A nicer woman would've offered her assistance in catching the animals, but I'd used up all of my niceness by playing the Virgin Mary against my will. So, I moseyed around the corner of the Dollar General building to sneak a cigarette before driving home. I'd have to bathe in mouthwash before I arrived, but it would be totally worth it.

Once safely in the shadows to the back lot and far from prying eyes, I lit my cigarette. I held it just in front of my mouth for a couple of seconds, reveling in the anticipation before closing my eyes and inhaling the nicotine goodness. Well, not goodness per se. My mother would have a conniption if she knew I still snuck two cigarettes a day. I could almost hear her admonition, "It wasn't enough for us to lose Corey to cancer, are you trying to kill yourself, too? What do you think *he* would say about it?"

It didn't matter what Corey said about my smoking because he had already shuffled off his mortal coil. He was in the clouds playing air guitar with Jimi Hendrix, having left me to pay off the bills and try to figure out how to move on without him. My hand inadvertently traveled to the side of my purse to pat the sealed envelope I kept there.

Okay. So it's possible Corey did have something to say to me about my smoking, but I couldn't bring myself to open the letter he'd handed me two years ago, so I would never know. As long as I didn't open that letter, then I still had a part of my husband with me. I used to tell myself that one day the pain wouldn't be so bad. Then I would open the letter, find my closure, and move on. But day dragged on after day and the acute stabbing pain of grief settled into a dull ache with the occasional sharp pang, so I left the letter alone, afraid I'd read something there that would open up the wound all over again.

Besides, the man had been delirious from morphine there at the end. His letter was probably an enigmatic haiku:

Buy flashlights and pie
Give yourself a fluffy pup
Cancer sucks skunk balls

I once asked him why "skunk balls." He had this convoluted thing about *stink* and *suck*, the latter of which he couldn't say around his mother—at least not until the end when he said whatever he pleased. But, in general, everything bad stank like skunk balls for him.

I still missed that man's way with words—even if he did tell me that smoking was a nasty habit that made my breath smell like skunk balls. Since so many things nauseated him, I got in the habit of gargling so much Listerine I could've been a spokesperson for the stuff. Still didn't get all of the smell or taste.

Looking down at my orange-tipped cigarette, the only light behind the Dollar General, that old familiar calm washed through me. I missed the heady early days when I got the calm along with a preternatural alertness. Oh, well, it was fun while it lasted. Now I survived on copious cups of coffee and my two cigarettes a day.

Ironically, I picked up the habit while Corey was getting treatments. Sometimes a treatment would run long, and I'd get cabin fever. Sometimes, my poor husband got tired of looking at me and sent me out of the room. One day—I can't remember who was sick of whom—I wandered past the smoking area. One of the nurses offered me a cigarette. It was one of those days when I wanted to feel something, anything. It was also one of those days when I wanted to be done with hospitals and tubes and bills and the smell, always the smell. So I took the cigarette, coughing my way through the first few drags but then feeling that nicotine rush that was kinda like coffee but not. Once I knew I could drink some coffee *and* have a cigarette to cut through the fog of my fatigue? There was no turning back.

Maybe subconsciously I had been thinking of following him into the great beyond. I certainly didn't want to keep taking down his notes for the impending funeral. He wanted pimento cheese finger sandwiches and Jack Daniels on hand—not that the two of those went together in the least. He suggested I see if Beulah Land could play show tunes, especially songs from *Chicago*. I didn't think "When You're Good to Mama" would play well at the Anderson Funeral Home, but I smiled and nodded and wrote it down anyway. Then he had the best idea: I needed to get several de-scented skunks as therapy animals for the mourners.

I took him home and reread the notes after he'd fallen asleep.

First, I laughed. Then I wept. Then I laughed again.

In the end, we went with a simple closed casket service. No skunks and no *Chicago*, but plenty of pimento cheese and some Jack on the sly.

I was down to the filter and wanting another cigarette, but no way was I going to give in. It was a point of pride that I now limited myself to only two a day. I tossed the butt on the ground and stomped on it to be on the safe side. I had my hand in my purse searching for my keys when I sensed a presence. I turned my head to see a creature with a long neck and pointed ears peering at me.

The llama.

Slowly the animal approached, her head held high. She stopped a foot in front of me and turned her head to the side as though studying me and finding me lacking.

"What are you doing here?"

I reached for the lead.

She took a step back.

"Deanna!"

The llama turned toward the voice and I jumped forward to grab her lead. We'd backed into the beam of the security light, and I noticed her ridiculously long eyelashes, and how her mouth pursed into a coy smirk. "Aren't you a lovely creature."

She lowered her head regally as though accepting a compliment from a peasant before sniffing in my general direction, snorting when she didn't find anything of interest.

Gabe ran around the corner, winded.

"Gabe, you are going to have to do a better job of corralling these animals," I said, hardly able to keep my expression stern. Deanna the llama gazed at Gabe with what could only be described as llama judgment.

"The livestock learning curve has been steep," he admitted.

I would've sworn he was blushing, but I couldn't tell for sure. To soften my teasing, I added, "I'm sure you'll get the hang of it."

"Yeah. Good thing you were skulking back here ready to stop her."

"I was not skulking!"

"Smoking, then?"

I crossed my arms over my chest. "No lectures from you."

"Your lungs, if you want to blacken them," he said over his shoulder as he led the llama around the corner of the building.

Lot of nerve he had.

Gabe pointed his head around the corner. "Also, I don't think cigarettes are any more biblically accurate than cell phones."

I looked down at the long robes I still wore. "Why do you think I was smoking back here? But, fine. Next time I'll bring wine."

"Excellent. My devious plan is falling into place." He disappeared around the corner, but I heard, "Hey, don't spit at me!"

The giggle bubbled up, then an idea. In my mind, I saw a Regency romance heroine sneaking out to the stables to smoke a cheroot. She could befriend a llama. Then the ginger hero with a beard would surprise her and scold her because smoking was decidedly not ladylike but—

Llamas didn't arrive in England until the Victorian Era.

Sure. That was one glaring problem with this scenario. It had nothing to do with the fact that I had imagined Gabriel Ledbetter as a hero.

Oh, what harm could it do to imagine?

At least I was finally daydreaming again. Sometimes I worried myself with how I could get through a day of stocking shelves and ringing up purchases without ever once slipping into a flight of fancy. Every other report card from my childhood had warned my mother I was prone to daydreaming, yet I'd lost that ability when Corey got sick. He'd told me not to, but my imagination didn't listen to him any better than I did. It was as though I'd had a lifetime quota of good story ideas, and I'd used them all up during the first quarter or so of my life.

I patted my cheeks. They ached ever so slightly from my smile because I wasn't in the habit of smiling all that often. As I drove home, my imagination returned to the last story I'd been writing. My most recent heroine would definitely be one to sneak a cheroot, and Gabe—because he'd taken over as the hero of the piece—eyed her suspiciously because he suspected she might have poisoned her first husband. As fictional characters did.

The story points rolled around in my brain, mixing and changing. My tiny smile remained.

No harm had ever come from a daydream.

Chapter 2
Gabe

"Why are you grinning like a jackass eating saw briars?"

"No reason," I said, even though I wanted to smack Julian for his ridiculous expressions.

At least no reason I'm going to discuss with you because it's illogical. Spock might even qualify that illogical with a "highly."

There was just something about my worldly Mary with hazel eyes and a penchant for smoking.

Nasty habit, but I couldn't help but think of her dry-witted "try the veal" and her amusement at our menagerie run amok. She wore no makeup, hardly smiled, and I loved how Ivy Long didn't present herself as something she wasn't. Heck, I'd let all of the animals run away again just to see her smile even if Julian had cussed a blue streak all the way back to the barn. Good thing his wife and daughter had ridden home in their own car.

Of course, according to my father, I was supposed to be *bonding* with Julian for some crazy reason. I'd given up on figuring out what Dad's motivations were. Hard to get a handle on the guy who'd sent you to live with his sister when you were only a baby. Sure, I'd come back almost every summer, but summers weren't long enough to figure out a person.

"You gonna stand there, or are you going to help me get these animals back up?" Julian asked.

"I'm working on it," I said, looking down at my ruined loafers before I shooed our assorted manger denizens back into their appropriate pens.

Why was I even here?

Helping Dad after his hip replacement surgery made sense, but Julian didn't need my help. He just liked to lord it over me that I didn't know as much about the livestock as he did. These days, I didn't even *need* him to help me milk the goats each morning and afternoon, but he showed up every day anyway.

But why?

I kept coming back to money. Somehow this hayseed had wormed his way into my father's world and figured out that Dad had real money. Most people had no idea that Dad was loaded. They called him Goat Cheese, while pointing their fingers and snickering at his "failed" attempts. Little did they know he'd traveled as far north as Wisconsin and talked to all sorts of experts before finding a local cheesemaker and creating a unique recipe now sold in some pretty exclusive places. Then Adelaide had figured out an ingenious way to make a honeysuckle soap that held its scent particularly well thanks to just the right amount of vanilla. She contracted with a little shop up the road to make the soap, and, of course, they used the milk from Ledbetter Farms. Couple those investments with the fact that Dad sat on over a hundred acres and lived on the cheap, and he had amassed quite a fortune.

If one subscribed to the theory of Occam's razor, then money was the only logical answer. It was hard to believe that someone I'd never known before could suddenly appear after all these years and make himself indispensable by handling a few chores and doing anything else Dad asked him to do. I should be grateful that Julian kept things running after Adelaide had passed, but that didn't mean I had to trust him.

Dad wouldn't be the first Ledbetter who'd been fooled for money.

I'd hoped he would go, but Julian leaned against the gate, a twinkle in his eye. "Know what? I think you're up to something."

"Maybe *you're* up to something."

His eyes narrowed, extinguishing the twinkle. "What's that supposed to mean?"

"Take it as you'd like. I don't know you from Adam and now this place can't run without you? I wonder why that is."

Julian looked away, confirming my suspicions.

"Just trying to help the old man out," he said softly, his eyes still looking out to the pasture beyond the barn where we stood.

"Uh-huh."

He looked back to me, his eyes locking with mine. "I ain't looking for a handout, if that's what you're implying."

The redneck doth protest too much.

"Well, that's good because you aren't going to get one if I have anything to say about it."

He spat on the barn floor. "Maybe I like ol' Lester, and I want to help him out since he got that hip replacement and doesn't have Adelaide around to assist him anymore."

"Could be."

"Maybe I question your motives coming back after having been away for so long. Maybe you're the buzzard circling around waiting for the inevitable."

It was none of his damn business that I was on something between a vacation and an unintentional sabbatical. "I'm taking a break."

He took off his cap to wipe the sweat from his brow. "Taking a break. Can't imagine why such a respected doctor would need to take a break or come slum it out here with us little folk."

My hands clenched into fists. "You need to go home now."

He squared his shoulders. "I'll do that, but if you're just 'taking a break,' then you need to steer clear of Ivy Long because she's been through enough already."

So he had noticed.

"And what does it matter to you what I do with Ivy Long?"

Julian snorted. "She hasn't smiled a whole lot in the past few years, but I don't want you to get her in the habit if you're going to run off to Memphis to keep living the high life."

His cow and horse stomped in the trailer as if ready to go home.

"What do you mean she hasn't smiled a whole lot?"

"Her husband died of cancer a few years back. Horrible time of it, he had. Third time it'd come back, I think. She hasn't been the same since."

"Well, I guess not."

"She hadn't worked in forever since taking care of him was a full-time job, but the bills were so bad our church must've had three spaghetti suppers to help them out. Then she went to work at the Dollar General."

I knew more than I cared to about medical bills, paperwork, and insurance. Sometimes I thought I wouldn't have needed a break if I'd been able to just see my patients and make them feel better. I liked working with children—well, most of them—and I enjoyed the puzzle of what was wrong and how to make it better. I didn't care for all of the paperwork, and I disliked some of the entitled parents in the area where I'd worked. Half of them wanted antibiotics every time Little Johnny got the sniffles. The other half had looked up everything on WebMD and thought they knew better than I did.

Then there were the parents who'd sued me.

Nope. Not thinking about that.

"Thanks for the info, Julian, but I'm not looking for a girlfriend right now, so neither you nor Ivy have anything to worry about."

He nodded. "Good. I'd hate to have to kick your ass."

What did it even matter to him? Anger simmered low in my stomach and threatened to come up with some acid reflux for good measure. "I'd hate to see you try."

We sized each other up. Julian might be stockier, but I had a black belt in Taekwondo. I'm sure he didn't see much more than the tall absent-minded doctor, but I could hold my own. I'd had to learn how back when I was the skinny kid with glasses.

He must've sensed I wouldn't go down easily because he took a step backward.

Or maybe he was thinking that beating up Lester's son wouldn't get him what he wanted.

I didn't know, and I didn't really care.

"Tomorrow at four thirty?" he grunted.

"Fine."

He climbed back into his truck and took off. Hooves scraped in the back of the trailer as the cow and the horse scrambled to keep their balance. The cow bawled to let him know she didn't appreciate his driving.

With Julian gone, I breathed much easier, even enjoyed the quiet.

Leaning against a post of the barn, I looked past the cinder block milking parlor to the farmhouse bathed in moonlight. Dad had told me the house had been built in the forties because the original structure from the late 1800s had burned down. He told me these stories to instill a pride of place in me, but it was awfully hard to be attached to the farm when he'd sent me away shortly after I was born. Never once had he explained why he'd sent me to his sisters, either. Memphis had always felt more like home to me than Ellery, but it hadn't been for a lack of trying. Both Aunt Vi and Aunt Lois had passed away, and I technically could've moved to the town where, as a boy, I'd always wanted to live. Unfortunately, in Ellery I stuck out like a sore thumb, the "city boy who playacted at farming"—that's what one old geezer had said to another when I went to the feed store the other day.

Since I was persona non grata in Memphis at the moment, too, I had no idea where I needed to be. Maybe I should look into California.

I flipped off the barn's light switch and headed for the house, giving myself a minute for my eyes to adjust to the moonlight. I didn't like walking around at night because I'd seen more than my share of copperheads and water moccasins, but walking around in the moonlight didn't seem to bother Dad or Julian. I'd likely never achieve their level of nonchalance when faced with the possibility of snakes, briars, or manure.

And my mind had come full circle to how the whole Julian thing didn't make any sense.

Maybe I'd ask Dad about it, make sure Julian wasn't trying to get something out of the old man.

With Adelaide gone, Dad hardly talked. The man used to spend hours on the phone collecting gossip, but now he let the phone ring. I'd swear he was shriveling up and dying before my very eyes, but he got up every morning and hobbled into the kitchen with his walker. He'd fix his bowl of Special K and then bitch about not having bacon because Adelaide wasn't around anymore. I'd offered to make bacon, but that wasn't the point: The point was that he wanted to acknowledge the gap in his life where his wife used to be. Complaining was the only way he knew how to do so.

When he did speak, he talked about selling the farm—or at the very least selling the goats—since he couldn't keep things up. I told him I had everything under control—especially since he'd foisted Julian on me—so he didn't have to make that decision. Then he'd say something about how I was going to go back to Memphis, and he didn't want to burden me with all of this.

You didn't have to be a doctor to see the signs of depression, but he wouldn't hear a word about it. Told me he didn't want any of my fancy pills. He had his cigarettes and his beer, and that was enough for him. To be able to see the diagnosis and not be able to do anything about it was beyond frustrating, but all I could do was lead the stubborn horse to some water.

Mind you, he hung on Julian's every word. Maybe I should get Julian to tell him to look into antidepressants. I could almost hear him now, "Look, Lester, these here pills will pep you up. Probably dill your pickle."

You're just jealous that Julian can make him laugh.

Could be. I had nerdy city boy humor, thanks to being raised by a couple of old maid school teachers who found dangling participles and misplaced modifiers to be great fun. I knew more than my fair share of dirty jokes, but I couldn't tell them with Julian's flare. Sometimes Dad would look at him and grin, and it only reminded me that he'd sent me away. Just once it would be nice if Dad acknowledged all of the hard work I'd put into medical school. The man had never once said he was proud of me. He'd complained about how so many young people were getting out of

farming, but I'd never heard him say word one about my being a
doctor.

Adelaide used to tell me that he bragged on me all the time,
but I couldn't believe it. I never knew her to lie, but she, like my
aunts, wasn't above a fib to save someone's feelings.

As I approached the house I could see Dad through the back
window. He sat at the old metal and Formica table eating ice
cream straight from the carton.

"You gonna want popcorn?" I asked.

"Already ate that. Needed something sweet to get the salt taste
out of my mouth."

We went through this every night. Either he started with the
ice cream and needed something salty to get the sweet taste out
of his mouth or vice versa. At least I had missed popcorn duty. I
knew I needed to listen for the pauses between pops and go on
instinct, but I wanted to follow the instructions on the bag. The
result? Burned popcorn.

"How'd the Nativity go?"

"All right," I said.

"Did you get back with my goats?"

"Yes, Dad."

"And my donkeys?" He put the lid back on the carton.

"And the sheep and the llama and a partridge in a pear tree," I
said, pulling out a chair because I might as well say what I needed
to say about Julian.

"Always did want a pear tree," he mused. "Mind getting me
some water?"

My ass had just touched the chair, but I got up anyway.

"Naw, the cold water," he said as I turned on the faucet.

If he asked one more thing of me, I might leave him at Julian's
mercy. Instead, I reached into the fridge for the half-gallon container that contained his "cold water."

I waited until he'd taken a sip before trying to talk again. "Dad,
I think this Julian character is after your money."

The old man's eyes bugged out and he almost choked on his
water. "He's not after my money."

"Then why exactly is he here?"

"He's here because I want him here." He slammed his water glass down so hard that Adelaide's collection of souvenir spoons rattled on the wall behind him.

"Have it your way."

I wanted nothing better than to slam something down on the table myself, but to do so would be a loss of self-control. So would showing any hurt that my father thought more of a random guy than his own son.

Chapter 3
Ivy

I sat in the dim glow of the security light studying the brick ranch I didn't want to enter.

Somehow, both my sister and I had ended up back in our childhood home with our mother. This time, of course, Holly was sure to grab what had been my bedroom because she claimed it had an extra square foot of space.

It didn't.

I suppose her old room felt smaller since its lone window faced north while my old room had windows to both the north and the east, but, my gosh, my sister was petty about such things. Now I had the room with one window, the one Corey and I had kept on the off chance someone from the foster care system might have another baby for us.

The room *was* darker, not that I would ever admit it.

I could still remember how, as a college freshman, I'd been so happy when I'd moved into the Memphis State dorm. It didn't even matter that my first roommate threatened twice daily to smother me with my own pillow. After years of living with Holly, I had been well equipped to deal with such people. Two weeks later, the resident assistant even commended me on my calm as we moved my stuff to another room with a new roommate who, presumably, didn't have the urge to smother me. My new roomie had hung so many Disney posters I was convinced I would find my own happily ever after or, at the very least, benefit from the housewifery of small woodland creatures.

I took her taste in movies as a good sign, and she ended up a bridesmaid in Corey's and my wedding.

These days, I identified more with my first roommate because smothering my sister had taken on a new appeal. She came and went at odd times, seemingly always underfoot when I didn't want her there and always running that cursed blender for some protein smoothie or the other. With any luck, she would already be asleep tonight.

I heaved myself from the car, stripping off my head covering and robes as I walked through the back door.

Not only was Holly not in bed, but she was taking clothes out of the dryer. She paused with socks still in hand and wrinkled her nose as I walked by. "Ugh. You gotta stop with the cancer sticks. I'm telling Mom you're bringing that nasty smell into the house again."

How to explain to my sister that I needed my cigarettes the same way she needed her elliptical? It couldn't be done, but I could tell from the light sheen of sweat on her face and chest that she had been exercising only a few minutes before. I also knew that she'd no doubt worked out while at the gym earlier. Rather than point out that I could tell Mom she was going too far with the exercise, I took our conversation another direction.

"Are you three or thirty-seven?"

She stuck out her tongue at me.

"Three it is," I said as I laid my clothes on the drying rack.

Holly picked them up between her thumb and index finger as if she were handling something straight from a sewer. "Look, you know how she feels about it and the fact that she's allergic to it, so why can't you stop?"

"Same reason you can't quit going out with assholes, particularly married ones?"

A slap to her face wouldn't have been as effective. Usually I brushed away her nonsense, but I was too tired to put up with it tonight.

"Touché," she finally murmured.

I plopped down at the dining room table, and ran my fingers over the uneven patches in the middle where the finish had come up, probably from putting down hot pots without thick enough potholders. Holly slid into the chair opposite mine, obviously oblivious to my secret desire to smother her.

"Why didn't you and Corey have kids?" she asked softly.

Her question cut me to the quick and then poured a little lemon juice on top. "What is wrong with you? Why are you asking me that?"

"No reason."

"No reason, my dimpled derriere. With you there's always a reason."

Holly held up her thumb and index finger, pinched them almost together. "There's an eensy chance I might be pregnant."

"And you were going to tell Mom about my smoking?" I bellowed.

"Seems like you did that yourself," my sister said with the serene smile of one who loved nothing more than to stir the shit.

"Fine. Whatever. What does *your* being pregnant have to do with why I did or did not have kids?"

Holly frowned, and I think it finally dawned on her that her question was insensitive at best and hurtful at worst. "I don't know. I wondered if you ever regretted not having kids or if you were happy just the way you are."

I laughed out loud. "Happy? Holly, I am going through the motions here. I've forgotten what happiness looks like."

If I didn't know better, I would think the human being sitting across from me had been switched at the hospital. Other than her resemblance to our mother, she couldn't possibly be my sister. She had blond hair, blue eyes, and freckles. I had brown hair, hazel eyes, and darker skin. She was athletic, and I was . . . not. She hated to read, and I couldn't live without it. Besides, *my* sister would know better than to shack up with a jerk of a man who also happened to be her employer. *My* sister would've used contraceptives. *My* sister wouldn't ask hurtful questions out of the blue.

Now, Ivy. You know that no birth control is 100 percent foolproof.

I ran my hand down my face. "I'm not talking about this with you."

"It's a shame. I would've been a great aunt."

Of course you would say that.

"For heaven's sake, you're only one year younger than I am!"

"Well, you know. I take care of myself," she said with a shrug. "I still have time. I'm not dead yet!"

"Well, you act like it."

I couldn't form the words through my rage. So what if I'd spent more time mourning than the average Victorian. Corey and I'd pledged to love each other forever, and I took my vows seriously. I couldn't bring myself to date. For one, it felt like . . . cheating. For another, I had no desire to saddle myself to another man who might die on me. Even worse, I could end up with a loser like all of the men Holly kept not dragging home.

Of course, it might be worth marrying a man for his money if I could get away from Mom's watchful eye and my nosy sister. All I'd ever really wanted was to move out of Ellery and see the world, but Corey's illness had dragged us back here. Now I barely kept enough in my checking account to keep from going overdrawn, and I had closed my savings account when the fees started cutting into what little I'd managed to save.

Meanwhile, my nosy sister had been talking to me this whole time, but I only tuned in to hear, "You're not going to meet anyone if you don't date, and you're not going to get a date if you keep wearing those wedding rings."

I looked down at my finger. I still wore the simple band and the tiny engagement ring Corey had given me, merely switching them from left hand to right. At the time, that eighth of a carat from a department store was all he could afford. More than once I'd considered selling it back for money to pay off the bills, but the pawn shop probably wouldn't even give me a hundred bucks. Corey's memory meant a whole lot more than that to me.

"Wedding bands don't seem to stop you."

Holly took in a sharp breath. "So, we're back to that," she said. "You really do hate me."

"I don't hate you!" I yelled. "I hate the things you say to me."

"Oh my stars and all of my garters! Are you two done with your little hissy fit?"

We both turned to where Mom stood between the spindles that separated living room and dining room and answered, "Yes, ma'am" in unison.

I immediately turned to my sister and held out my hand. "Pay up."

Holly reached for a tiny purse that was hanging off the back of one of the dining room chairs, but she paused. "Why do I have to pay up?"

"Because I was the last one speaking."

"Oh, Lord. Here we go again," Mom said. She came by and snatched up the five-dollar bill Holly hadn't quite relinquished. "This five is mine because you both started it, and I have finished it."

Holly and I had decided long ago to make a game out of all the times we made Mom resort to some variation of "oh my stars." She prided herself on her education, but when she was tired or angry, she started talking like Granny Bess and couldn't quite get rid of that hilarious phrase. Whoever got Mom to say the phrase had to pay the other five dollars. In this case, she was stuffing the five inside her robe.

"Are you putting that in your cleavage?" Holly asked.

"Someone needs to get a little action around here," Mom said as she headed into the kitchen. "You two girls brush your teeth and go to bed."

Holly and I exchanged a rare look of solidarity. We were far too old to be put to bed.

"I'll go to bed as soon as I take a quick spin on the elliptical," my sister said.

"Little miss, you yourself told me that exercising this late at night isn't healthy," Mom said.

"I'd be willing to bet you've already been on the elliptical to-night," I said softly.

Holly cut her eyes at me. I raised an eyebrow in return to remind her that she had other secrets I could spill.

"Then you definitely need to go to bed," Mom said. She drew Holly into a hug and stood on her tiptoes to kiss her cheek. I held my arms open to receive my hug and kiss—from Mom. The only thing Holly could kiss was my butt, and I was pretty sure she'd say the same of me.

My sister dutifully plodded down the hall, but I stayed behind.

"You go on to bed, too," Mom said. She stood in front of the kitchen sink.

"Mom, I know what you're up to. Heck, get me one, too, if you don't mind."

She waited for the sound of Holly's bedroom door to close then she took the bottle of Jack Daniels out from beneath the sink. When we were kids, she'd kept it in the cabinets above the refrigerator; now she kept it a little lower because her back hurt, and she didn't feel like dragging one of the heavy chairs over to the fridge. She took two juice glasses and poured us each about half a glass full—a little over a shot, I'd imagine. Those glasses had once had a pattern of bright oranges all around them. Now, the oranges were long gone, leaving only clear glass behind.

"You already smoke. How many vices do you need?" Mom asked.

The whiskey burned my throat going down, and I grimaced. "I don't plan to pick this one up permanently."

"That's good." Mom studied her glass of amber liquid as lovingly as I sometimes held that first cigarette of the day. When people talk about the genetics of addiction, I think they're on to something. If only I could've taken Holly's addiction to exercise instead.

No, I didn't want to have traveled the road she traveled to get there, and the damage done to her internal organs probably wasn't much different than the damage I'd been doing to my own.

Mom downed her whiskey in one gulp and didn't even make a face. "You think you girls will ever learn to get along?"

"Doubtful," I said. "We're just turned differently."

"Or maybe it's that you're too much alike."

Holly and me alike? I chuckled at the thought of it.

Mom's gaze pinned me to the old china cabinet behind me.

"Look, I didn't have two children so they could fight all the time. I had two children so they could take care of each other."

I downed the last of my whiskey, and she took both of our glasses to the sink.

"Don't stay up too late, will ya?" she said as she headed down the hall, turning off lights as she went until only the dining room light shined on me.

I sat in the chair and studied the house around me. Only two weeks from Christmas and we didn't have a single decoration. The kitchen wore its same yellow and beige linoleum, faded in the dim light of night as if hibernating until summer. To my right a set of spindles separated dining room from the living room, a dark and paneled room that could look cozy or claustrophobic, depending on my mood.

We used to put the tree in front of the window. Mom wasn't much on Christmas, but she'd humored us when we were little by putting up a scraggly fake fir. A nail hung at the top of the doorway between the spindles where one whimsical year she'd put up mistletoe. No men came over except our uncle Edgar, so the mistletoe had never made a return appearance.

At the far wall of the living room sat the old wood stove. She used to hang our stockings from the mantle above it. She probably didn't even know where our stockings were now. Sometimes, when we were little, she would spread out a ragged olive drab green towel on top of the rarely used stove and then put a little Nativity scene on top of it, but I didn't know what had become of that set. Holly had once put a series of ceramic penguins to the side as if the arctic birds had wandered to the Holy Land to see the Christ child.

No telling where those little penguins had gone, either.

For a split second I thought about journeying up to the attic and looking for decorations, but I squelched the idea. I'd stopped decorating long ago, and Mom had worked almost every Christmas because that meant she would get time and a half. We'd learned to treat Christmas Day like any other, sometimes celebrating before or after with the few presents we had for each other.

Have Mercy. I would have to start shopping soon. I usually put it off until the last minute.

I'd heard stories about these grand family gatherings. I'd seen the movie and television version, but the Long girls had never had much to give—not since my father had managed to get himself run over back when I was two. I couldn't even count how many Christmases my mother had received no gifts at all except for whatever Holly and I could make out of construction paper and the requisite fruit basket from Uncle Edgar.

There was that urge again, the desire to make Christmas something better and brighter, but my butt remained planted to the chair. I was so . . . tired. Surely I'd had Christmas spirit before Corey got sick and before I had to work retail during the holiday season—nothing like being on your feet all day and not being able to close the store because one customer couldn't decide between the red shirt and the blue one.

Mom, Holly, and I had never been particularly good at giving gifts, but Corey had been worse. One year he'd given me Jenga. He, of all people, should've known I didn't like to watch things come crashing down, that the sound alone made me flinch. Then there was the year he got me Milli Vanilli's *Greatest Hits*. I still had no idea what that had been all about.

My hand reached for the purse that I'd hung over the back of the chair, but then I pulled it back. I wasn't about to open that letter. Nor was I going to decorate for Christmas and set us all up for yet another disappointment. For half a second I considered writing about my cheroot-smoking heroine and the hero Gabe had inspired. Instead, I went back to my room for yet another night of reading someone else's book rather than writing my own.

Chapter 4
Gabe

The phone rang at five a.m., vibrating in my pocket and jolting me awake. As a resident I'd gotten in the habit of sleeping in a T-shirt with a pocket so I could have my phone on me because, otherwise, I didn't wake up.

I could only recognize the number as a local one, and I didn't recognize Julian's voice until his third hello.

"Wait. You want me to do what?"

"I need your help with a couple of cows."

A couple of cows? I felt like paraphrasing McCoy: I'm a doctor, not a veterinarian. "Why would anyone need cows at this time of the morning."

"Come on, City Boy. Dad said you could do it since he couldn't."

I muttered something about how I'd show him a city boy and was already putting my jeans on when I tossed the phone on the bed, his laughter still echoing from underneath the comforter. I grabbed a shirt and a ball cap and ran down the stairs. Then I stood and looked at the two pairs of shoes at the back door. There were Dad's boots, a full two sizes too small, and there were my loafers, still stained from the night before.

I cursed as I put my loafers on and walked outside to wait for the asshole who woke me up.

"Julian, what the hell?" I asked when he drove up the gravel drive pulling a trailer.

"There are some cattle that kinda need rustling, and I could use your help."

"Kinda? Isn't stealing cattle a hanging offense?"

"Well," Julian said as he took off his cowboy hat long enough to scratch his head. "Being as the sheriff is going with us, I think it'll be okay. Now, let's go!"

"If you've got the sheriff, I don't see why you need me," I said once I'd closed the cab door.

Julian grinned at me. "I promised your daddy I'd show you a good time while you were here, didn't I?"

God, I hated this man. He oozed schadenfreude at having awakened me and didn't even have the common courtesy to bring coffee.

About fifteen minutes later, I was trying to figure out how to shoo the second emaciated Jersey into a trailer while Julian and the lanky Yessum County Sheriff, Len Rogers, laughed at me. "You could lend a hand rather than laugh, you know."

"Nah, rounding up cattle is a life skill," said Julian.

Life skill, my ass. In my forty-two years on the planet, I'd never once needed to know how to round up livestock of any description. I'd also never once needed to know the prologue to *The Canterbury Tales* in Middle English, but I still had a few lines of that stupid mess in my brain. Come to think of it, quoting Chaucer might be the way to get the cow to head into the trailer and away from me. " 'Whan that Aprille with his shoures soote . . .' "

"Are you speaking in tongues, City Boy?"

Great. Now the sheriff was calling me by that awful nickname. I resisted the urge to push both him and Julian into a patch of poison ivy on the other side of the road because then I'd be forced to help heal them, and I wasn't in a healing mood. Instead I flipped them the bird. Their laughter, more so than my clapping or Chaucer quoting, startled the last sluggish cow into plodding up the ramp and to the trailer where her sister already stood.

"Why are we doing this again?"

"Well," Len said. "We got this complaint about these here cows being malnourished. At first I thought it was some city fool who didn't understand that dairy cows are naturally going to be leaner than beef cows, but she kept calling, so I came out here and started counting ribs. When I counted one rib too many, I told the owners they could give up the cows or they could go to court. They chose to give up the cows."

I turned to Julian. "And what does this have to do with either of us?"

"Didn't you wonder why most of the Nativity menagerie is coming from your daddy's farm? He likes to take in strays, and your pal Julian here likes to help him."

He paused before saying the word *pal*, and I wondered what he was up to. I didn't trust Len or Julian any further than I could throw them.

Len cleared his throat and muttered something about having other places to be. He was hiding something. That much I knew.

Julian and I rode in silence to the barn, and I helped him shoo the two cows into a paddock with the sheep.

"Now, who's going to milk these cows?" I asked, remembering how Len had mentioned they were dairy cattle.

"I guess you are," Julian said with a smirk.

"If you're so damned cheerful in the morning, then you can come do it."

"Well, if it needed doing, I might. I don't think these gals are going to produce much. That one's a heifer, and the older one has been neglected. She'd have to calve to need milking."

I could punch him for his condescending tone. "Good to know, Smartass."

He shrugged. "You're the one with the fancy education, City Boy."

"I know kids, not cows." I paused to think of what I was going to call Julian in response. *Asshole* had appeal, but it wasn't quite the right response. *Country Boy* lacked imagination. *Redneck* had its own connotations. *Hick* only had one syllable. I was left with *Hayseed*.

"Hayseed?" He laughed. "That the best you could come up with?"

"Redneck asshole has a certain appeal."

He considered my words, his smile fading. "Reckon both of those apply, too."

I felt a momentary twinge that I'd gone too far.

I got over it.

Once we'd coaxed the cows into the pasture, Julian turned and said, "You don't have to milk these cows, but we'd best tend to the goats."

As much as I wanted to tell him to stuff it, the milking did go faster with two sets of hands, and he still knew the best order in which to lead them in. Once inside the milking parlor, I filled the troughs with feed, and he sent the first ten goats, securing their necks between the bars. They didn't care since they were eating.

We went about the business of cleaning teats and hooking up the milkers that would send the goat milk to a tank in the next room. Adelaide's protégé, Monique, would come in later to make cheese and set aside milk for the soap makers. She handled everything that happened after the milk left us.

After the fourth and final round of goats, my stomach growled loudly enough even Julian heard it.

"You go on to the house, and I'll clean up and lead them out to the pasture," he said as he lightly smacked the last goat on her rump to get her to leave the parlor through the out chute.

"You sure?" No clue why I felt guilty since he'd been the one who'd dragged me out of bed to chase cows.

"Yeah, I got this."

Part of me wanted to stay and prove to him that I had this routine down just as well as he did. The other part of me wanted bacon and to finally have a cup of coffee to stave off the headache threatening to bloom.

Besides, I needed to chat with dear ol' dad about volunteering my services.

Chapter 5
Ivy

The next morning I sat on the back stoop savoring my morning cigarette when Holly slammed the back door into my back.

"Ow!"

"What are you doing out here? Oh. Smoking."

I rolled my eyes, any enjoyment from my cigarette seriously diminished. "Don't you have some miles to run or some smoothies to drink?"

But should Holly be running if the "eensy chance she was pregnant" was more than eensy? Of course there was that woman who'd won a marathon ten months after giving birth. She'd run through her pregnancy, hadn't she? As long as Holly had been exercising, surely a short run wouldn't hurt her.

"You're still here?" I asked my sister since I'd gone through an entire mental debate and deemed her capable of running whether pregnant or not.

"Yeah, but first I had something to ask you."

Ho boy. The wide eyes, the almost pout—sure signs that my little sister wanted something. "Yes?"

"Could you pick up some Christmas decorations while you're at work?"

I stubbed out the cigarette, my enjoyment soured by my sister's request. "I don't want to decorate for Christmas."

Why did we have to go through this every year?

Because of the Christmas of 1981, you idiot.

Sure, sure. That was my last-ditch effort to catch the eye of a certain jolly man in a red suit. I'd heard rumors of his nonexistence, so I'd secretly mailed a letter to the North Pole with my request for Princess Leia, then set about decorating for his arrival. Mom had merely shrugged. She worked so hard back then, and her feet ached with the beginning stages of the plantar fasciitis that would plague her for the rest of her career. She didn't mind if her almost eight-year-old decorated the house and made slice-and-bake cookies.

She did mind Holly's exuberance for tinsel icicles for the tree, but that was another story for another day.

"You are such a Scrooge!"

"No, I'm not. Unlike Ebenezer, I don't have any desire to decrease the surplus population, thank you very much." I simply didn't want to go to the trouble of decorating anything for anyone.

"Here it is the eleventh of December, and we still haven't so much as put up the tree. What kind of family does that?"

"One that's smart enough not to go to a lot of trouble for three working adults."

Holly started pacing the little concrete path between the back stoop and the edge of the house. "Look, I know that you and Mom don't have the best Christmas memories, but why wallow in all of that instead of trying to create new, better memories? This will be Mom's first Christmas since she retired. We can start over."

"Mom and I are set in our ways."

Also, you got to have a bit of Christmas magic. I saw to that. Now my work here is done.

"You are the most stubborn person I know!"

"I take it you're not in the habit of looking in the mirror?"

She made a sound that was half scream and half grunt, and a tiny bit of perverse joy blossomed beneath my rib cage.

"Use your employee discount to grab some things. I'll put them up," Holly said.

I cleared my throat.

"Please. Would you please get some decorations?"

"I'm not putting them up or taking them down."

We stared at each other, knowing that this was a bald-faced lie. Every year we had some variation of this conversation, then Holly would put something up, and I would end up taking it down about a week before Valentine's Day because I couldn't stand it anymore.

"I will take them down this year. Promise," Holly said. "Oh, and get ornaments. We accidentally broke at least half of them last year."

Accidentally? We? Would we call it an accident if, say, I dropped the box from the attic, relishing the lovely crashing sound as the box hit the floor, and the ornaments shattered upon impact? I did utter a belated "oops."

Man, that had been a mess. I hadn't counted on the box falling open halfway down. I'd almost got caught vacuuming up the last slivers with Mom's beloved Hoover, too.

Holly crossed her arms. "Fine. I'll even chip in thirty dollars. Will you just get some new ornaments and some lights that actually work?"

Sure. Or I could try replacing the bulb I had taken out last year because I knew removing one would turn the whole strand off. Maybe I threw that light bulb away. . . .

Come to think of it, if Santa had a list, I was sure to be on the naughty side. Probably right under the Grinch.

The idea didn't make me feel as remorseful as it should have.

"Ivy, please?"

My fingers twitched. Something about these sisterly chats always made me want another cigarette. "Okay, okay. Ornaments and lights, but that's where I draw the line."

She grinned just as light from the rising sun hit her shortly cropped blond hair, reminding me of when she was nine and I was ten. We had to cut all of her hair off that summer because she went to sleep chewing gum and got it all tangled up in her long lustrous hair. She made such a mess of it that her options were a mannish cut or a huge chunk of hair missing at the nape of her neck.

Mom had cried when they cut her hair. Holly'd fallen in love with that haircut and kept it boyishly short ever since.

"Any chance you could get some icicles?" she asked.

"No! You know how Mom feels about those things," I said. We'd lost the vacuum cleaner before the Hoover to multiple strands of silver tinsel that someone *cough* Holly *cough* didn't pick up from the floor before running the thing. Ever since, the pesky foil demons had been verboten.

"Please?" She poked out her lip and batted her eyelashes.

"Are you serious? You know that puppy dog face does *not* work on me."

Usually.

"Just think about it. And a snowman! Can you find a snowman? Maybe one for the lawn?"

"You're acting like the Dollar General in December isn't sold out of everything."

"Come on, Ivy, work your magic, please?"

"I have no magic."

"You do. I know you do. I remember the bicycle."

I gasped. She wasn't supposed to ever find out about the bicycle I had so desperately wanted for myself—at least I didn't think she ever knew how much I coveted that gorgeous banana seat bicycle with its airbrushed electric-blue to fluorescent-pink paint. All the better that it didn't have the prissy streamers. I did not want the prissy streamers. "How did you find out about that?"

"Mom told me a few years ago," Holly said softly. "She told me that you won the bicycle at the Christmas Bazaar raffle, but that you wanted me to have it because, you know, I still believed."

And I didn't believe because I'd caught Mom sewing faux Care Bears late one night. At the memory of how Mom had come home from a twelve-hour shift to sew Care Bears, my eyes misted up. She'd just started working the longer shifts, which meant more time for us on her off days, but the longer hours were killing her.

I had peeked around her master bedroom door that night because I couldn't identify the hum of the sewing machine. She never saw me, but I saw the empty bears turned inside out and lying there deflated. A week later they came to us on Christmas Day. Holly had hugged her Cheer Bear immediately, while I gazed down at my Grumpy Bear, putting two and two together only to come up with one hundred and three. Mom asked what was wrong, but I didn't tell her that I'd wanted Cheer Bear. I muttered something about the pillow not being the real thing and then stomped off without looking her in the eye.

My heart burned with the shame of how I'd disparaged those bears she'd made with love. The least I could do would be to pick up some tree decorations for my sister.

No, you already paid that debt by giving up your bicycle the following year.

But still.

"Fine, I'll get your stuff."

"You don't have to be so grumpy about it."

Dammit, is that why I got the Grumpy Bear?

I couldn't tell her about the bears, so I said, "I'm never going to live that bicycle thing down."

"Live it down? It's the nicest thing anyone has ever done for me," she said. "Oh, and I'll get the mistletoe."

"Mistletoe is the last thing we need around here," I said. "There's no one to kiss us—unless you want to kiss each other."

"You never know," she said as she bent over to kiss my cheek. "Gotta go for that run. Then I'm going to drink a smoothie—since you were so interested earlier."

She ran around the house toward the two lane country road where we lived, a road that had practically no shoulder.

"Run a couple of miles for me. But be careful! People drive like idiots!" I yelled, doubling over into a cough. Maybe my two cigarettes a day were affecting me more than I thought.

The quiet of the morning irrevocably disturbed, I entered the house for a cup of coffee and a muffin, still not ready to go to work.

Mom sat at the table. "I've had this in my purse for over a week. I keep forgetting to give it to you," she said.

I took the envelope, immediately recognizing the company name on the front.

"Aren't you going to open it?" Mom asked. Her expression was far too bright for whatever the envelope contained. Besides, I didn't like to open envelopes that might mean goodbye.

Better to rip off the Band-Aid in this case.

I opened the envelope, which was much too thin to contain anything exciting, and drew out my sales report including royalties for my lone book. There was a check this year made out to me for the staggering amount of twenty-six dollars and twelve cents.

I laughed to keep from crying and passed the check over to my mother.

"Well," she said.

Well, indeed.

Ha, and that was the sort of snippet that I used to save for my books, an understated response to a sad and somewhat ludicrous situation—perfect for the Regency romances I used to write.

Romance.

I had written precisely one.

"Are you ever going to turn in your second book?" Mom asked.

I closed my eyes and took in a deep breath, holding it for a couple of seconds before letting it all whoosh out. "What's the point?"

"Meeting your obligations! That's the point!"

"Corey didn't meet his." My words tasted bitter, and I shouldn't have said them.

Mom reached across the table to take my hand. "I know, dear, but you signed a contract."

Pretty sure widowing me was the ultimate breach of contract.

After Corey's sickness my publisher had kindly given me not one but two extensions, but I still had nothing other than three quarters of a book about a duke who was masquerading as a vicar. What had seemed like fun at the time now felt . . . silly.

"You made a promise," Mom said softly.

I forced my eyes to meet hers. These are the sorts of things that she never said to Holly, who, best I could tell, only kept her promises to her blender and elliptical, but me? I was supposed to keep my word. "It's too late. There's no way I can finish the book before January third."

"Of course you can," Mom said.

"Mom. I don't even remember what I wrote." I didn't care what I wrote. I didn't believe in Santa Claus or universal signs or happily ever after.

Not anymore.

"At least think about it?"

My eyes blinked one, two, three, four times.

"There. I thought about it."

Chapter 6
Gabe

"Well, I only wanted him to show you a good time!"

I buried my face in my hands to grimace before wiping my face clear of any expression and looking up at my father. "For future reference. I don't think rustling cattle at the butt crack of dawn is a good time."

"Huh." The old man sucked on his cigarette and tapped his fingers on the table.

Remorse hit me. Maybe if my world consisted of moving between the living room and the kitchen with the help of a walker, maybe then I'd consider rescuing cows fun. Doubtful, but maybe. The man did love his goats. Yesterday, he'd asked about all of them by name and then gotten irritated when I couldn't remember which was which.

"But, son, they don't look exactly alike, and each one has a different number on her chain!" he had said.

Never mind the fact they were all white and looked the same to me. Dad launched into a diatribe about ones who had odd udder attachment or nubs where their horns had been or were a little bowlegged.

They were . . . goats.

Julian knows all of their names.

I busied myself getting a cup of coffee.

I wanted to ask again why Julian was close enough to learn all of the goats' names, but I'd probably get another nonanswer. I'd never seen my father take help from anyone or offer help to anyone over the summers I'd stayed with him. Instead, he seemed to see life as more of a competition. I'd seen him downright gleeful that he'd managed to get a cow or goat or lawn mower at some ridiculously low price and was going to be able to turn a profit later.

Caffeine brought me back to life, coursing through my body until I felt my eyelids peeling back. "Just don't sign me up for any more early morning livestock trips."

"Fair enough."

We sat there, one sipping and the other smoking, not sure what to say to each other next. The ringing doorbell came as a relief.

"I'll get it," I said, as though that weren't a foregone conclusion. Little did I know I would open the door to . . .

Chickens.

Standing next to the homemade cage that contained at least four chicks stood a young woman with greasy hair and a fussy toddler on her hip. "Please, sir, I heard tell you're a doctor. I can't afford to pay you any money, but I do have these chickens."

What the hell? Is this the nineteenth century?

As much I wanted to shut the door and pretend chickens had never appeared on my front porch, I had that pesky "first do no harm" thing to think about. I looked over my shoulder to make sure Dad wasn't trying to hobble outside. He was ridiculously nosy like that. When his walker stayed put and I heard the click of his lighter, I knew he was staying inside for another smoke. "Let me step outside, and you can tell me what the problem is."

The young woman took a ragged breath and sniffled.

"So what happened?"

"She snuck into the kitchen while I was cooking. I didn't see her there, I swear." Her eyes shone glassy with unshed tears.

Could she even be twenty yet?

"I didn't want to tell nobody lest they take her away from me."

"No one's going to take her away from you," I said gently, even though I didn't know for a fact it was true. "Just tell me what happened."

"She—she reached around my leg to hug me while I was trying to get the cornbread out of the oven. I thought it was the dog, and I swatted her sweet little arm. It landed against the stove for a minute, only a minute." Her voice cracked. "I snatched her right up and put her arm under the cold water, but now it looks like this."

She tried to hold out the child's arm, but the girl turned into her mother's chest, whimpering.

"So it's a burn. Now what's your name, er, Mom?"

"My name's Olivia," she said before clamping her lips together as though she'd betrayed herself. She didn't trust me not to tell the authorities. That much I could see.

"All right, Olivia, who's this you have with you?" Had to keep her talking, get the child's name to try to build some trust. Normally, I would've given the toddler my stethoscope, but it was packed away upstairs.

"Her name's Taylor."

"Taylor, sweetheart, I need to see your arm," I coaxed, finally securing a hand and pulling the arm out enough to see a nasty sore with read streaks emanating toward the elbow.

Infection. And that infection wasn't going to get better without some help. "I want to help you, Olivia, but you need to take her to a doctor who can prescribe antibiotics."

"But I ain't got no insurance!"

Oh, I had thoughts on insurance, not that anyone was listening. "If you go to the emergency room, they can't turn you away. Especially not with her arm looking like this."

"I can't afford the emergency room." Tears cascaded down Olivia's face and a bubble of snot peeked out of her nose. "Them creditors are still hounding me for the time I broke my foot three years ago."

I ran a hand through my hair in frustration. Technically, I *could* write a prescription because all of my licenses and insurance policies were up-to-date. That said, I didn't have all of the supplies I needed to properly clean the wound, and writing this one prescription could set a very dangerous precedent.

I looked at little Taylor. She clung to her mother, who was little more than a girl herself. The child held out her arm at an awkward angle to keep the sore from hitting anything, making a constant sound that was somewhere between a cry and a moan. I put a hand on her forehead, and I didn't need a thermometer to tell me that she had a fever.

First do no harm.

"Wait here." I rushed upstairs to the leather satchel I'd hardly touched since coming to Ellery from Memphis. Sure enough, I had a prescription pad from my old practice, a practice that continued on without me. I paused for a moment but then grabbed a crinkled twenty from the dresser, too. After asking about Taylor's weight and any possible allergies, I chose the antibiotic best for such infections, then did the mental calculations to determine dosage before adding Silvadene.

I ripped the prescription from the pad and held it out along with the twenty. "This should cover the cost of both the cream and the antibiotics. Follow the instructions carefully and make sure she eats something with the Keflex and that you keep her burn bandaged. The pharmacist can help you find the right gauze."

"Thank you!"

"Don't thank me yet. She'd be better off if a doctor could wash that wound out thoroughly. At least see if someone at the Ellery clinic will do that for you."

"I don't—"

"I know, I know. Go see Dr. Malcolm and tell him to put it on Dr. Ledbetter's tab." I didn't know Dr. Malcolm well enough to know whether or not this would work. Sometimes doctors could elect to waive fees, but they couldn't do so too often or Medicaid would want to know why all of their patients couldn't be free, too. Better for me to pay for it out of pocket, just in case. "I'll call and let him know you're on the way."

I gave her my I-am-a-doctor-and-you-must-do-this stare, hoping that she would take me seriously. "Are you going to be okay to drive?"

She swiped at her eyes and nose and nodded affirmatively.

"Please don't feel like you have to leave me your chickens," I said with a smile, not wanting to insult her gift. "I didn't even have to go into the office for this one."

"Yes, sir, but you took time out of your day to see us after I imposed on you in your own home, so you keep those chickens. They oughta be good layers."

Well, at least the rooster Julian had rescued last week would be happy to have some hens around.

"Oh, and Olivia?"

"Yes?" She'd already put Taylor in her car seat and now leaned over the driver's side door.

"Let's keep this between the two of us, shall we?"

"Yessir."

She took off down the driveway, gravel flying behind her beat up little hatchback. I paced the porch. Sure, everyone knew that I was a doctor, but I never thought anyone would show up at my father's door. I had better call Dr. Malcolm before the mother and daughter arrived.

A receptionist answered the phone, a welcome change from the automated phone tree I usually reached when making calls. She put me on hold with a jazzy big band version of "Jingle Bells" while I waited for the doctor. I looked through the window of the house, frowning at the utter lack of decoration. Lester Ledbetter simply wasn't a sentimental man. He had no time for the frivolity of Christmas.

"Gabriel Ledbetter, you make this quick. My waiting room is full of folks."

I explained the whole situation about who I'd sent and why, to which the older man responded, "I don't have to tell you that you did the right thing, but it'd be even better if you'd open up shop over here instead of wasting your time playing with your daddy's goats."

"I don't think—"

"That's the problem with your generation: You don't think. You all ran off to the cities to practice and make the big money. Now we're running short on doctors here in the sticks. I'm not going to live forever, you know."

I didn't see where it was written anywhere that I needed to re-place Dr. Malcolm, but I knew better than to say so. On one hand I was more than a little ticked that Dr. Malcolm would imply that I was selfish, stupid, or both. On the other, I knew I'd stayed in Memphis partially because the pay *was* better. In the back of my mind I hadn't considered practicing in Ellery for another reason:

I'd never thought I would be welcome.

Chapter 7
Ivy

Being the chump that I was, I spent my break picking out new Christmas decorations even while I thought how satisfying it would be to watch another round of delicate little ornament balls shatter. Maybe this year I'd drop them from the attic one by one. I indulged in a vision of sitting at the top of the pull down stairs and letting each ornament bounce down the ladder rungs until it shattered.

I'd have to buy a whole other vacuum, though. I wasn't going to risk the wrath of Genevieve Long.

After the boxes of ornament balls, I picked up a string of lights even though I'd fixed the ones from last year after breakfast. Well, I got them to turn on, but I could only find the bulb that made them flash. I took that bulb out and tossed it in the trash. I was not about to put up with blinking lights for the rest of the month.

I even found a snowman for the lawn. It'd been put in the back because its box had been damaged to the point that I could see the wire frame. I talked Mavis into giving me another 10 percent off on top of the employee discount. I think I could've talked her into twenty-five, but I didn't push it. I was doing us both a favor by clearing it out so we didn't have to fill out the "damaged merchandise" paperwork.

The rest of my afternoon passed without incident. We had

more customers than usual, but a lot of people had traveled into Jefferson to do their Christmas shopping at the mall. Personally, I wasn't sweating it. Thirteen days? I had plenty of time.

"You headed out to the Nativity?" Mavis, my manager, asked. I think she'd been born with that look of disapproval on her face. Based on some of our customers that afternoon, I couldn't blame her. On occasion, she would reward us all with the richest, most beautiful laugh I'd ever heard. On those days, her smile would reach all the way to her deep brown eyes—those were usually the days her youngest son visited. He always dressed sharply in his Marines uniform. It killed Mavis to have him off who knows where and quite possibly in harm's way, but she was so proud of him for getting his college education through ROTC.

Today Mavis wasn't smiling, so I hastened to answer. "Indeed, I am."

"Still can't figure you for a Mary," she said, but now there was a hint of a twinkle in her eyes to let me know she was teasing.

"Tell my mother."

There came that rich laugh. "You know, Genevieve and I do go *way* back."

"I know. You tried to talk her out of marrying Daddy."

Mavis shrugged. "Well, I was right, but I was wrong. I can't imagine your mama without you and your sister, so I'm just going to say that the Lord does work in mysterious ways. Now get out there and oversee the birth of Jesus before I make you work overtime."

As much as I didn't mind time and a half, I did mind the aching of my feet, so I went into the back and changed into my robes, then took my belongings out to the car. I considered bringing my phone so I could listen to my own music. What were the rules so far as Mary and ear buds anyway? I decided it wasn't worth risking the wrath of Miss Idabell. Besides, my Joseph might be back, and he might have interesting things to say.

In the end I put my phone in the car and locked it before walking around the side of the building, down a worn path through weeds. I often took this short cut to the employee parking lot.

Sometimes I'd meet someone on that path and we'd stand and smile awkwardly, neither one of us wanting to step into the knee-high grass.

Usually, I caved and stepped into the itchy, tall weeds.

There was probably a metaphor there, but I didn't want to examine it.

When I reached the front of the building, I turned right and walked across the parking lot to the empty lot adjacent to the Dollar General. Blessedly, it didn't have high weeds because Julian had brought his bush hog over to cut everything around the makeshift stable. The cars and the animals kept the rest trampled down. The way Julian had set everything up was pretty ingenious: Cars from the main highway could turn to pass the stable and then follow the ruts on the other side of the new Dollar General building and finally behind the building through the employee parking lot to a side street that could take them either back to the main drag or to the backside of town and beyond. A lot of folks circled the store, then parked in front to either take pictures or run an errand. No telling how many sales the Dollar General owed to Grace Baptist Church. I kinda wanted to ask Mavis how this year's sales compared to last year's, but then she'd start talking to me about management. Best I could tell hourly was better because managers were expected to work more hours for a set amount of pay—especially during the Christmas season.

I took a minute to drink in the empty stable and to cleanse myself of commercialism before the shepherds, Wise Men, or Julian and his menagerie arrived. The sun set behind me, something that was great for the people looking at the scene but not so good for those in the scene. Even so, it would be gone soon, and it did bathe the stable in a nostalgic pinkish glow.

"This is going to make one incredible picture," someone said behind me. I turned around to see Lydia Hill toting a ladder with a camera around her neck. As one of three full-time reporters, she had to be coming to take a picture of the scene for the *Ellery Gazette*.

"Slow week?" I asked.

"No car crashes—thank goodness—and no one has taken down an impressive buck this week, so you get to be on the front page."

I chuckled. "Unless there's a car crash or someone bags an eight-point buck in the next thirty minutes?"

Lydia smiled. "You won't be bumped for anything less than a twelve pointer. Promise."

I pointed at her. "I'm holding you to that—and no car crashes unless the jaws of life are involved."

She threw up her hands. "Fine. But if another possum parades around the Piggly Wiggly, then all bets are off."

I sighed. "I can't beat that. It's even alliterative."

"Speaking of, I'm going in to buy a Dr Pepper. Want anything?"

"No, I'm good."

Lydia disappeared inside the Dollar General, and I looked at the empty stable before me. Soon it would be full of people and animals. Corey had been agnostic, but I couldn't join him in doubt. Too much design, too many unexplained happenings in the world.

He'd shake his head and give me his crooked grin. "You and your signs and serendipity and celestial master plans."

I'd shrug and then we'd argue over good and evil because he didn't believe in those concepts, much less angels and demons. He'd say to me, "Ivy, you're a rational, logical person. How can you believe any of the craziness in the Bible, especially virgin births and people being raised from the dead?"

"Well," I'd say. "I like to call it my 'I'm a writer and I can't make this crap up' theology. I can create a story about a duke who's pretending to be a vicar who marries a widow who turns out to be a virgin because I can *make* all of that make sense. What I can't imagine is how anyone could make up a story about a poor virgin girl who gives birth to a prophetic carpenter who dies on a cross and then comes back to life three days later because he's actually the son of God."

"Yeah, but that doesn't mean the story of Jesus is true. The whole thing is ridiculous."

Then I'd lean in and hold Corey's cheeks between my hands. "How did the tale of a virgin birth survive all of these centuries?

How did the tales of a man who heals lepers and talks to adulterous women remain? Water to wine? Fishes and loaves?"

"I'm sure it all made sense at the time," he would scoff.

"Well, imagine someone writing during biblical times. Imagine that man—because we both know he was a man—writing about a group of women going to the tomb and getting news of the Messiah first. What *man* from that era would've given such an honor to *women*? I can't explain it. I can't tell you there haven't been some errors in translation over the years, but I believe in prayer and I believe the story of Jesus because—"

He'd roll his eyes and nod as he said, "You're a writer and you can't make this crap up."

Then I'd kiss him and whisper a prayer for his healing.

But that healing never came unless you wanted to count the ultimate healing of the human condition that put him in heaven. I had a hard time speaking to God for a while there toward the end. It was excruciating to watch my husband suffer.

Man, Corey would've gotten a kick out of me as the Virgin Mary, though. Knowing him, he would've frequently whispered about certain situations that disqualified my virgin status. I would've reminded him he hadn't been complaining at the time. I chuckled at the thought.

Huh. I'd been smiling. I'd remembered my late husband with more fondness than grief.

Wouldn't it be funny if Corey could somehow let me known he was okay?

I snorted. If he did send me a sign, would that qualify as a Christmas miracle?

I reached for his last letter—just to reassure myself it was still there—but I'd left my purse in the car.

That's when I heard the baby.

Chapter 8
Gabe

"You gonna help me with this or not?"

I looked up at Julian and considered telling him I wanted no part of anything he did including, but not limited to, his crazy drive-through Nativity.

Then I thought of Ivy. Silly to think I owed her anything, but she didn't want to play Mary any more than I wanted to pay Joseph so leaving her alone seemed like a crap thing to do. "Yeah."

We worked in silence, shooing llama, alpaca, donkeys, beagle, and sheep in with the cow and the horse. Then the rooster hopped in.

"Really? Do we need another animal? There's no room at the inn."

"Oh, let CJ come along," Julian said. "He's a civilized rooster." *Why not? We're only a hippo and a giraffe short of a zoo.*

Romy and Portia sat in the back seat of the double cab, and the little girl held her rabbit again. Next thing I knew Julian would add an elephant.

I climbed into the cab while Julian picked up hay and other supplies.

"I heard about the other morning," Romy said from the back seat. "I'm sorry about that."

"At least I didn't fall for the snipe hunt."

She giggled. "He didn't ask you to tip those cows, did he?"

I turned to look at her. "Nah. Everybody knows you only tip cows at night."

Julian jumped behind the wheel and started the truck. "Did Romy tell you the good news?"

"Julian—" she started.

"We're going to have another baby!"

And I would want to know this . . . because?

"Congratulations," I said with all of the enthusiasm I could muster, which, apparently, wasn't quite enough because Julian's grin disappeared.

My eyes instinctively traveled to the rearview mirror where I caught sight of chubby-cheeked Portia and her bunny. Her earnest expression was all Julian, but her wild black hair and dark eyes were Romy made over.

I tried to imagine what Brittany's and my daughter would've looked like. I couldn't even imagine Brittany pregnant.

"Yep, she peed on a stick while we were off getting those Jerseys."

"Julian, I don't think Gabe wants to know *all* of the details."

I turned around to look at Portia this time. She grinned at me. "Imma be a big sister!"

"I bet you're going to be a great big sister."

"Yep."

Such modesty, too.

"Daddy says you're my uncle Gabe."

I shot Julian a dirty look. We weren't close enough for me to be an honorary uncle to his child. I'd almost punched the man twice.

His ears turned bright red.

Good. He needed to be embarrassed. No doubt he'd been making fun of me in front of the child. I was surprised she hadn't called me Uncle City Boy. Maybe I could get her to tell something else on him.

"Uncle, huh?" I said, careful to keep my voice even for the sake of the child.

"He said maybe you'd take me fishing someday with him and Grandpa," the little girl said matter-of-factly, her eyebrows lifting in a way I'd seen many times before only I hadn't seen the resemblance until now.

Holy shit.

It all made sense.

All of this forced contact between Julian and me, the insistence he wasn't after Dad's money. My mouth went dry, and my heart caught in my throat.

Julian was my brother.

Chapter 9
Ivy

I tiptoed toward the manger, but the fussing stopped. So I stopped. The sun had almost disappeared and a chill had set in.

What if this stable were haunted?

Yes, Ivy, the ghosts of woodshed past have placed their own baby here to remind us of the Christmas story and scare us all on the straight and narrow.

The fussing came again, this time devolving into a low cry.

Definitely not a ghost.

Maybe.

I tiptoed closer and a decidedly human baby lay in the manger. His chubby arms had come free of his swaddling—a Sesame Street blanket—and he waved them as if trying to get someone's attention.

"Oh, look at you. What's a nice fella like you doing in a place like this?" I asked as I scooped the child up. He stopped fretting long enough to look up at me with enormous blue eyes as if to say, "And you are . . . and I would know you from?"

"You like that bouncing, don't you?"

He didn't so much as crack a smile, but he fixed me with an intense stare.

I remembered something Corey had once said. We'd been in

hospice, and he'd grabbed my hand out of the blue. "I wish I'd given you a baby, Ivy."

My blood ran cold at the memory. Hadn't I just been thinking about my husband sending me a sign?

But if he were going to send me a sign, then he would've remembered our conversation about children and how he had always wanted to have a child far more than I had.

He could've sent a puppy for starters.

Then again, he always did think he knew best.

"You don't happen to know a guy named Corey, do you?"

The baby's expression went from stern to grinning, his chubby arm breaking free of the blanket and waving around for emphasis.

"You know, you kinda look like him the last time I saw him. He didn't have much hair, either."

That smile disappeared into a frown. His lower lip jutted out as if he was ready to cry.

"I'm sorry, I didn't mean it like that. He was a handsome fellow, you know."

"Who are you talking to?"

I whirled around to face Lydia, who'd returned with a Coke for me even though I'd told her I didn't want one.

"And what are you doing with a baby?" she asked, causing me to jump out of my skin and almost drop the baby.

"I, uh, someone left him in the manger, and he was crying and—"

"Don't touch him! What if the police need fingerprints!"

"Lydia, it's a baby, not a murder weapon."

"Still, we're going to have to call the police if someone has abandoned a baby."

The child turned instinctively to my breast, calm but rooting. My Mystery Jesus was hungry. "Do you see anyone?"

Lydia walked around the manger and stopped on the other side from where I stood. "I see a small bag over here, but I'm pretty sure we shouldn't touch *that* in case there are fingerprints."

Who knew Lydia had such an obsession with forensics? Maybe

she watched entirely too many cop dramas on television or something.

"Do you see a mother?" I asked as I bounced the baby and slowly turned around, looking for any signs of a parent. "Or a father?"

A faint scratching sound made me look back to the driveway in time to see a piece of paper floating along the asphalt of the parking lot. "Can you grab that note?"

Lydia ran after the sheet and then stomped on the edge to keep it from flying away. She stooped down to read it. "Please take care of my little girl."

"That's it?" My arms drew the abandoned baby closer. How could anyone leave such a dear behind?

"That's all the note says."

Surely, the note didn't mean me?

Of course not, and why would it? This wasn't a Christmas miracle. It wasn't a sign from my husband. Someone had abandoned a baby and had no idea how this all worked. I had some idea because Corey and I had been trained as foster parents. We'd been on the foster to adopt list, but we'd already had one turn. I knew darn well that parents vied for babies like these, abandoned but healthy children who'd never have a memory of a birth parent. Often babies this young didn't have someone who would come calling before parental rights had been terminated; parents could adopt without having to fear losing a child they'd grown attached to.

Unless those parents happened to be as unlucky as Corey and I had been. We'd taken placement of a little boy with the hopes of adopting him. Everything had gone so well right up until about three weeks before parental rights would've been terminated. The mother showed up, completely sober with a new job and a support system in place to help her take care of Byron. We'd had to live through supervised visits and reunification.

Then I'd watched that mother take her baby back from us. I'd told myself to be happy the two had been reunited, but I'd made the mistake of falling in love with chubby-cheeked, pensive

Byron. At night when he would wake me, I would quote his name-sake, "The night hath been to me a more familiar face." That was all I could remember, but I had hoped my Byron might grow up to be a poet, too.

He'd be in preschool now.

I looked down into another pensive face, this one belonging to a little girl.

"You're in good hands until the police get here. How about that?"

Lydia called nine-one-one. Next, the police would take her to the hospital to be examined. A case manager would find the next name on the list and call that family. There would be hearings and court dates and breath holding until those lucky parents could give this sweet child a home.

I bet those parents were named Lance and Courtney. They lived in a four-bedroom house in a great neighborhood with a fenced-in backyard for their golden retriever. No doubt Lance made enough money for Courtney to stay home with the kids—or maybe she brought home the bacon and he fried it up in the pan. Either way, they would take in this baby girl and learn to love her.

Or the baby's mother would show up.

"Ivy, what's the matter with you? Why are you crying?" Lydia asked, bringing me out of my reverie.

"It's just so sad."

"I know," Lydia said from where she still stood on the note. "I can't believe anyone would leave a baby out in the open like this, either."

Lydia thought I was crying for the baby, but I was crying for the imaginary parents who would love this child and then have to give her back. Lance and Courtney, despite being figments of my imagination, would've been such great parents.

My unexpected charge fussed in my arms, rooting with more insistence. "Lydia, we have to get into that bag. The baby's hungry."

"This is going to be a great front page story: Mother knows people would show up for the Nativity scene, leaves child with woman slated to play Mary," Lydia mused, too caught up in her own thoughts to have heard me. "I mean, could there be a better place to leave a baby than with a bunch of church folk who are celebrating Christmas?"

With a relative? A hospital? A super-competent babysitter? I could think of a few. "What did the dispatcher say?"

"That they'd be here in less than fifteen minutes. I told them to hurry because we have a baby on our hands."

A hungry baby at that. Maybe we could make it another few minutes?

Julian's truck pulled into the lot, and I glimpsed Gabe in the passenger's seat.

He's a pediatrician. He'll know what to do.

Chapter 10
Gabe

"Uncle?" I managed to choke out.

"Yep," Julian said.

"I told you that you two should've told him first thing," Romy muttered under her breath.

"Uncle Gabe?"

That would take some getting used to, but I forced a smile because my niece was precious and didn't know—or need to know—anything about the crazy things adults got up to. At least not anytime soon. "Yes, sweetie?"

"You gonna take me fishing like Daddy said?" The way she said her daddy's name with reverence told me she'd believe anything he told her.

"I might. Do you think I'm going to be a good uncle?"

She turned her head sideways and crinkled her nose as she studied me. "I think you'll do."

Romy coughed or pretended to cough in order to hide her nervous laughter. Julian might turn purple before we reached the Nativity scene. It'd serve him right if he did. He could suffocate for all I cared, just as long as he waited until we arrived safely before he did.

"Well, this is all a surprise to me. What do you think uncles should do?" I asked.

"Take me fishing and buy me ice cream." She stopped to think about it. "And get me a really nice Christmas present."

"Portia," Romy hissed, her cheeks now pink, too.

"I see. What about your new baby brother or sister?"

Her sigh came far too world-weary for a little girl. "I guess he can come, too."

"He?"

"It's a boy," she said.

"Now, Portia, I told you it could be a boy *or* a girl," Romy said, her voice still shaky, but her tone indicating she was relieved to be back in familiar territory.

"It's a boy," the little girl repeated. "And we're going to be good friends. When he learns to use the potty like I do."

For some reason the enthusiasm of the little girl—my niece—caused a chunk of my anger to dissipate. She was so excited at the prospect of having a sibling and here I was mad as hell. Ironically, when I was her age, I'd prayed Dad would take me home and marry a new mommy and give me a baby brother. All these years I'd thought those prayers unanswered.

Maybe God had seen fit to give me a part of my wish.

But Julian? Really, God?

Even if I couldn't stand Julian, I owed it to Portia to be a good uncle, didn't I? And to her little brother? Or sister?

Wow. An uncle.

That was another thing I'd given up on since divorcing Brittany.

Dammit. Now I probably owed it to Julian to at least *try* to be civil.

But not tonight. I'd stew in my juices tonight.

Julian pulled into the Nativity scene and turned to say something. I cut him off. "Have fun unloading the livestock. Bubba."

"Now, you wait just a minute, you—"

"Julian," Romy said from the back. "Little pitchers have big ears, remember?"

He scowled at me and then got out of the truck, resigned to doing all of the work himself.

"Uncle Gabe?" Portia said as I was about to open my own door.

"Yes, sweetheart?"

"You gonna spend Christmas with us?"

That girl had to get all of her sweetness from her mother. Either that or she was thinking about that "really nice Christmas present," but I didn't think so. "That depends. Are you coming over to your grandpa Lester's?"

"For supper," the little girl said. "But we gotta go to Grandpa Hank's for dinner."

"Well, I will be there at Grandpa Lester's." And I suppose I'll have a Christmas present for my niece—coal and switches for my father and . . . brother.

It just didn't sound right.

"Promise?" she asked, holding out her pinky.

It got a little dusty in that truck cab as I linked my oversize pinky with her tiny one. "Promise."

I had to get out of the truck and blink my eyes several times after that. Behind me I could hear Romy saying, "Portia, baby, you remember what I told you?"

"I gotta stay still while the cars are coming through, and that it will be long and boring, but I can pet Leonard."

"That's right."

Suddenly, my new best friend was standing beside me. "Were you bored last night, Uncle Gabe?"

"A little," I said, not wanting to tell the whole truth but also not wanting to lie. "It's not that exciting, but you gotta figure it wasn't that exciting for Mary, Joseph, and Jesus, either, once all of the shepherds and angels left."

"And Wise Men."

"And Wise Men," I echoed.

"Mama says Leonard and I have to be quiet."

I didn't think the rabbit was going to have any trouble keeping quiet. My brand-new niece, however? That was another story.

"How old are you?"

"I'm going to be four in March."

My niece was quite precocious, probably gifted. I puffed up a bit at the thought before remembering I'd had nothing to do with her smarts. "Quite the vocabulary you have there."

"I can already read," she said proudly.

"You'll have to read me a book one day soon, then," I said.

She grinned at me, but then Romy called for her.

Someone put a hand on my shoulder, and I turned around ready to punch whoever it was.

Julian. No wonder the desire to punch was so strong.

"Gabe?"

"We're not having this discussion now," I said.

We might not have this discussion ever.

He shuffled off, and I told myself not to feel guilty for not helping him. I'd leave right then and there except for the fact I hadn't driven. Even so, the idea of heading back to Memphis a few weeks early had never been more appealing.

I needed a quiet evening with no more surprises. I would sit there with Ivy and think about what to do next as the cars rolled past. I rounded the corner of the stable, almost running into Ivy. The last rays of evening sun gave her a halo, and there was something about the twinkle in her eyes, the slight parting of her lips.

We stopped a foot apart, and the bundle in her arms wriggled. She looked down at her armload of swaddling and then back up at me, and I sucked in a breath. My Mary held a living, breathing baby. I had never seen her smile reach all the way to her eyes. My God, how had I missed her beauty?

"Hey, Gabe. Guess what I found?"

Chapter 11
Ivy

"Um, that appears to be a baby," he said before adding, "And I should know. Are we method acting tonight?"

"No, someone left this sweetheart in our manger."

His smile faded. "Do you mean to say this baby was abandoned?"

"Pretty much. There's a note over there asking someone to take care of her, but that's all we have."

Gabe flung off his robe and rolled up his sleeves. "Well, let me check the little lady out and make sure she's okay."

I hesitated, then kicked myself for being silly. The man was a pediatrician, for heaven's sake. I handed over Mystery Jesus and my arms immediately felt the loss.

He cooed to the child and manipulated her arms and legs gently, feeling all over her little body. No doubt there were all sorts of reflexes he had to check, maybe the fontanelle. I couldn't remember. . . .

"She appears to be healthy, but—"

"Hungry?"

He laughed. "We might have a tiny Hulk on our hands if we don't feed her soon. How about I'll change her diaper, and you can fix a bottle?"

"Deal."

"Fingerprints!" Lydia shouted as I rifled through the diaper bag.

"Oh, lighten up. We have to feed and change her."

"Well, I'm not moving."

"Great, they can take prints from the note you're standing on and won't need any prints from this bag."

I found a bottle with powdered formula at the bottom, so I ran for the break room kitchen. Then I panicked.

Did I use water from a jug? Water from the faucet? Warm water? Cool water? Did I need to sterilize anything? Why couldn't I remember these details from my first tour of duty with Byron?

Blessedly, Mavis, grandmother of five, sat at the crumb-coated table eating a quick supper. "What are you doing?"

I explained the situation to her, and she only paused for a minute. "A baby? Outside?"

"I know, right? Doesn't this formula need to be heated?"

"Girl, no. That's asking for trouble. You want to have to heat up formula every time that baby gets hungry?"

"Oh, I don't plan to *keep* her. I'm just looking out for her until the police arrive."

"Mm-hmm."

"Seriously. Why would I want a baby?"

"You wouldn't," she said between bites of Lean Cuisine. "But it would be just like you to get caught in the middle of this because a baby is the last thing you need."

"I wouldn't make *that* bad of a mother!" At least I thought I'd done a good job with Byron—especially since it was Corey who'd talked me into foster parent training.

She arched an eyebrow.

"Fine. Whatever. Thanks for the advice," I said.

I power walked back to the manger, and Gabe opened his arms. Somewhere in the diaper bag, he'd already found a burp cloth, so I had nothing to do but sit on a bale of hay and watch. Our Mystery Jesus latched on to the bottle as though it'd been a week since she'd eaten. Based on her chubby arms and legs, that couldn't have been the case.

"She's about three months old and appears to be well taken care of," Gabe said. "And— Why is that woman taking pictures?"

"Oh, that's Lydia. She came from the paper to take pictures of the Nativity. I think she's got the scoop of the year tonight."

"Well, she might want to move. Doesn't she see the ambulance coming?"

I shielded my eyes against the headlights coming straight for us. "She's standing on the note and doesn't want to touch it in case there are fingerprints. She didn't want me to touch the baby for the same reason."

Gabe muttered something that didn't bear repeating, and I had to admit Lydia was being particularly theatrical. Then again, she had originally wanted to be an investigative reporter before she ended up in a small town, reporting on car accidents, dead bucks, and miscreant possums.

He chuckled as an afterthought. "Well, now this little lady has both of our fingerprints all over her."

The ambulance pulled around Lydia and her ladder, with a police car behind.

EMTs along with the new police chief walked over. To my left, Gabe chatted with the EMTs while he burped the baby over one shoulder. He did so with ease, and I marveled. The minute he rolled up his sleeves and took the child, it was like seeing him for the first time—probably because he was finally in his element.

"So you're the one who found the child?" I turned to look at Chief Gattis, who'd taken out his notepad and was looking at me expectantly.

I nodded but before I could speak, Lydia yelled, "I found this note!"

Gattis nodded to the officer who was with him, and the younger man walked over and put on gloves in order to rescue Lydia by picking up the note.

"Did you see anyone leave the baby?" Gattis asked, bringing my attention back to him.

"No, sir. I picked her up, and that note floated away. Then we found the diaper bag under the manger. We tried not to touch it any more than we had to, but the baby was hungry and needed a change."

"So you fed and changed the child?"

"Of course. Well, Gabe did. He examined her, too, because he's a pediatrician." All I did was bounce her. "My late husband and I were foster parents. We only got to host one baby before Corey's cancer came back, but I'm qualified. I promise."

Gabe turned to look at me. He'd heard that?

And why had I told the chief that? I guess I didn't want either of them to think I was completely incompetent even though it didn't matter what they thought. Besides, without Mavis, I'd probably still be standing in the break room looking from the sink to the jug of water I'd taken from the shelf on my way back, so maybe I wasn't that competent after all.

I looked over Gattis's shoulder to see Gabe surrendering our Mystery Jesus to the EMTs.

He was going to put that baby in an ambulance with strangers?

Gattis had to repeat his question because I was awfully close to asking to ride with the baby.

Gabe's eyes locked with mine. I took a step toward the ambulance but then Gabe held up a hand, then tossed his robe to Julian and trotted toward the ambulance. He banged on the back door just as the ambulance took off, but they stopped and let him in. I exhaled in relief.

"You okay, ma'am?"

I swiped away a few tears. "I'm fine."

I'm ridiculous, but I'm fine.

I turned back to Gattis and answered all of his questions, telling myself that the child was in far more capable hands than mine.

At long last the chief was satisfied with my answers, and I turned around to survey the scene, trembling from the waning adrenalin. I needed to focus on something else. Tonight's Nativity had two donkeys this time as well as two goats. A three-legged beagle bounced around us, barking and wagging her tail until she smelled something. Then she put her nose to the ground and hopped along as she followed a trail around the corner of the stable.

"We meet again," I said to the llama. She stepped aside to show me her mini-me.

"Is that a baby llama?"

Babies, babies everywhere.

"Alpaca," Julian said. "Deanna was fussing about leaving Teresa behind. She's very maternal about her alpaca. It's a long story."

I kinda wanted to hear it, but Miss Idabell was flitting around close to a conniption because the police had held up her production. Without Gabe, Bethlehem was an estrogen-oriented place these days. Julian and Ben had to feel outnumbered.

I moved over to the llama to get out of the way and patted her neck until Star reached over and slurped my arm. I turned my attention to the black cow with the white face.

"Ew," I said as I petted her anyway.

"That means she likes you," Julian said as he led a palomino to the other side.

"Daddy! Bunny!" Portia, ran up to him with her arms full of rabbit. He carefully swung her up, rabbit and all.

"Don't you squeeze Leonard too hard, now."

"I won't. I love my bunny," she said as she rubbed her cheek against the bunny's soft fur.

Then I saw the rooster.

"Really, Julian?"

He put his daughter down and turned to me. "Look, we were running late and then the llama wouldn't leave without the alpaca, and Portia wouldn't leave without the rabbit. Little Ann was baying at me and chasing the truck. Then CJ decided he sure as heck wasn't going to be left behind."

Even as I tried to reconcile the rooster, whose name was apparently CJ, to that already odd menagerie, Portia shifted the rabbit under one arm and reached into her pocket to pull out a few grains of corn that she tossed out to the rooster.

Something bittersweet tugged at my heart. I'd probably never have a spunky little girl who fed roosters.

"Well, I'll be damned," Julian said. "*That*'s why that rooster follows her around."

"Where'd she get that corn?"

"I don't know, but I bet it's a place that has snakes, and, once I tell her that, she'll stay away in the future," he said with a smile.

"Places! Places! The cars are beginning to line up!" Miss Idabell, our fearless coordinator, called. She had a clipboard. I stifled a giggle at the vision of a list on that clipboard: Mary. Check. Llama. Check. Tripod beagle. Check.

"Where is Joseph?"

"He rode with the baby."

She sighed as though Gabe had done the most inconsiderate thing ever. "Julian, come be Joseph. Ben, go be a shepherd."

"That sheep does *not* like me and neither do the goats," Ben Little, local lawyer, said from his perch as a Wise Man.

"Man, the goats *love* you."

"Shut up, Julian."

"Mr. Little, you be Joseph. Now we need another Wise Man."

"I'll do it!"

We all turned to see Lydia who had been snapping pictures of Portia and her bunny.

"Robe's around the corner," Miss Idabell said.

Ben settled in across from me. "Hey, all of the Wise Men are women."

"And this surprises you?" Romy asked.

Someone in the line honked his horn. Then another person. And another.

"The nerve," Miss Idabell said.

"It'll be fine once they read the paper," Lydia said as she stepped into place. "Someone be sure to take my picture before we go home."

"I'll take one now," Miss Idabell said with another long-suffering sigh. "What's one more minute at this point?"

I smiled for the camera, but the scene didn't feel right. Gabe had left, and the manger was empty. We didn't even have the demonically cheerful Cabbage Patch Kid someone had placed in the manger the night before.

I clenched my fists, not sure what to say to Ben and unable to stop worrying about the baby I'd found now that I sat still and had plenty of time for my mind to wander.

It's okay. Gabe is with her. You know they'll find a good family to take care of her.

Even so, to be left alone at Christmas? How bad did it have to be for that mother if she left her child in a manger just hoping for someone to come along and do the right thing? Maybe she'd at least watched from nearby, kinda like the story of Moses's sister watching from the bulrushes.

Well, at least my part in this adventure is over.

Chapter 12
Gabe

When I got to the hospital I had to surrender the baby to the staff. I'd known this. I had no privileges at Jefferson General. Even so, I paced the hall, not sure what I would do next. I wouldn't be able to get a cab to drive me two counties over. I didn't have Ivy's number. I could call Julian, but I was still not ready to contemplate how we were brothers and too mad at my father to call him even if he'd been able to come get me.

You're going to have to call one of them eventually.

Not if I could help it. I'd think of something. If it weren't so late, I'd *buy* a junker to get me home.

I read every magazine in the waiting room, then talked another doctor into letting me visit the baby, but she was asleep. Once I was sure the Nativity scene had closed up for the night and that Julian had had time to get the animals home, I pulled up his number and tried to get my finger to touch it.

My finger wasn't keen on the idea.

About that time a young Asian woman showed up with her laptop bag and her phone. Before I saw the bag and the phone I'd thought she was a teenager, but, no, she was a petite woman in a low-cut green velvet dress. Thanks to my ex-wife, I knew enough about hairstyles to know that her glossy black hair had been expensively drawn up. She also wore diamond earrings and sported professionally manicured nails. Her shoes had a red sole, the kind of ridiculously expensive footwear Brittany always fussed over.

Red soles meant a hefty credit card bill, and I didn't miss those soles or the ridiculous bills they'd created.

"Did you leave a Christmas party?"

"I drew the short straw," she said with a wry smile as she opened her laptop, and took out some paperwork I recognized. I did a double take because her outward appearance didn't pair with being on call or working for the state.

"Social worker, I'm guessing," I said as I sat down two seats from her.

"Case manager," she corrected, giving me a once-over. Apparently she wasn't all that impressed with what she saw because she went back to work.

To a young woman fresh out of college I did probably look ancient. I told myself I wasn't going to say anything else, but then she kicked off her fancy shoes, and I couldn't let that slide. "Whoa! Don't take your shoes off."

"Excuse me?"

"I'm sorry, that came out a bit sharper than I meant for it to. I'm Dr. Gabriel Ledbetter. I strongly recommend that you put your shoes back on because you definitely don't want to get a staph infection. I know hospitals look clean, but germs aren't easy to see, so it's better to be safe than sorry."

All of the color drained from her face for a moment, but she recovered nicely, shoving her feet back into the pumps.

I held out my hand, and she shook it but answered reluctantly. "I'm Chelsea Stapleton, and this is, ah, my first call, well, ever."

So, I was right. Fresh out of college. Now as to what Chelsea Stapleton was doing in the field of social work, I didn't know but I could guess.

"You must be here for the baby we found in a manger in Ellery."

"You're kidding. An actual manger? You were there?"

"I was playing the part of Joseph in the Nativity," I said. "Mary found her—if you would believe that."

She smiled but then her face narrowed in suspicion. "What are you doing here, then?"

Good question.

I thought of the peace in Ivy's eyes as she approached me with the baby, then the panic as the ambulance rolled away. "I wanted to make sure our wannabe Baby Jesus got to the hospital okay."

Chelsea nodded and turned back to her laptop. After a few minutes, she looked up at me. "As a doctor, I guess you've done this before."

"Only once," I said. I'd been an intern at a Memphis hospital back then. The baby had been outside for too long and didn't make it, but I didn't want to tell Chelsea that. She'd discover enough sad stories if she stuck with her career long enough. "I wish I could tell you that this will be the last time you get a call while at a party, but I'd hate to lie to you."

She bit her bottom lip. "I'm trying to remember everything I need to do for an abandoned baby. It's not a situation I've run across yet. I haven't run across *any* situations all by myself yet."

Ivy mentioned being a foster parent.

The words tumbled out of my mouth of their own accord. "You know, the woman who found the baby has been a foster parent in the past. She might still be in the system."

"Really?"

Oh, I knew better. I didn't know all of the particulars, but I knew there was a protocol to foster care and probably a waiting list. What was I doing? I didn't know that Ivy wanted to take care of this baby. I only wanted her to have the opportunity if it would make her as happy as she had seemed earlier tonight.

Chelsea chattered on about convenience, her big brown eyes dancing. Apparently, she had been at her boyfriend's company Christmas party and they were giving away a car at midnight, but you had to be present to win. Well, that and she had borrowed her boyfriend's car to get to the hospital because she was in need of that car they were giving away.

I had to admire her youthful optimism.

I didn't have the heart to tell her that she didn't stand a chance of making it back to that party on time.

She tapped away merrily on her laptop. I should tell her to look for another name, to look for a waiting list. I should, but I couldn't seem to make myself do so.

Meanwhile, Chelsea called Ivy's cell phone number. When it went to voicemail, she disconnected the call. "I guess I'd better find another person."

"Maybe she was fumbling with her phone. Why don't you try one more time?"

Chapter 13
Ivy

By the time I got back to the house I was exhausted and beyond grateful I had the next day off. I was running late because I'd stayed to help Romy and Julian put all of the animals back into the trailer, but my job had mainly been chasing Portia around to keep her out from under livestock legs. Chasing Portia meant chasing the beagle and the rooster and telling her to be sweet to her bunny.

I sat out in the driveway, too tired to even swing my legs out of the car and walk into the house.

But you've got to bring Holly her goodies.

With a groan, I forced myself out of the car and to the trunk where I'd stashed all of the Christmas regalia. I put purse on my shoulder, plastic bags over each forearm, and the large flat lawn snowman box under my arm. That thing had best work because it was a bear to carry around.

Holly met me at the door, and I could tell she'd been up to something. "What did you do?"

"Nothing, I did nothing!"

Her protestations of innocence rang false. My little sister couldn't keep the grin from her face or the pink from her cheeks, two sure signs that she had been up to something.

"Saran wrap on the toilet?"

"Gosh, I'm not thirteen anymore."

I cut my eyes at her to remind her the last time she'd pulled that stunt she was well over thirteen.

"And it's not April Fool's Day."

"You didn't put salt in the sugar bowl again, did you?"

Holly sighed. "I only made that mistake *once*. Now I'm well aware of how seriously Mom takes her coffee."

I looked up, down, all around. Then I spied the box of icicles on the counter.

"You didn't."

"Oh, but I did," she said with a huge grin.

"You're going to make the tree look tacky *and* kill another vacuum cleaner?"

"No, I won't!" She put her hands on her hips in righteous indignation.

"Settle down. I brought all sorts of things for you," I said as I offered an arm that was laden with plastic bags.

"Is that—?"

Of course, she took the snowman and left me hanging with all of the bags. I sighed and laid them out on the counter. "Lights. Ornaments. Garland. Wrapping paper. An ornament that's Santa on a Treadmill."

"Love!" She cried, putting down the snowman box so she could hug me.

"What are you two doing?" Mom asked.

"Ivy got me all sorts of Christmas decorations," Holly said, clapping her hands together.

"She got you *all* of this?"

"Every last bit. Playing Mary has rubbed off on her. I think I see a halo."

"Well." Mom looked from the box of icicles to me and back to the box. "I see a little devil, and you can take that box of his instruments of torture right on back to that store where you work because I'm not going to have either one of you ruin my Hoover with this nonsense. Furthermore—"

"Mom."

"Futhermore, it makes the tree look tacky and—"

"That's what I said! *Mom*—"

"Don't you 'Mom' me, young lady! I can believe your sister would do such a thing, but *you* know better."

She continued in that vein, recounting in detail the strands of tinsel wound around the beater bar, then the smell when the beater bar got so clogged that it caused some inner mechanism to burn up. Holly snickered in the corner rather than fess up to her shenanigans. The whole thing could've been a scene from our childhood: I did something nice. Holly didn't. I got in trouble for it. Finally, I'd had enough.

"Mom, Holly bought the icicles. I bought everything else!"

Mom stopped and looked at Holly for confirmation. "Did you really?"

"Yes, ma'am."

If I'd hoped Mom would turn on Holly and chew her out the way she had me, then I was bound to be disappointed because, instead, she said, "Everything that I just said to Ivy? Take that and apply it to you. Take that mess out of my house, and if you break my vacuum cleaner, then you can buy me another. I'm going to bed. Y'all behave. For once."

Even after several years of watching similar scenes play out, my mouth hung open. I wanted to rail about the unfairness of it all, but I couldn't find the words. I stood staring at the empty hall where Mom had disappeared, then to Holly, then to the icicles.

Then Holly burst out laughing.

"You!"

I lunged for her, but she evaded me, curse her perpetually physically fit self.

"You should see the look on your face," she said. In my attempt to catch her—and do what, I didn't know—we'd switched sides of the table.

"Yeah, how's it looking right now?"

"Like you want to kill me."

"That's cuz I do."

"But you can't," she stage whispered. "Then we'll both get in trouble for being too loud."

"Apparently, I'm the only one who ever gets in trouble around here," I said through gritted teeth. "Since I'm far closer to forty than thirty, I'm tired of it."

"Oh, she gives me grief, too!"

I had to scoff at that. "Tell me one time when you got in trouble and I didn't."

"There's . . ."

"You won't be able to think of it."

"But . . ."

"Just run."

She took off for the back door, and I followed her. The night had turned off cool, and I could see my breath as I chased my sister. I knew I'd never beat her in a foot race, and, sure enough, my lungs were already gasping from the slight effort I'd expended. But I knew something that Holly didn't know: She might be speedy, but I was sneaky. Sure enough, she ran around the house, and I backtracked, tackling her just as she was about to make her first lap.

Since I outweighed her by a great bit, I could stop her by sitting on her, and that's what I did.

"So you've got me, now what? I can call the police and charge you with assault and battery if you hit me."

True. I hadn't chased her since we were teenagers at the oldest, and I had gotten in trouble for the shiner I'd given her.

Then there was the possibility that she could be pregnant. "Oh. Are you okay?"

"What?"

"The baby," I whispered, looking left and right.

"If there is a baby inside me, I'm sure it's well cushioned," she said.

"Good," I said. Before she could respond, I tickled her.

"For the love. . . . Stop it!" she gasped.

I dug my fingers into her side just hard enough to be uncomfortable and ticklish at the same time but not hard enough to leave a mark. She stopped squirming. "No, really. Stop. I hear your phone."

From my back pocket Beyoncé sang about the "single ladies," a parting gift from my husband who had thought it would be funny once I was "back on the market." I reached back for my phone, then stared at it, but it had quit ringing.

I didn't recognize the number, but whoever it was had called twice.

When it started ringing again, I jumped out of my skin and almost dropped the phone before answering. "Hello?"

The world went a little fuzzy as someone named Chelsea explained the situation of an abandoned baby to me. I already knew about that particular situation and that specific baby. I stumbled to my feet and heard myself say, "Yes."

"What are you doing?" asked Holly.

"I honestly don't know."

Chapter 14
Gabe

I didn't realize I was clenching my fists and holding my breath until I heard someone say hello. I let all of that held breath whoosh right out.

Chelsea explained the situation. Then there was silence and finally a *yes* that I could hardly hear.

The young case manager's face lit up as she started spelling out details to Ivy, and I got up to pace because I was tired of sitting.

But I *could* get a ride home from Ivy if she were coming to the hospital. Then I could avoid Julian and my father a little longer. I waved at Chelsea. "Ask her if she can take me home when she comes."

Chelsea did as I suggested and nodded affirmatively.

I plopped down in one of the chairs, amazed by how uncomfortable it was. Next I watched Chelsea work her magic as she called someone from the court office, who called a judge. Twice she tried to call another case manager to make sure she was doing the right thing. Neither of those managers picked up.

Finally, she sat back and checked her watch. "I'm not going to make it by midnight, am I?"

"Nope."

About that time her phone rang. I could hear the angry male

voice from across the room. Finally, she said, "Look, Kyle, this is what I do. It's my job. Kyle?"

She looked up in disbelief. "He hung up on me."

"Boyfriend?"

She nodded in exasperation. "He's ticked that I have his car so he can't leave without me."

"I've been there a few times," I mused. On more than one occasion I'd left a party or a show because I was on call, and I'd been on the receiving end of the angry voice of someone who had to find another ride home. No matter how many times I suggested that Brittany and I take separate cars, she never listened.

"I have got to get my own car," Chelsea said.

"You probably could if you pooled the resources from selling your earrings and your shoes," I said, immediately regretting it. I should mind my own business. Sometimes I blurted out easy solutions when they came to mind, forgetting others hadn't asked for my help.

She laughed. "You noticed? Both were early gifts from my parents. They offered to get me a car for Christmas, but I'm trying to make it on my own."

"At the risk of giving you more advice that you didn't ask for, why don't you take them up on it? I'd feel better knowing you didn't have to deal with this Kyle guy."

She put her phone in her lap so she could massage her temples. "Oh, I think he and I are through this time. No matter how many times he tries to apologize for this one."

I hoped she stuck to her guns. "My wife used to call me like that."

"Used to?"

"She left me. Said I was never home and that I never had time for her."

Her eyes met mine. "That's what Kyle says!"

"Well," I said. "If he can't appreciate what you do after a few months of being together . . ."

"Then he's not the guy for me," she said softly.

I nodded. "Yep."

Her phone blared "All I Want for Christmas," and I looked at the television on the waiting room wall where Santa Claus appeared to be on trial in an old black-and-white movie. I tried not to listen in on Chelsea's conversation with Kyle, who'd developed a more contrite attitude once he remembered he had neither keys nor car.

When she hung up the phone, she turned to me. "I thought you were a real pain at first, but I'm glad I ran into you, Dr. Ledbetter."

"Well, I'm glad I ran into you, too, Ms. Stapleton. I wish you great success in your new career."

She wouldn't be as glad when she found out that I'd nudged her down the path of fudged protocol. Even I had to admit my behavior had been, as Spock might say, "highly illogical." I couldn't say what had gotten into me. Maybe I was still off-kilter from finding out I had a brother.

Or from really seeing Ivy Long for the first time.

"Gabe!"

Ivy tackled me with a hug, and I swear she looked almost ten years younger than she had the first time I met her.

"Still able to give me a ride home?"

"Of course!"

I introduced her to Chelsea, who spread out only two pieces of papers. Ivy drew out a manila folder full of her own. They chatted and compared notes. Ivy hesitated only a second before signing her paperwork.

When I left to get a couple of Cokes because Ivy had been yawning, she was asking about WIC vouchers for formula. As I returned, Ivy was hugging Chelsea to within an inch of her life. Chelsea made her goodbyes and sent a nurse to bring us the baby.

"Sure you don't mind taking me home?"

"Not at all," she said. "Thank you for riding with her to the hospital. I guess you could tell I was nervous?"

"Maybe a little."

"You think I'm silly, don't you?"

"My aunt Vi didn't raise any fools. I'm not answering that."

"Well, that's a cop-out," she said as we walked together toward the hallway where we could see the nurse approaching with Ivy's new charge in one of those bucket seats that could also serve as a car seat.

"Well, look at you two standing underneath the mistletoe," the nurse said.

Ivy and I both looked up, then at each other. Color drained from her face and she took a little step back.

I swallowed hard but couldn't get rid of the lump in my throat. *She doesn't want me to kiss her. Duly noted.*

"Think you can install this, Dad?" asked the nurse as she transferred the bucket seat and then handed me the base for the car.

"Sure," I said even as Ivy was saying, "Oh, he's not. I mean, we're not—"

The nurse had left. She didn't care about mistletoe or if we were a couple. She had better things to do.

"I'm sorry, Gabe. I didn't mean— Oh, can I just take that?" Ivy asked as she held out a hand for the car seat, her cheeks pink.

"I'll take it," I said. "You lead the way to the car."

Chapter 15
Ivy

Way to go, Ivy.

I'd bungled the whole thing about the mistletoe. I had only meant to step backward because I didn't want Gabe to feel like he had to kiss me because some nurse we didn't know said something, but I could've sworn I saw hurt flash in his eyes for a second before he schooled his expression into something inscrutable.

He hadn't said a word all the way home.

Maybe he was just tired. It was well after midnight now.

Gabe snored once and leaned against the window.

Oh, thank goodness. He's not just giving me the silent treatment.

I'd been so surprised about getting the call to take in our little Jane Doe. I still didn't know if I'd made the right decision, but I'd gone with my gut for the first time in a very long time.

Then my gut had told me to stay put in that doorway, but my brain had told me to back up.

It'd been so long since I'd had any sort of intuition; I didn't even know what I was doing. Not with the baby in the back seat. Not with whether or not I wanted to kiss Gabe.

Kiss Gabe? What would Corey think?

Oh, who cares what Corey thinks? He's off playing celestial poker with Harry Truman and Winston Churchill.

Well, that and he'd once told me to hook up with a doctor next time. He'd said, "It pays better *and* you can have the healer instead of the healee."

Oh, Corey. I would've already wanted to smack him for not taking any of this seriously.

When it came to my bundle of joy in the back seat, though, I needed to get serious. Even if the placement only lasted a week tops. My little charge deserved a good Christmas whether she would remember it or not.

Gabe snored softly, but my mind kept working. Even though tiny, the child needed her own bedroom. That *had* been my room up until a couple of months ago when my sister showed up. I had added Gabe to the paperwork of people who were allowed to care for the child, but I would need to find an appropriate daycare in addition to Mom and Holly. He'd have to pass the background check, technically. Then I needed to write down the information on the car seat since it was a loaner, to get more formula first thing in the morning, and then to look into the WIC vouchers. I'd soon need new diapers, but I had a few left. They'd yellowed, but, according to Google, the aging shouldn't hurt. Holly was washing baby clothes and blankets and sheets.

Drat. I bet the wipes had dried up and—

I'd driven home. I'd been so wrapped up in my thoughts that I'd driven home.

Gabe awakened with a start and yawned.

"Oops. Uh, want to help me get her settled before I take you home?"

"I can do that."

I still couldn't read his expression, so I slid out from behind the steering wheel and had to remind myself to open the passenger side door behind me. I released the bucket seat from the base, and Gabe grabbed the two diaper bags, the original one and another that clearly had come from a formula company. My heart beat ridiculously fast. I was forgetting something. I knew I was.

Ivy, you have to calm down.

I did have to calm down.

One thing at a time. You're getting ahead of yourself.

First, the baby. I would get the baby settled in, and then I would worry about whether or not I'd offended Gabe. But then if I asked him if I'd hurt his feelings, would that make me seem conceited? This was almost as bad as high school, and—

First, the baby.

We walked in to an assembled play yard, complete with the bassinet portion and a little changing table over one side, thanks to Holly. The diaper wipes I'd bought several years ago had indeed dried up, but there were enough in the diaper bag to take me to the morning. The diapers still smelled fresh, and I had enough formula to get us through the night. When we'd walked in, we'd passed a load of sheets, blankets, and burp cloths dancing in the dryer. Mom had long since gone to bed, but Gabe, Holly, and I stood over the baby, watching her as if she were the most exciting thing ever.

"Do we know what her name is?" I asked.

"Nope," Gabe said. "Once the police did their thing with the diaper bag, I went all through it. Not so much as initials on the bag to help us out. They did say they might be able to identify her by her footprint."

The television was on in the background, and *It's a Wonderful Life* had reached the part where George Bailey was "fixing" Zuzu's flower and putting the dead petals in his pocket.

"Zuzu," I said.

"Zuzu?" asked Holly.

I pointed at the television. "Why not?"

"So many reasons," she said with a yawn, "but you do you. I'm going to bed."

"I thought you might give Gabe a lift so I could keep an eye on the baby. On Zuzu."

Holly looked down at the sleeping baby and back up to me. "I don't think she's crawling out of that thing anytime soon, so *you* drive him home."

"But the baby—"

The baby—as well as anyone else in a three-mile radius—had

picked up on our argument. Now she was crying. I scooped her up, and some sensation in my belly tightened.

Gabe pulled his phone from his pocket to see the time and frowned. "It's probably time to feed her again."

"Think you can wait until I change and feed her?" I asked.

"Sure," he said. "I'll make the bottle while you change her diaper."

I turned to sweet Zuzu. "Hush now. We'll change you and feed you."

My sister yawned again. "Great. Glad we've got that all sorted out. Good talk. I'm going to bed."

"Holly," I said in warning.

"Oh, and you're welcome for putting together the play yard and finding all of the things in the closet and putting on a load of clothes."

Dang it. I hated it when she had a point. "Thank you, Sis."

She waved off my thanks as she disappeared down the hallway.

"What do *you* think about Zuzu?" I asked my new charge once I'd changed her diaper. She fussed at me, her little mouth turned downward, but I didn't take her too seriously because I don't want to talk about much of anything on an empty stomach, either.

"I'll be right back," I said as I moved her from changing area to bassinet so I could dispose of the diaper and wash my hands. I acted quickly because I wanted to be the one to feed her.

"I think Zuzu is a cute name," Gabe said when I returned.

"Thank you," I said as I slapped a burp cloth over my shoulder. He handed me the baby and then plopped down on the sofa.

Zuzu.

It suited her. I couldn't look away from those chubby cheeks, the huge eyes with long lashes, the impossibly perfect little fingernails. She finally fell off the bottle, her eyes closed and her little mouth still working every now and then even though she no longer had the bottle. I wanted to let her sleep, but I knew better.

"No sleepy time yet," I whispered. "We have to burp you."

I patted and patted that child's back, but she wanted to keep her gas bubbles, thank you very much.

"Gabe," I whispered, hoping he could give me advice on another burping position.

"Gabe?"

He answered me with a snore.

I searched my memory banks for alternate burping positions and tried what I could remember until I managed to elicit a burp of epic proportions.

"Good girl," I murmured before shifting her into my arms and gently rocking her until she fell asleep. At one point she clenched her fists and looked up at me but then her eyes closed and her arm relaxed and gently fell. I placed her in the bassinet and turned around to see Gabe sleeping soundly.

I probably should've said something when he stretched out earlier. Now I didn't have the heart to wake him up.

Instead I took a couple of quilts from the linen closet at the end of the hall, one for me and one for him. As I covered him with one of my grandmother's quilts, I noticed a cowlick over his forehead. Corey had always kept his hair in something close to a buzz cut, but Gabe let his auburn hair wave. The man who lay on my couch with his neatly trimmed beard, that unruly lock over his forehead, looked like the antithesis of my first husband. I reached for that strand of hair and stopped myself.

I shouldn't.

You should wake him up and take him home.

According to my phone, it was almost four in the morning. I really, really didn't want to have to drive myself back alone and risk falling asleep at the wheel now that my adrenalin had spiked and dissipated, leaving me sluggish.

The baby behind me sighed, and my own eyes fought to close. I gently brushed back the lock of Gabe's hair, but it flipped into its original place, of course.

Surely it would be okay for him to stay a little while longer, to get some sleep before I took him home in the morning.

After turning off the lights, I moved over to the recliner and snuggled under my own quilt before pulling out the footrest and leaning back. From my spot in the recliner, I could see my purse there on the floor beside the diaper bag.

I bet Corey's letter doesn't say anything about this situation.

No, but it had been a long time since I'd been this content, and I was willing to close my eyes and let it be.

Chapter 16
Gabe

"Oh my stars! There's a man in the living room—and a baby?"
Who the heck used that expression anymore?

Since I was in that twilight space between sleep and consciousness, I first thought someone had turned on the television and that the voice had come from a sitcom. No laugh track, though. Then I heard the thud and wondered who was dropping things in the kitchen.

Wait. That *thud* was coming from the wrong area to be the kitchen. I was in the wrong place on the wrong couch.

The baby.

I must've fallen asleep at Ivy's house. Based on how she'd backed away from me last night, I'd truly made a bone-headed move.

I had a vague recollection of lying down on the couch and thinking that wasn't a good idea since I'd be hard to wake up once I was asleep. My reasonable side had been too tired to argue the point, though.

I sat up straight, my body checking in to tell me I had a headache, a crick in my neck, and not anywhere near enough sleep. In front of me, the baby—Zuzu—slept in the bassinet contraption. When I looked to my right and down the hall, I saw the soles to a pair of house slippers. The person they belonged to lay on the floor.

I reached her in seconds, checking all of her vitals, then searching carefully for any broken bones. No, she'd fainted. The woman moaned. Finally, her eyes fluttered open, and she screamed.

"Wha—?" Ivy asked groggily from the recliner behind me. I wasn't the only heavy sleeper, it seemed.

The baby let loose with a howl.

"Knock it off!" someone down the hall yelled. Ivy's sister, Holly, I presumed.

"Mama?" Ivy peeked over the arm of the recliner, then jumped down to sit on her mother's other side. "Are you okay? What happened?"

I couldn't help but smile. "I don't think she was expecting Zuzu or me. She fainted."

"Do I need to call nine-one-one?" Ivy asked.

Her mother's eyelashes began to flutter, and her pupils were the same size and not overly dilated. "I don't think so."

Mrs. Long looked up at me. "You're not him. Thank God."

"No, I'm Gabe Ledbetter." *And I'm confused as to which "him" I am not.*

"Oh, you're Lester's son, the doctor."

"That's me."

"You seem a strapping fellow. Can you help me up?"

I stood and extended a hand to Mrs. Long before turning to Ivy, forcing myself to meet her eyes. "I think she'll be fine. You get Zuzu."

"I thought I heard a baby," Mrs. Long said as she massaged the back of her head.

"That's because you did," Ivy said from where she leaned over the bassinet, changing a diaper.

"A baby? What in heaven's name is going on around here?"

"Long story," Ivy said as she handed the baby to her mother and went to wash her hands. Older lady and baby each stared at the other with an expression somewhere between bewilderment and curiosity.

Mrs. Long instinctively began to bounce the child. "I'm very sorry, Gabe, but my mind played tricks on me. I saw you there on the couch under that old quilt and for half a second I thought you were my late husband."

So that was "him." Good to know.

Wait. Ivy's mother was a widow, too? What were the odds of that?

As if sensing I might be about to ask a question she didn't want to answer, Mrs. Long changed the subject. "How's Lester doing with his hip?"

"He should graduate to a cane any day now."

"That's good, that's good," she murmured, now entranced by Zuzu.

She hadn't called Dad by that ridiculous Goat Cheese nickname, and I silently thanked her. She wore a caftan in a bright tie-dye pattern. Adelaide had loved those, too, but preferred floral patterns. No Christmas was complete unless she'd received at least two.

Holly stumbled down the hall. Ivy held out her hand to her sister and said, "Pay up."

Holly muttered something under her breath that rhymed with *witch* and took a five from her pocket to slap into Ivy's hand.

"What's that all about?"

Mrs. Long rolled her eyes and allowed me to guide her to a chair. "I have worked very hard to get rid of my accent."

I could tell because now she almost sounded like a midwestern news anchor.

"But if I'm tired or mad or surprised, then this one expression about stars and possibly garters slips out. Obviously I did a poor job of raising my children because they have made my slipups into an ongoing contest. If one of them can make me say that phrase, then the other has to pay up."

"The other day we argued at bedtime about hating each other," Holly said cheerfully.

"The other day?" I echoed at the same time Ivy grumbled, "More like every day."

"It's a ridiculously common occurrence," Mrs. Long said while Ivy prepared a bottle.

'Then you must have a lot of money circulating," I said.

Holly shrugged. "We mainly pass the same five back and forth. Unless . . ."

"Unless what?" I asked as Ivy appeared, shaking the formula and gesturing for her mother to hand Zuzu over. She shot a dirty look to her sister and shook her head no.

Holly forged ahead into the conversation anyway. "If Ivy can get me to say that expression or vice versa, then the payoff is a fifty."

I whistled. "That's pretty steep. So let me get this straight: If one of you says 'oh my stars,' then the other gets a US Grant?"

"Yep," said Holly.

"Never going to happen." Ivy shifted the baby into a burping position.

"Never say never." Holly's mouth curved into an almost evil smile.

Ivy turned to her mother. "Would you mind making a pot of coffee? Then we can talk about why Gabe and a baby were in the living room."

"I'll get it," Holly said. Ivy's eyebrow rose in surprise, but Holly bounced into the kitchen and put on a pot of coffee before mixing up something green in the blender.

Once she'd finished making noise, Ivy told her mother about finding the baby the night before and then going to the hospital to pick her up. She left out the part where the nurse mistook us for a couple.

"Are you the father?" Mrs. Long asked, her eyes shrewd.

"No," I sputtered. That didn't even make sense. "I was there when Ivy found Zuzu."

And I had a hand in the baby being in Ivy's custody, but no one needed to know that.

"Zuzu? What kind of name is that?"

"One that I picked out to use until we find out her real name," Ivy said, her pats eliciting a burp from the baby.

"Told you it was a stupid name," Holly said through a yawn.

"I don't understand. Why did they give the baby to *you?*"

"I'm not really sure," Ivy said with a frown. "Maybe because I found her?"

Or because I meddled in a young caseworker's affairs. Whichever.

Mrs. Long's questions continued like rapid fire. "Well, how long is she going to be here?"

"I don't know."

"I knew we had to prepare for the annual home visits, but you said you never expected anything to come of it."

"Well, I didn't," Ivy said. "After Byron, I didn't think I'd get another chance. Even this time, I think it's temporary."

"You think? You don't know?"

Before Ivy could answer, Mrs. Long turned on me. "And you just happened to be at the Nativity scene and then the hospital and now on my couch?"

"Mom!" Ivy shouted.

Holly snickered.

I smiled because doing so when a parent questioned me tended to disarm them. Today was no exception. "I rode with the baby to the hospital without thinking about how I'd get home. Ivy offered to give me a ride, but she was so preoccupied with everything that she drove straight here. Then I fell asleep on the couch while she was feeding the baby."

"Uh-huh," Mrs. Long said before turning to Ivy again. "The next time you plan on bringing a man or a child into this house I will need a heads-up."

"It all happened so fast, and you'd already gone to bed."

"Oh, don't give me that. One minute you and your sister were carrying on about tinsel, and the next thing I know you've brought a strange baby home. And after I told you to behave."

Wow. Might be time for me to leave. Hard to believe an adult child would let a parent talk to her like that.

My phone buzzed, and I saw that it was Dad before I answered. I considered putting my phone back into my pocket, but I might as well face the music.

"Where are you? The goats need milking. Don't tell me you ran away from home just because—"

Yep. Hard to believe an adult child would let a parent talk to him like that, indeed. "Dad, I didn't run away from home. I'm an adult and don't have to—"

"Well, I hope that piece of tail was worth scaring your old man half to death."

I put my hand over the receiver, hoping none of the ladies heard his insult. "I think I need to step outside to take this."

Chapter 17
Ivy

Once Gabe closed the door behind him, I turned back to my mother. "Mom, I'm a grown woman, and I would appreciate it if you wouldn't chew me out in front of my friends."

And that sentence sounded exactly like something I would've said as a teenager.

You can come home again—just not as an adult.

"*Friend*, is that what we're calling it these days?" asked Holly as she waggled her eyebrows.

Mom ignored us both. "This is temporary, right? You aren't seriously keeping this baby, are you?"

"I don't know. Is Holly keeping—?"

Holly shot me the dirtiest look, and I had to improvise on the fly. "Her Cheer Bear. Because Zuzu might need it."

My sister scowled in outrage. "She can't have my lovie!"

"Again I ask, thirty-seven or three?"

Mom put a hand on my cheek and physically turned my face so I was looking at her instead of my sister. "Ivy Genevieve, are you keeping this baby?"

I handed Zuzu a crinkly cloth book. "Corey and I were on the foster to adopt list," I said as I sat back down at the table. "I'm still on that list, but this is probably a temporary placement until they can find a couple who's looking to adopt."

She closed her eyes. "Thank goodness."

"What do you mean, 'thank goodness'?"

She fixed me with a stare. "You can't seriously think it's a good idea for you to adopt a child, can you? You're barely making above minimum wage."

"The state helps," I said, omitting the part about how state funds go away the minute you officially adopt.

"I just think you should wait until you're more . . . settled."

I spewed my coffee, almost choking on an involuntary laugh. "Settled? Some people would argue I'm a little too settled."

Two years ago, we'd moved in with Mom—until Corey had gone to hospice anyway. I needed help taking care of my husband, and I didn't want to live in the Memphis house that reminded me of Byron anymore. Even now there were boxes in the closet I hadn't unpacked. I wanted to leave, but I also hadn't found the where-withal to make enough money to make such a move possible.

"Now, Ivy, I don't want to see you hurt the way you were when that other baby—"

"Byron. His name is Byron."

Mom waved her hand in a gesture that reminded me of Granny Bess. "I remember how you felt when Byron's mom showed up. What are you going to do when they find a more permanent situation for Zuzu?"

I swallowed hard. "I'll have to cross that bridge when I get there. At least this time I am wise to the fact that Zuzu will probably be going to another home."

"Well, I hope to goodness you know what you're doing," Mom said.

Zuzu saved me from responding by taking care of her morning constitutional with an unladylike grunt. I was so concerned about getting the baby changed I must not have heard Gabe coming back in.

"Hey, I gotta go," he said as he leaned over my shoulder while I was finishing up with the diaper. For a second, I thought he was going to kiss me on the cheek. No, I'd missed that opportunity. He was simply checking on the baby.

"Seems to me you're always just in time to miss the diaper change," I teased.

He scooped up a freshly changed Zuzu. "Yet another part of my devious plan. I didn't go to evil medical school for nothing."

"Is that what I did wrong? Skip out on *evil* medical school?" I asked as I disposed of the diaper and washed my hands. Again. Hand washing was, apparently, going to be a big thing for a while.

He never answered. Instead I found him making faces at Zuzu until she smiled.

"I gotta go, little lady. You be good," he said to her. She made a sound somewhere between a giggle and a gurgle, and my heart squeezed in on itself as I took in the tableaux of the tall handsome man holding a tiny laughing baby.

"So soon?" Mom asked.

Holly and I looked at her and then each other, using our sister telepathy to ask, *Didn't she move pretty quickly from "Bring my smelling salts—it's a man!" to "So soon?"—complete with fluttering lashes.*

Apparently, she'd been taken in by the sight of man and child also.

"Afraid so," Gabe said as someone honked a horn outside. He transferred Zuzu into my arms and hesitated only a second before heading to the door.

"I still don't know how you're going to take care of this baby and go to work," Mom said the minute the door closed behind him.

"The same way millions of other mothers do." I didn't sound too confident and, honestly, I had no idea how many—if any—accredited daycares were in Ellery. Surely Mavis could accommodate me for a week or two.

During December? Yeah, right.

Or I could finally get off my lazy butt and look for a job commensurate with my education.

I'd settled on the Dollar General because I needed something to do after Corey passed. Or, more accurately, Mom called Mavis to get a job for me because I couldn't seem to make myself leave the house to look for one. Not one of my prouder moments. Mavis and Mom had known each other since playing together as children, and Mavis had offered me a job as a favor to Mom to get me off the couch and away from HGTV shows about houses I couldn't afford, complete with couples who bickered over stupid stuff instead of being glad that they had each other. She didn't mean for me to work for her for quite so long, but inertia was a powerful thing. No external force had set me in motion, so, once Mavis and I had come to an understanding, I'd gone into the Dollar General five days of every week for the past four years, punching my clock and doing my job.

Of course, I hadn't been the *best* employee. Mavis had told me three strikes and I would be out, and I was on my second strike already. In my defense, that first year had been particularly hard. I'd had a relapse last year but managed to put myself back together and hadn't missed a day since.

"And what if this arrangement is somehow permanent? How are you going to afford childcare on a retail salary?" Mom asked.

My stomach squeezed at the thought, the kind of inner somersault one felt in the first throes of love. Letting Zuzu go wasn't going to be pretty, but I couldn't afford to fall in love with her, either. "The state helps, and I'll start looking for a new job. *If* that happens."

I bounced the baby. Her eyelids had grown heavy once again. It was hard work for such a little baby to laugh and smile like she had. "Besides, you raised us all by yourself, and we turned out fine."

Mom snorted. So *that*'s where Holly got the habit. "Oh, yes. I did such a great job of raising you that you're both right back here."

Her bitterness took me aback.

"I can move out if you want me to."

She reached across the table and grabbed my hand. "No. I don't want you or your sister to move out. I guess I'm trying to say that motherhood is complicated and that I probably shouldn't be your role model."

"Mom—"

"Come on, Ivy. You know we had lean times and shitty Christmases. And that was with a nursing degree! Yours is in general studies. What are you going to do with that?"

"General things?"

"Smartass."

"I come by it honestly."

She muttered under her breath, then added, "I suppose you still have me and Holly on all of your paperwork?"

"Yep, and I'll see about a daycare, too."

"Is the state going to watch the baby if all of the daycares are full?" Mom asked.

This wasn't a possibility that I'd considered. "Well, I was hoping you and Holly could help me since it won't be for *that* long."

"Don't ask me," Holly said as she breezed back through the kitchen to put her cup in the sink and then head out the door for work. "My schedule is all over the place."

I opened my mouth to ask Mom, but she cut me off. "I'm too old to babysit."

She'd signed the paperwork. This couldn't have been that much of a surprise for her, and it wasn't like I was asking her to watch the baby so I could go take a mud bath and then get my nails done.

"I bet you'd watch a baby for Holly."

Mom gave me the arched eyebrow of doom, her mouth a thin line and her nostrils flaring. When she spoke, her voice was dangerously calm. "What would make you say a thing like that?"

I laid Zuzu down in the bassinet to avoid her stare. Might as well go ahead while we were airing our grievances despite the fact it wasn't yet December twenty-third. "You let her get away with everything."

"I do not!"

"Mom. The other night you ripped me a new one when you thought I'd bought icicles. Then Holly fessed up, and you told her to remember the tongue lashing you'd given me."

"I didn't see the need to repeat myself."

"But I got in trouble for something I didn't even do, and that has been happening around here forever—especially since we were teenagers."

She cleared her throat. "I want you to think about what happened when you and your sister were teenagers."

As if I could forget. The year Holly turned sixteen, she had complained about a sore throat, and our pediatrician had taken Mom aside and whispered his suspicions. Sure enough, Mom caught Holly throwing up after supper when she thought we'd both gone out for a walk. Holly and Mom yelled at each other from one end of the house to the other, and I sat on the front porch cringing at how well their yelling penetrated the brick wall behind me. Holly ended up going into rehab for bulimia. Mom cried the whole time she was gone, and I avoided her as best I could.

Then when Holly came back, she could do no wrong because Mom was afraid she'd relapse.

Honestly, I was afraid my sister had recently transferred her bulimia to excessive exercise based on the late-night elliptical sessions that had become more and more frequent. But even if she had, she was a grown woman. What was I supposed to do with her?

I cleared my throat. "Mom, I understand that you don't want to upset her, but don't you think it's time to take off the kid gloves? Is it fair for you to yell at me for the same thing you didn't yell at her for?"

"I didn't see the need to repeat myself," Mom said, failing to see the irony in how she'd just repeated herself.

"Well, you didn't even apologize to me, and I told Holly that morning that I would get everything she wanted *except* those icicles."

"Did you?"

"I do pay attention, you know."

Mom grabbed my hand. "I know. I'm sorry I yelled at you last night."

The apology should've made me feel better, but it didn't. I felt a little worse, to tell the truth, because Mom might be apologizing for the night before but she wasn't apologizing for any of the years that had come before.

"Mom, taking care of Zuzu means a lot to me. I don't know why, and I don't know for how long. Could you please help me?"

She sighed. "I suppose I can help you."

"Well, I wouldn't want to put you out or anything."

"Look, little miss, I did not ask to have a baby in the house. I am old, and I do not feel well."

Her response surprised me. Mom didn't feel well? "But you're only sixty-six."

"Well, I feel like I'm ninety-six. That's part of the reason why I want you to quit smoking."

And we're back to me.

"I know it's not easy, but you don't want to be this out of shape, do you? And you need to find a job where you don't have to stand so much so your feet don't aggravate you. After all those years as a nurse, my heels are killing me. I can hardly walk—"

"The doctor said—"

"I do not care what that doctor said. I'm not going under the knife unless I absolutely have to. You forget: I used to work in a hospital and would like to avoid any kind of open wound there if at all possible."

"Fine. I'll talk Holly into watching Zuzu," I said with a sigh.

"Don't you overburden your sister. I'm already worried about her exercising too much."

So, Mom had noticed. Not only had she noticed my sister's overboard exercising, but she was still more willing to help my sister than to help me.

You don't have to take this.

But I did. Where else would I go?

I had to swallow my pride and ask for help until I could find a better job.

"I wish Holly had gone into something other than nutrition and personal training. It keeps the girl stewing," Mom said, running her hands one over the other as she stared at some point well beyond me.

Holly, Holly, Holly. It was always all about Holly.

Funny, really. In the Christmas song, they mention the holly first. For years, my little sister couldn't understand how I was the oldest. If her name came first in the song, then she should be the oldest. At least she was the most important—that much she had already figured out.

"Mom, Holly will be fine. Maybe it will give her something else to think about other than exercising."

"That would be good," Mom said, her expression brightening. "Well, maybe it will be nice to have a baby around the house again."

Resentment rose like bile. Oh, sure. *Now* taking in the baby was a good idea. If babysitting would benefit Holly, then Mom was all for it. Taking care of Zuzu for me wasn't enough.

Heck, Mom might've mentioned how having the baby around the house might be an inspiration for me to quit smoking. Or to get that better job. Or to cannonball into the dating pool.

I thought of the look on Gabe's face when I backed out from under the mistletoe. I didn't need to get back into the dating pool because I'd obviously forgotten how to swim.

I couldn't do anything about the dating or the job, and today didn't look like the day to quit smoking.

Funny, I'd missed last night's smoke in all of the drama and hadn't thought about my morning cigarette until I started talking with Mom about my sister.

Now, I craved it almost as though I needed two to make up for last night, too. "I'm going out for a smoke. Watch the baby, will ya?"

"This is how it begins," she grumbled, but she didn't recite her litany of all of the reasons I should quit smoking, one of her favorite diatribes.

I should be glad, but her silence screamed that she didn't love me as much as she loved my sister, which was a crazy thing to feel, but there it was. I grabbed my purse and walked quickly outside, careful not to let her see the tears sliding down my cheeks.

Chapter 18
Gabe

"Morning, Bubba."

"Do you have to call me that?" Julian pulled the truck on the main road and headed toward home. Well, toward that place where my father lived anyway.

"As long as you call me City Boy, then you will be Bubba," I said through a yawn.

"Fine."

"I guess I should be glad I have someone else to do dear ol' dad's bidding now."

Julian snorted.

We rode in silence the rest of the way and even sat in the truck for a few seconds after he killed the motor. Interesting. He didn't want to have this discussion, either. Good to know.

"Might as well get this over with," Julian said.

"Sure. Just as soon as you help me milk the goats."

He muttered under his breath but helped me get all of the goats up and milk them, and I had the pleasure of knowing both he and Dad were stewing in their own juices. I still wasn't quite sure how I felt about all of this, but at least it made sense for Julian to be hanging around.

Or it would've made sense if he and Dad had told me the truth right off. Finally, we'd taken care of the goats and checked on the other animals, so we headed inside to the little farmhouse I should've called home. Dad sat at the Formica table, his walker to the side. He'd been through a ridiculous amount of cigarettes.

His bottom lip trembled with rage. "Look here! I don't need to worry half the night—"

"Dad, I'm over forty. Save it."

His mouth snapped shut, and I half regretted what I'd said because he'd actually admitted to worrying about me, and that was new and exciting. Julian and I eyed each other. Who was supposed to sit where in this dysfunctional family dynamic? Growing up, Aunt Vi, Aunt Lois, and I each had our own seat, more through habit than declaration. I'd never had my own seat here.

Maybe it's high time I pick one.

I chose the seat across from my father, and Julian sat on the end.

"Dad, you have some explaining to do."

The old man squinted as he took a drag on his cigarette, looking from Julian to me and back again. "So, I'm guessing you've figured out that Julian here is your brother."

"Figured it out? I had my niece tell me last night. Kinda hurts that the two-year-old found out before me."

"She's three," Julian said.

"I don't care if she's thirty-three. The least you could've done was tell me before you told her."

Julian studied the floor.

"Oh, don't be so hard on the boy. Didn't either of us know until three years ago. Came as a bit of a shock," Dad said.

I slammed my hands down on the table. "You've both known for three years? Unbelievable."

Julian shrugged. "He didn't want me to tell you yet."

I stared at the younger man and now I couldn't see anything but family resemblance. Dammit, I looked a lot like these two jackasses. Maybe I'd keep this beard forever so no one else could see the similarities around the mouth and chin. Not much I could do about the nose. At least I had red hair instead of Julian's blond or Dad's white that was once almost as dark red as mine.

"I wanted to see if you two would get on before I told you."

Dad stubbed out his cigarette with his left hand while his right fingers danced nervously in front of the pack.

"What difference does that make? If we're related, we're related!"

Dad shrugged his shoulders. "Seemed like a good idea at the time."

I started to say, "Like the goats?" but I didn't. The goats actually had been a good idea at the time.

"I don't even understand how any of this is possible. I thought Adelaide didn't have any children and Mom died not too long after I was born. What the hell?"

"Well, I, uh, got . . ." Dad paused to clear his throat, and his leathery face took on a reddish tinge I'd never seen before. "It's complicated."

Complicated? According to Adelaide, it wasn't complicated. During the summers when I stayed with them, she'd entice me into the kitchen with cookies or cake or pie. I listened to all of her stories somehow understanding that she was trading sweets for companionship. She knew no young man could resist food.

One of her favorite stories to tell was the one of how she and Dad had met. She'd gone to Burger Paradise with her friends, and a group of guys had gathered there. Lester walked up to the cash register while she was paying for her burger and fries and said, "You're the woman I want to marry."

She'd taken one look at the wiry man with the already wizened face and laughed.

He'd said, "You can laugh now, but I'm not joking."

He'd brought her flowers, talked her into going to the fair with him. One night he'd even serenaded her, singing Elvis's "Can't Help Falling in Love" while strumming a guitar beneath her window. They'd married a month later.

Surely he didn't.

As unlikely a romantic hero as Dad was, I'd clung to Adelaide's story, inwardly smiling at the twinkle in her eye as she described Dad's off-key singing complete with her own warbly imitation. I didn't want that homespun love story to have been sullied. "Please tell me you didn't cheat on Adelaide."

"I would never," Dad sputtered. "I was kinda lost there for a while before I met her, though, I will tell you that."

Well, I couldn't toss stones at that particular glass house. I'd been a bit lost when I found out Brittany was cheating on me with the orthopedist. Oddly enough I hadn't missed her much recently—the idea of her, sure, but not her.

I leaned back in my chair and tried to imagine how I would've felt in Dad's shoes.

I couldn't.

Losing Brittany had left me lost for about ten weeks, not ten years, and I guess that should've told me how much he loved my mother versus how little I'd loved my first wife.

The first two weeks I'd spent all time not at work on my couch. The next couple of months I'd made up for lost bachelorhood by going out with several women, some of whom had come home with me. When that last one asked for a drawer after only two dates, I was over playing the field.

And I hadn't run around impregnating women.

"Now, son, if you're worried about your inheritance—"

"Whoa. Stop right there. I'm not concerned in the least with any inheritance. But I do have a question: If you're so keen to take in Julian, why didn't you send for me when you remarried?"

Dad's eyes bugged out.

"Just thought I'd ask while we're spilling family secrets."

Julian, who'd had the good sense to stay quiet up until this point, said, "It ain't like he raised me. Like he said, we only found out three years ago."

"Look, I come home and all of a sudden the two of you are awfully tight. He treats you more like a son than he's ever treated me."

Up until I said the words, I hadn't realized that even more than the deception, the feeling that Lester Ledbetter could be a father to someone, even though he'd chosen not to be mine, was what hurt most of all.

Sure I'd spent summers with Dad because Aunt Vi and Aunt Lois felt I needed a male influence, but Dad and I had never been close. Talking to Adelaide had always been easier. Quite a shame she'd passed on because she would've been able to unravel all this mess in such a way that didn't leave us emotionally raw and disjointed.

A slice of her chocolate pie wouldn't have been remiss, either.

"I guess Julian and I are more alike," Dad said finally.

"Well, whose fault is that?"

We stared at each other, neither one willing to give an inch after my last comment.

Julian shifted in his chair, and the creaking noise reminded us he was there. "It took me and Dad a while to get used to the idea, so I kinda wanted to get to know you before we broke the news."

"Ever consider how we could've gotten to know each other together? Maybe let me be surprised and awkward alongside the two of you?"

My half brother had the good grace to look away.

"There isn't another brother, is there? Or should Julian and I prepare for a third stooge?"

Dad's gazed downward, his eyes locked on his packet of cigarettes. He still hadn't answered my question about why he'd never sent for me. I could only guess he was happy to finally have a manly man country boy for a son instead of the uppity doctor son who'd been raised by his sisters to be too soft.

At least he had someone to go hunting with since I'd never taken to the sport. They could haul hay and swat mayflies together, maybe go on a father-son bonding trip to the feed store to get a salt block. In the future, they could definitely rustle cattle at dawn together.

This is why I'd told myself to stay in Memphis. As much as I'd wanted my father's approval, as much as I preferred country air to city pollution, I'd never fit in. Something about knowing the universe had sent my father a younger son who could do all of those country things, though, really chapped my hide.

"Keep your secrets, then," I muttered, leaving both father and brother at the table to think about what they'd done.

Chapter 19
Ivy

Thank goodness it was one of my two days off. Since Zuzu was in foster care, I had help through WIC, but I still had to make some calls and run some errands to get everything set up. I happily bounced her while on the phone or bundled her up as we ran around town.

She seemed a little fussy to me, but I had to admit I wouldn't be too pleased at having been abandoned, then poked and prodded in the hospital before being deposited with a stranger. Her forehead didn't feel warm and she had only a little mucus—not enough for me to brave the bulb syringe.

Corey had wielded the syringe when Byron got a cold. If eliminating snot had been an Olympic sport, my husband would've medaled. I smiled at the thought and reached into my purse for his letter, but I only touched it. I couldn't make myself open it.

When we got home from our outing, I fed her and put her down for a nap, thinking I might put myself down for a little nap, too. When I got my phone out of my purse, though, I saw I'd missed two calls, one from New York and the other local.

In my first voicemail, my beleaguered agent, Datya, had called to remind me that my final deadline was January third. I didn't want to call her. The second message informed me a social worker, one Yolanda Gibbons, would be coming to see me soon and to call her in the meantime if I had any problems.

I didn't want to call her, either.

Truth be told, I never wanted to call anyone anymore. After years of wrangling with insurance companies over incorrect bills—some of them the day after Corey's funeral—I didn't like talking on the phone anymore. Just as I'd nodded off, though, the traitorous device vibrated, and I saw that it was Datya calling me again.

Persistent, one reason I liked her.

I started to end the call and send her to voicemail, but then I thought of what my mother had said. *You made a promise.* I gritted my teeth.

Might as well face the music—or the printing press, as it were. "Hi, Datya."

Silence, then a sigh. "Know why I'm calling?"

"My renegotiated delivery date is January third?"

"Bingo. Any chance I'm going to have a manuscript on my desk?"

"Probably not?"

"And you realize that it will be considerably harder to sell your work in the future if you don't turn in this book?"

"I know."

"Okay, then."

More silence. "I'm sorry, Datya. I don't think I'll ever be able to write another book. I'm only weighing you down at this point."

My agent laughed, but there was no mirth to it. "Oh, Long. You're also not creating a lot of work for me, either. Maybe someday you'll change your mind and write me another great story."

Yeah, a story I wouldn't be able to sell without giving the publisher a right of refusal first. After missing a deadline with multiple extensions, said publisher would be less than amenable to even looking at my work.

Come on, now. Datya would find a way.

Yeah, but I shouldn't put her in that position.

Tears rolled down my cheeks at the thought of my agent's loyalty. "Thank you. Really."

"I can't begin to understand all that you've been through, but it would be a shame to quit now. Are you sure you can't turn in that second book to buy you some breathing room? Even if it's still a little rough around the edges? Maybe if they turn it down, then at least you'd have fulfilled your contract."

"I don't know."

"Come on now, didn't you have a chunk of that book written? The one where the duke pretended to be a vicar?"

I shook my head vehemently, forgetting that Datya couldn't see me. "Yes, but that book is crazy and it needs to never leave its coveted spot underneath the bed. I should've never pitched that idea."

"Ivy. You were over two-thirds of the way through with it. The first chapter is at the end of your last book."

"Read my lips: no new vicar story pages. That story is a train wreck. It's—"

Just the sort of thing no one would ever buy.

So it'd be like *The Producers*. A little. I slapped the arms of the recliner. "Datya, you're a genius."

"I know! Aren't you glad I have a mind like a steel trap? Wait. Why am I a genius?"

Zuzu cried—apparently, on the list of stupid things I'd done, slapping the arms of a leather recliner less than two feet from a sleeping baby ranked only slightly lower than writing a historical romance about a rake pretending to be a vicar.

"Is that a baby?"

"Yes," I drew out the word as though doing so would keep Datya from asking a follow up question. I should've known better.

"Why is there a baby?"

"Um, I may or may not be a foster parent to said baby."

I heard a thud on the other end of the line. I hoped it wasn't Datya's head hitting her desk, but I wouldn't take any bets on it.

"Okay. Look. It's the thirteenth of December. You have twenty-one days to finish that story and get it to me so I can get it to them, and they can think we're both clinically insane."

"But what if they decide they want to publish it?"

"Then yay. The goal this time isn't to make a sale, but I can't stand the thought of your being locked into contractual red tape because you missed one deadline. Not after everything else you've been through. Besides, finishing this one might be what you need to get you back into the habit of writing historical romances that someone *will* want to buy."

I put the phone between ear and shoulder and picked up the baby. "Datya it's *awful.*"

"Hon, that's really not your call to make."

"I don't know if I can do this and take care of Zuzu and work around this hectic Christmas schedule."

"But it's also Hanukkah. May your midnight oil not run out so we have another miracle on our hands."

Oh, it would take a miracle for me to finish this book, much less to sell it. Then again, Datya had once told me that her name meant faith or belief in God. The hair on the back of my neck stood up, but I refused to see this as a sign.

You don't believe in signs anymore, remember?

My self was finding that harder and harder to remember.

There were a hundred reasons why I should've said no, a tiny infant not the least among them, but I heard myself say, "Okay."

"Okay? So crazy vicar book will be on my desk by January third, right? No. January first."

"That's New Year's Day!"

"And? I need time to read it before I send it in, and that's pushing it."

"Fine."

"Don't overthink this, Long."

"But overthinking is what I do best," I said automatically.

"Today's a good day to stop, then. Ciao."

I said my goodbyes, realizing that overthinking was what I *used* to do best. Then I'd gone through a few years of not thinking much at all. I disconnected the call and flung the phone to the couch before whispering, "Zuzu, what have I gotten myself into?"

* * *

Zuzu had no answers for me, but she did take a long afternoon nap that allowed me to bring out the old manuscript and flip through it. Unfortunately, my long neglected laptop appeared to be dead. I had hoped a low battery would be the culprit, but there it say in the corner of the dining room, plugged in but doing nothing.

Someone banged on the door, and I looked up to see two silhouettes beyond the curtains that covered the windows of the back door. One of them was too tall to be my mother. I sucked in a breath at the murmur of a voice distinctly lower than that of my sister.

Sure enough, Gabe followed Holly in, the two of them laughing over something. Did everyone have to like her better than me? About that time, Zuzu whimpered, and I waved at the two, hurrying to the play yard. I caught his woodsy winter scent even before I felt his presence behind me.

"Thought I'd check on Zuzu," he said.

"She's a little fussy, but appears to be okay," I said, backing away so he could pick her up. "Why don't you change her, and I'll get a bottle."

He chuckled. "I see what you did there. But you're on."

As I walked into the kitchen I cut my eyes to Holly, who leaned against the counter drinking water. Through sister telepathy I asked, *What is he doing here?*

She shrugged in response.

While I fed the baby, Gabe said nothing, but restlessness rolled off him.

"What brings you over? Besides checking on the world's cutest baby?"

"Mainly wanted to see how you and Zuzu were getting along," he said.

I didn't ask him to elaborate on the other reason he'd dropped by because he clearly didn't want to talk about it.

"Well, I guess I'd better go," he said as Zuzu finished her formula and I moved her to a burping position over my shoulder.

I instinctively stood to see him to the door. Zuzu burped, and

I shifted her into more of a cradled position. Gabe stopped in the doorway between the spindles, studying the piles of manuscript laid out on the dining room table. "What's this?"

"Oh, that's my book," I said.

"You're a writer? That's so neat."

I moved to stand beside him. "I foolishly promised I'd try to fix it before the year ended."

"Aw, snap. You two are under the mistletoe."

We both looked at Holly over by the sink, her smile entirely too smug. "Come on now. You know what to do."

Wondering if Gabe could possibly be as embarrassed as I was, I chanced looking up. Sure enough, his cheeks shone faintly pink above his beard.

Then again, my gut had told me to kiss him last time, and I should've listened.

"Well, I guess a tradition is a tradition," he said.

He leaned closer, and my eyes naturally closed. The world moved in extreme slow motion, my heart beating ninety to nothing.

But then my lips lightly brushed a beard that was quickly moving past, and I opened my eyes in time to see him gently kiss Zuzu's forehead.

Of course.

How could I be so stupid? Why would he kiss me, the weird widow who smoked when he could kiss the adorable baby and still satisfy Holly's pot stirring?

"See you this evening," he said, his eyes not meeting mine. I stood frozen in mortification under the mistletoe. Not only had I just embarrassed myself but I also had to be at the drive-through Nativity in less than two hours.

God, I want a cigarette.

Or maybe a Valium.

"Yeah, this evening," I said to his retreating back.

I put Zuzu down, still vibrating from embarrassment and no small amount of nicotine withdrawal. I grabbed my smokes, a lighter, and the baby monitor and headed for the back door. Holly stood with her arms crossed at the back door.

"What?"

"Just wanted to see if you were okay."

"No. I'm not okay."

"I'm sorry. I didn't mean to embarrass you. Really."

"Well, that's what you did. Now can I have a smoke before I have to go face the man who thinks I'm too repulsive for so much as a kiss on the cheek?"

"The way he's been looking at you, I thought he would kiss you. I was trying to help," Holly said.

"Apparently you're not good at interpreting looks. Now let me go and please watch the baby."

She stepped aside, but I paused before opening the back door. "On a scale of 'didn't even notice' to 'I can't be in his presence ever again,' how bad was it?"

"Oh, he noticed."

I groaned.

Outside I savored my cigarette, drawing it out as long as I possibly could in the hopes of stopping the shakes and the silent tears that streamed down hot cheeks. So much for quitting today.

Chapter 20
Gabe

A tiny swath of my cheek tingled from where Ivy's lips had touched my cheek and then my beard. Not really. I knew physically there was no way I could still be feeling her kiss, but mentally and emotionally? That was another thing altogether. I half wanted to throw up at the thought of her embarrassment when I kissed Zuzu instead.

Why didn't I just kiss Ivy on the cheek? Now she thought I had something against her. But I didn't. She'd so clearly not wanted me to kiss her at the hospital. Besides, it felt weird kissing another man's wife.

Another man who is dead. Gabe, what is your problem?

So many problems. Holly had caught me off guard, and I'd only stopped by the Long residence to avoid going home because I didn't want to put up with Dad or Julian. Now I'd managed to alienate the one person who could've provided me with sanctuary from those two.

I pulled into the driveway and banged the truck's steering wheel, but I couldn't get the moment out of my head. She'd closed her eyes, her trusting lips parting ever so slightly, but then I'd thought of her wan face at the hospital. I almost kissed her cheek, but then I saw the baby and went for her forehead, thinking that a much safer bet. Maybe Ivy didn't want to kiss me. Had her sister ever thought of that? Now I'd embarrassed us both and we still had two nights together at the Nativity.

Maybe I should find someone else to play Joseph.

Don't be a coward, Ledbetter.

I needed to take my lumps and finish my commitment. Honestly, wasn't Holly the one to blame? Neither Ivy nor I even realized where we were standing until she pointed it out. It was an excellent argument for not putting up Christmas decorations, that much I knew.

I jumped out of the truck, slamming the heavy door behind me, pausing because I'd jumped right out of the frying pan of idiocy into the fire of awkward situations. I did not want to enter that house.

But enter it I did, and my reward was a sweet whirlwind running down the hall and throwing herself into my arms with the trust of a child who knew nothing yet of the stupidity adults could concoct.

"Uncle Gabe!"

"Hey, how's my favorite niece today?" I asked as she kissed my cheek, then turned her head so quickly that her hair ran through my mouth.

She wanted down, and once there, crossed her arms and looked up at me with her face screwed up. "How many nieces do you have anyway?"

I fought back a smile. "One."

She thought about it for a second and then grinned and hugged me around the legs before running outside.

When I entered the kitchen, Romy was leaned against the counter with a glass of water in her hand. "Thanks for not taking out any of this on her."

"I couldn't do that," I said.

"For the record, I told both of them that they should tell you as soon as the DNA test came back." She fixed a stare on Dad, who studied the refrigerator.

"You're still going to the Nativity, right?"

Oh, yes. Between my new brother and the woman I've unintentionally spurned, it's sure to be a blast. "I guess."

"Well, thank you for not backing out. Although"—Romy paused, wincing as she picked her words—"if you want to be on time, you might want to help Julian with that chicken coop he's making."

"Chicken coop?"

Dad finally spoke, his voice rusty. "Got some chickens, didn't you?"

"Ah, yes."

"Can't keep 'em cramped up in that cage, you know."

Not being an expert on chickens, I hadn't given it much thought. I sighed. Apparently, I was going out to the barn to help with a chicken coop.

Romy nodded her head in the direction of the barn.

"Fine. I'm going."

As I got closer to the barn, the pounding of the hammer got louder and louder. I told myself not to close my eyes every time the hammer hit because I didn't need to give my father and brother any other excuse to make fun of me. I found Julian and the frame to a modest chicken coop to the left of the milk barn under a poplar tree. I tamped down some jealousy at the idea that he'd built this coop from scratch; that required a different skill set from mine but an important one nonetheless.

"I guess I should say thank you," I finally said.

"Least I could do," he said.

He'd finished the frame, so I picked up the roll of chicken wire that was leaning against the trunk of the tree. I held it in place while he stapled. We were halfway around the coop before he said, "I'm sorry I didn't tell you first thing."

"Thank you."

"If you're going to be mad at someone, be mad at me instead of him. Especially right now."

"What do you mean right now?"

Julian looked up at me in surprise. "It's his first Christmas without Adelaide."

I had to give my new baby brother that. I'd been too wrapped up in myself to really think about what that might mean for Dad.

Julian went back to work. "He's not happy about his hip, and he doesn't even want to talk about Christmas. Adelaide did all of that. Wouldn't even take the Christmas cookies Romy brought. He's been talking about selling the goats again, maybe even the farm."

Everything clicked into place. I'd thought Julian was trying to usurp my place. Instead, he'd seen a lonely old man who was giving up on everything and had tried to keep things running for him. "I never have thanked you for keeping the place going until I could get here."

"You're welcome," Julian said as we moved to the third side. "Lester's a lot better than the asshole who raised me, so I figured it was the least I could do."

There was that phrase again—*the least he could do*. I could think of plenty of people who could, and often did, do less.

"I mean, it's not like I've got a fancy degree or anything."

I laughed. "And I wouldn't know where to begin with a chicken coop."

He grinned a little. "Then maybe we're not as mismatched a pair as we thought."

"Maybe."

By the time we'd finished with the chicken wire and added a roost and some nesting boxes, I had another question for Julian. "What do you mean, Dad thought about selling the goats and the farm?"

"Oh, he thought it wasn't something you'd ever want, but I could see he didn't want to do it. He's got every one of those goats named, you know. Then I found the llama and alpaca, and he got a kick out of them, so I picked up a sheep and those two donkeys. You helped me with the cows."

"He didn't even see those!"

Julian smiled. "Naw, but he sure did get a kick out of my story about how you shooed them into the trailer. Laughed so hard he went into a fifteen-minute coughing jag."

A little of the "City Boy" made sense. I still didn't like it, but I could see Julian using my ineptitude to amuse our father in an attempt to cheer him up. He'd also mentioned that he didn't have a "fancy degree," so no doubt he felt as defensive about my education as I'd been feeling about his country boy skills.

"What are you going to do with all of these animals?"

"I don't know," Julian said with a shrug. "I couldn't stand to see them suffering, and we didn't have any room over at our place because Uncle Charlie's contesting the will, and I've lost my share of the McElroy place. Hank's land is pretty full, and Lester didn't seem to mind so . . ."

"So you started a sanctuary?"

"Must run in the family since you're the one who took in these chickens."

I laughed. "But that was an accident."

Not only that, but it had cost a fair amount of money to get the materials for that coop, and the chicken feed had looked like it would add up over time. If it cost that much for a few chickens, how much more did it cost for the goats and donkeys and llamas and . . .

"Where do you get the money to feed all of these animals?" I asked.

"I cut a lot of hay over the summer, and I mean a lot of it. Romy was complaining about being a hay widow. Maybe that's why it took so long for her to get pregnant. Between the haying and the wife's demands, I was one exhausted sonuvabitch." Even as he said it, contentment oozed from him, and I was seized with an irrational jealousy for a man I'd despised not ten minutes before.

"Too much info, Bubba." That twinge of jealousy made me use the moniker he didn't like, but it still came out softer than I'd intended.

He pointed at me. "You need to get yourself a good woman. I know there was a time I thought I didn't need one, but I was wrong."

"Can I get that on tape? I bet Romy and I could both use those last three words."

"City Boy," he said with a laugh. "I will not tell you a lie. A good woman makes everything better."

"I had a woman," I finally said.

"I'm guessing she wasn't a good one or you'd still have her."

"Good call." I cleared my throat because I didn't want to talk on this subject anymore. "Thank you for building the coop. Really."

"You're welcome."

We might not be best friends, but we'd taken a baby step beyond civility.

I sensed a presence behind me and turned around to come face-to-face with the llama leaning over the fence, her chin almost on my shoulder and her alpaca at her side.

"It's like she has a mini-me," I told Julian.

"They both want apples. You'll be their best friend if you dice up some for them." He tossed a pocketknife and then the apple he'd brought out with him.

Apples. I could do that. I scratched the llama's head. "You said you didn't like to see animals suffer and that you brought them all here to amuse Dad, but where did you get a llama and an alpaca?"

Julian sighed. "See, these jerks a few counties over thought they were going to make all this money with an alpaca farm. They got Deanna there to be the herd protector, and she took her job seriously. She wouldn't eat until all of her little alpacas did. She patrolled the perimeter of the fence to kill off snakes and scare off other predators."

"What happened to the other alpacas?" I asked as I sliced up the apple, feeding the pieces to one and then the other.

"Oh, they sold all of them. The new owner didn't want a llama, and Teresa was hiding somewhere when they rounded the others up. No one found her until the new owners had left. So then poor Deanna mourned the loss of her herd. Loudly. When she found Teresa she guarded her so fiercely that the owners called ol' Pete Gates, but he doesn't like llamas so he called me. Idiots who owned them didn't understand that Deanna was simply doing her job. Took me forever to win her trust. I felt like the damn llama whisperer, but then one day she took to the halter, and the little one did, too. I brought them here, and here we are."

It was hard to be mad at my brother when I had this ridiculous vision of him sitting in a pasture somewhere in the lotus position communing with llamas. From the beginning I'd misread him. He wasn't out for money, and he was smarter than he looked—especially when it came to animals.

I sliced up the last of the apple, but now I had a sheep, some goats, and even one of the donkeys approaching. "I can't decide if I'm a modern Dr. Dolittle or if I'm living an awkward alternate universe version of *Green Acres*."

"Neither. You just have an apple."

"Yeah, yeah," I said as I scratched the donkey's head. I couldn't tell if it was Donna or Dawn. I was going to have to get the donkeys ribbons similar to the chains the goats wore so I could tell the two apart.

You've lost your mind, Gabe.

"How'd you get the rest of these animals?"

"Well, lots of people think they want to farm and then they change their minds. Or, in the case of those jennies, Dad bought Donna as a foal to look after the goats. Dawn came with the sheep. Both she and the ewe were so poorly I was afraid they would die, but I nursed them back to health."

Huh. Maybe medicine ran in the family, too.

"Maybe you ought to open a rescue farm, set it up as a tax-exempt organization."

Where had that come from?

"A what?"

"A 501c3 tax-exempt organization so you can collect money to help you pay for these animals." If we took video of Julian telling the stories of how these animals had been mistreated, then showed them as fat and sassy as they were now, then people would be willing to help fray the cost so my new sister-in-law didn't have to be a hay widow.

The man in question took off his hat and wiped sweat from his brow, more from habit than from the weather being warm enough to cause sweat. "I don't know, City Boy. That sounds complicated."

"I'll look into it for you," I heard myself say.

He nodded, but his expression suggested he didn't think much would come of my offer. "Let's milk the goats, then get the animals into the trailer for tonight."

I nodded, and we headed for the barn.

How had I gone from a sought-after pediatrician to a guy who milked goats and worked for chickens? From now on I'd even be thinking about bringing chunks of apple out into the pasture to share with my favorite llama. I considered buying ribbons for donkeys. Now I was about to put on robes and play Joseph in a faux Nativity.

And you're having more fun than you were in Memphis—even with your new super-secret brother and the woman you didn't kiss.

Maybe *fun* wasn't the right word, but I felt more alive.

I touched the cheek Ivy's lips had grazed, wishing I could go back in time and kiss away that look of hurt.

But, yes, definitely more alive.

Chapter 21
Ivy

I killed the engine and looked in the rearview mirror only to realize that rear-facing car seats meant I couldn't see Zuzu. I could, however, hear her.

"Think I can do this, Zuzu?"

She gurgled in response.

"That's easy for you to say. He actually kissed you."

She cooed this time.

"Don't rub it in, but I suppose I should try to salvage what's left of my dignity, huh?"

Her babble ended in a fuss, and I got out of the car since delaying the inevitable would do nothing but make me late. Lydia wanted a picture of the baby in the manger, and Mom couldn't babysit until after ten because it was Bunco night. Holly wasn't answering her phone, and I could only hope she was off making good choices. Gabe couldn't have watched Zuzu even if I'd been willing to ask, so I'd made the executive decision to bring Zuzu along to play the part of Jesus.

When I reached the stable, Lydia was already there with hands on her hips. Blessedly, Gabe was not.

"Oh, look at you," she said to Zuzu, who smiled for her as if she sensed this was her big moment. Lydia took pictures of the baby in the manger, then the baby in my arms. By the time she finished, everyone else had arrived, and Julian was leading the animals to their places. Aside from a nod, I ignored Gabe.

The canned carols started, and cars rolled past. Zuzu surprised us all by falling asleep.

"I hope this doesn't mean she won't sleep through the night," I muttered, careful that my head didn't move enough to disrupt the tableaux for those driving by.

"She'll be fine," Gabe said.

I said nothing. He might be a medical professional, but I neither wanted nor needed his advice.

"Ivy, about earlier today—"

"Pipe down, you Nazarenes!"

Romy was kidding, but I was grateful for an excuse not to continue the conversation. She yelped, and I could guess Julian had goosed her again. He'd traded places with Ben so he could stand behind his wife and had been known to pinch her posterior if she became too much of a stickler for the rules.

Meanwhile, the llama had taken quite a shine to Ben and kept nudging him while Kathy the goat circled him, occasionally nibbling the edge of his tunic.

When we finally took a break later, Ben found Julian. "Look, cowboy, you have to be a shepherd and handle your animals. That goat is getting a little too personal with me. The llama, too."

Julian grinned. "Yeah, but Deanna likes you, and she is a very discriminating llama."

"Whatever. Hand me my crown. I'm sending you back to your livestock."

I turned to Romy. "Do you think this is how the first Nativity went down?"

"I'm not sure you could get more cantankerous than those two," she said, walking over to a large orange cooler with a spigot to get some water. I thought about doing the same, but I didn't want to leave Zuzu. Also, Gabe stood over there.

I had hoped he would stay with the others until time was called, but he came back early and took his place across from me. "About earlier—"

"What about it?" I asked with the best smile I could muster.

"I didn't want you to think—"

"Oh, I haven't given it a second thought."

I hoped my pants didn't catch fire from the lie.

"Really?"

"Really." No need to let him think he'd bothered me.

He opened his mouth to say something, but Zuzu chose that moment to wail, then passed the gas bubble that must have awakened her. Gabe started to speak again, but she dirtied her diaper. "Hey, Miss Idabell? I know it's time to start again, but I need to change Zuzu's diaper. I should probably take her home, too, since it's pretty chilly tonight."

Miss Idabell threw her hands up. "Never work with children or animals they say. Here I am trying to work with both. Can you find someone to hand her off to? We can't do this without a Mary, and I don't have an extra shepherd to move over to the Wise Men and—why does this all have to be so difficult?"

Out of the corner of my eye, I saw Holly talking to Lydia. Not only did I see Holly, but I remembered something: My sister had always wanted to play the part of Mary in the children's program at church. The one year she was finally set to play the mother of Jesus was the year she came down with the chicken pox and had to stay home. Instead of handing the baby to Holly, I could have Holly play my part. "I might have someone."

"I don't care who it is as long as you make it fast."

I scooped up Zuzu and moved as quickly as I dared to the awning of the Dollar General where my sister leaned against the building. Lydia had moved over to the cooler but was still in earshot. "Baby sister, how would you like to play Mary?"

"Uh, okay?"

"It's either that or change this poopy diaper."

"I don't care for these choices," she said.

"Look, I don't have time to argue. I need to take care of Zuzu and Miss Idabell needs a Mary."

I looked into her eyes with what I hoped was a pleading expression of *please don't make me go back out there and sit next to the man who didn't kiss me, especially since you're the one who orchestrated the whole scenario that shattered my self-esteem.*

She nodded. "Mary, it is."

Sister telepathy was alive and well if one look could convey so much and get Holly to agree without arguing.

"Hold Zuzu, will you?"

Holly held the baby out from her body as if the child were toxic. "Wait. I don't know how to be Mary."

"Well," I said as I pulled my robes over my head. "I have good news and bad news. The good news is you only have to sit there. The bad news is you have to figure out how to look beatific while you do it."

"Very funny."

Once out of my robes I whispered, "Any word on whether or not you are 'with child'?"

"No, and thank you for reminding me."

"You need to take a test," I said.

"I have. And you don't need to be so loud. Isn't there someone else who could do this?" she asked even as she put on the robes.

"Just do me this solid. Gabe is trying to 'explain' things, and it's painful," I said as I took the baby, careful to both support her head and not redistribute the contents of her diaper. "Besides, you wanted to play Mary in the fifth-grade play but didn't get to. Here's your chance."

My younger sister studied me. "You remember that?"

"I was afraid Santa was going to get me confused with you and not leave me any toys because you pitched such an unholy hissy fit."

"I did not!"

Since it was a knee-jerk response, the byproduct of years and years of bickering, I simply waited.

"Fine. I did."

"Yeah, you did. It's a wonder we still have glass in the house after all of your shrieks."

"Stop while you're ahead," Holly said as she drew the head covering over her hair. "You *were* being nice."

She dashed out and took her spot before I could tell her not to get used to it.

I sighed and looked down at my towheaded baby. "I'd ask what they've been feeding you, but I already know the answer to that. How about we find a place to clean you up?"

I thought Zuzu might fall asleep in the car on the way home, but I was mistaken. Her big blue eyes remained open, her sweet Cupid's bow mouth twisted into a grimace. She'd even begun to fuss off and on. I tossed both purse and diaper bag over my shoulder, then tried to release the car seat from its base without having the bags come flying around and hit the baby. How did moms do this without feeling like a total bag lady? Also, the next time a bag slid off my shoulder and landed hard in the bend of my elbow, I was going to drop an eff bomb because that sudden pressure hurt like a sonuvagun.

"Now, now," I told the baby as I juggled carrier and bags to find the house keys. Mom still wasn't back from Bunco so the back door remained locked. At least it was easier to maneuver the car seat through the garage since it was empty. Finally, I found my keys and juggled all of my bags so I could unlock the door.

First the citrus and spice potpourri assailed me. Then I noticed the garland draped in loops from the kitchen ceiling. A mound of decorated sugar cookies sat on a plate in the middle of the dining room table.

Holly—because it had to be Holly—had decorated the entire house. She'd cut snowflakes from typing paper and put Mom's antique train around the bottom of the tree. She'd hung our stockings from the mantle over the old wood stove, and there was the Nativity scene, complete with errant penguins!

Then I really saw the tree.

If I had been thinking that my sister was a selfless and mature soul, I had to reverse that opinion because the Christmas tree was so covered in icicles that I couldn't even see the ornaments. Mom was going to lose her mind when she saw it, and this time I planned to pop some popcorn and enjoy the hell out of it.

Chapter 22
Gabe

When Holly showed up with a blithe "Today the part of Mary will be played by . . ." I chuckled. I also missed Ivy, which made no sense because I should've been relieved. I'd been trying to apologize to Ivy all night, but I couldn't find the words because I didn't know what I was apologizing for.

"Thanks a lot for putting me in an awkward position earlier," I said under my breath, trying to be quiet enough that Romy wouldn't yell at us this time.

"Not my problem you didn't have the good sense to kiss her."

"Maybe she didn't want to be kissed and maybe I didn't want to kiss her—you ever think of that?"

"No. I thought it would do Ivy some good to get even a peck, something to build up her confidence."

"Why?"

"The woman hasn't gone on a single date since Corey passed," Holly said, her voice a little too loud.

Romy cleared her throat, and we sat in silence.

"What are my chances of a mistletoe mulligan?" I asked finally.

Holly chuckled, but without mirth. "No way she's standing under mistletoe with you again."

I sighed deeply and we listened to a warped version of "Carol of the Bells" as cars passed.

"I guess it's just as well," Holly finally said. "I wouldn't want you coming through here and charming her with your hipster beard and your way with babies only to run back to Memphis and take up with a model or something."

Hipster beard? Take up with models?

In all fairness you did that second one once.

"I'm not a hipster!"

"But you did hook up with a model, I bet."

"Yeah, but it didn't last. You happy?"

Her smile faded. "Not really."

We sat through an awful instrumental "Do You Hear What I Hear?" before Holly added, "She will probably need your help again with the baby, though. I don't know what she was thinking."

I didn't know what she was thinking, either. Or what I was thinking. With anyone else I would've told them already that I didn't work for free, but I suppose it was, as my half brother would say, the least I could do.

When I trudged into the farmhouse that evening, I was ready to go to bed, but Dad called from the living room. "Could you pop me some popcorn? I need to get this ice cream taste out of my mouth."

So that's how we would play it.

We were going to return to our usual routine of my doing for him and his not answering my questions.

I put the popcorn in the microwave and reached into the fridge for a beer. I'd earned a beer.

I considered letting his midnight snack burn, but I couldn't stand the smell of burnt popcorn, so I was a dutiful son and poured the perfectly popped Orville Redenbacher into a bowl and dropped it on the end table beside my father. I was already on the second step when he called to me.

"Just a minute there, Gabriel."

I turned around in time to see him click off the television.

"There are some things I reckon I ought to tell you."

When I plopped down into the couch, I sloshed my beer a little.

Dad looked at me as if he wanted one, but I didn't offer to go get him one.

"Well, Dad?"

He hesitated but then took as deep a breath as he could before blurting, "You were born around Christmas, and your mother and I couldn't decide what to name you."

My mouth ran dry. Dad never talked about Mom.

"She wanted to name you Joseph. I wanted to call you Lester Junior."

Thank you, Mom.

"The Sunday before Christmas the preacher read that passage in Luke about how it all went down in Bethlehem, and we looked at each other when he mentioned the angel Gabriel. The way your mama's eyes lit up, I knew I couldn't argue with her. Lucky for me I liked the name all right, and I think it suits you."

So we were going to do this. We were finally going to do this.

"Well, you were born on the nineteenth."

"Yep. A week from now."

Dad reached for his wallet in his back pocket, wincing as he twisted his body and torqued the still sore hip. He took out five crisp twenties. "Go buy yourself something nice. You know I don't shop."

I blinked at him, but finally reached out and took the money. "Thank you."

Since he'd always sent money for my birthday, the moment shouldn't be so awkward, but I'd never been in Ellery on my birthday so my present had always come in the form of a check. Except when I was truly little, though. Aunt Vi and Aunt Lois had taken the money to buy presents for me back then. Up until fifth grade, I thought my dad really knew me well. That's when he admitted that he sent money and didn't know what Teenage Mutant Ninja Turtles were, and he sure hadn't bought me any damn turtles. My two aunts had to confess, and the gig was up.

Just the beginning of a long line of disappointments from him.

Please don't give me money I don't need instead of telling me my story. Please.

He cleared his throat. "So you were due on Christmas Eve and your mama had the whole place decorated as if Santy Claus himself was coming see you. When she went into labor, we knew it was a little early, but we didn't think much of it. Your mama was never one to complain, and she'd only been to the doctor once or twice. Her mama told her that she didn't need to waste her money on appointments before the baby even got here. She'd had all her babies just fine, and she was sure your mama would, too."

"But she didn't," I said, feeling that old nausea that came from realizing my birth had killed my mother. No one had ever given me this much detail, but when I did that family tree project in third grade, I could see that my birthday was two days earlier than my mother's death day. Aunt Vi and Aunt Lois told me it wasn't my fault, but it was hard to believe them because I knew they would do anything to protect me. For years, I'd told myself that Dad sent me away because he blamed me for taking Mama from him, but then he married Adelaide and still didn't send for me. I decided he must not like me all that much.

"No, she didn't." His voice cracked. "I should've told you all this a long time ago, but I didn't want to relive it."

"You don't have to tell me if you don't want to," I said, even though I wanted to know. Desperately.

"It all ties back to your question to me, so I'm gonna tell it."

I nodded.

"Well, your mama was only nineteen and the prettiest little thing I'd ever seen. While she was pregnant, she just glowed. After you were born they finally let me in to see the two of you. She looked a little tired, but I still thought she was the most beautiful woman in the world. We had at least one good moment there with me holding her and her holding you. Then the doctors took you back to the nursery."

Dad stopped speaking and raised a trembling, gnarled hand to swipe at some tears. "I was going to stay right there beside her."

Maybe I didn't want to hear the story after all.

"And she—she told me to go on home because I smelled like cows. Said I needed a bath and a good soft bed instead of that hard chair in the corner. She was worried about me, you see. She'd been through labor for a long time, but she was still worried about me. The nurses had told her about how I was wearing out the waiting room carpet, so she knew I hadn't slept a lick."

He gave up on trying to catch the tears.

"So I went home. While I was sleeping soundly, she went into all of these seizures. They called me in the middle of the night, but she was gone by the time I got there."

We sat in silence. My forgotten beer was warm. His popcorn had to be cold.

"I went down to the nursery—because that's the way they did things back then—and I looked at you in your little bed. All of the other babies were squalling and red-faced. You slept through the whole thing, this calm little creature that was half me and half her. You didn't know you'd lost your mama.

"I knew I should take you home and at least try to take care of you, but men didn't do that sort of thing, and I couldn't afford to hire someone to take care of you while I worked. I was at the factory back then, and they didn't pay much. So I called my sister, Vi, and she and Lois came down to help me. They had been planning to come help your mama anyway.

"One day I came home, and Vi was rocking you and singing a lullaby. I looked at how good she was with you, and I knew I couldn't do anywhere near as good, much less any better, so I let her and Lois take you back to Memphis to raise you as their own."

For the first time, probably because I was even older now than he had been when I was born, I saw the situation from his perspective. My dad wasn't a pediatrician. He'd been a farmer and a factory worker his whole life. He wasn't even yet twenty-five, a widower with a newborn.

He cleared his throat. "So Vi and Lois took you and did a better job raising you than I ever could have. I went to work and came home, worked and came home for years. I left up the Christmas tree your mother had put up for about eight years. Then one summer, Vi brought you to stay for the whole summer instead of just a few weeks, and she wasn't going to stay this time."

I remembered that summer, the first time I stayed with Dad by myself. He and I didn't say a lot. I read a lot that summer once he discovered how much I liked the library. Then we'd bond over old *Andy Griffith* episodes, and I'd pretend that he was Andy and I was Opie, even if our relationship never did get that close.

"Vi told me to take down that tree."

The tree! The pathetic Scotch pine with its dusty ornaments and icicles. I had almost forgotten about that tree—probably because it disappeared the summer I was eight. There had been three presents to Mom under that tree, too. I wondered where they'd gone, but I didn't dare ask. What did one do with Christmas presents if the intended recipient passed away before they could open them?

"I told her I couldn't, and she gave me what for. She told me I needed to step up and be a better male influence in your life, and that it was high time I stopped moping around. I told her to take down the damn tree if it meant that much to her. She started taking ornaments off, and I headed out the door to kick around the barn because I wasn't going to be a part of it. When I came back, the tree was gone."

"But I was still here."

"Yeah, she and Lois headed back to Memphis that afternoon, and I didn't know what to do, so we went to Burger Paradise. You wanted a banana split for supper."

"And you said you didn't see why not." I chuckled at the memory. We'd eaten that banana split in harmony. He liked the strawberry, and I preferred the chocolate. Then we shared the vanilla, the pineapples, and the bananas.

"That summer I thought about sending for you permanently," he said.

My heart thumped double time. For that moment I wasn't a forty-something doctor. I was the same eight-year-old who'd stood on the steps of his aunt's home in Memphis watching taillights and wondering why his daddy didn't want him.

"We did all right, you and I. You took to your chores pretty well, even. But then I went to Vi's house and saw the fancy neighborhood where she lived. I asked her about the schools, and she told me they were the absolute best. She had this nice clean house and lots of toys and new clothes for you. She and Lois could give you a whole bunch of things I couldn't. I'd never learned to cook, or I was too lazy to do it right. Vi would fix you proper meals and make sure you didn't go off to school without a good breakfast. So even though I felt like I was getting it together and could make a home for you, I knew I couldn't make that nice a home for you, and I left you there."

Tears pricked at my eyes. "I'm sorry I doubted you, Dad."

He turned to me, his beady eyes fierce. "They did always treat you right, didn't they? Vi and Lois?"

"Yes, Dad, of course."

He leaned back in his recliner. "Good, good."

We sat there for a few minutes, and he finally said, "Don't reckon I want this popcorn after all. Think you might get me a beer before you go to bed?"

I knew a dismissal when I heard one, but I took the bowl of stale popcorn and brought him back a beer instead.

Chapter 23
Ivy

I'd fallen asleep in the recliner with the baby on my chest, but the slam of the back door woke me up.

"Oh, Holly! Did you do all of this?" Mom must've come in from Bunco at the same time Holly came back.

"Sure did," my sister said, a little too proud of herself.

"It must've taken you forever—are those sugar cookies?"

"Yep. I used Grandma's old recipe. Why don't you try one?"

"Oh, I don't— Holly Renee Long, did you put all of those icicles on that tree?" Mom managed, despite a voice muffled from a mouth full of sugar cookie.

I sat up as carefully as I could and shushed them both.

Holly adopted a sotto voce. "If I said Ivy did it, would you believe me?"

Mom gave her the eyebrow of doom. She opened her mouth to speak, but I pointed to the baby. She, in turn, inclined her head toward the back door. Soon I could make out her voice, but not what she said, as she chewed my sister a new one.

I'd been positive that Holly's comeuppance would bring me joy. Now I felt bad because she had worked hard if she'd done both the decorations and baked the cookies. Surely it was worth cleaning up a few icicles for that. Instead of joy, I felt the opposite—

especially when Holly tromped in and plopped down on the couch across from me.

"There. Are you happy?"

"About what?" I asked in the loudest whisper I dared use.

"I got bawled out. Thought you might take some joy from that."

"Honestly? It wasn't everything I'd hoped it would be and so much more."

We sat in silence for a long while. Mom bid us a gruff good night and hobbled back to the bedroom still muttering to herself. She was determined to ignore her plantar fasciitis, but years of neglecting the condition had led to her current inability to walk without pain.

"Thanks for decorating," I said, wondering if I could somehow transfer Zuzu to the bassinet because I was sweating in the spot underneath her. Also, I needed to pee.

Diapers for mothers to wear—that's how I would make my millions.

Holly muttered something noncommittal, and I made sure to catch her eye. "No, you did a lovely job, and you were right about how decorating would make us all feel better. I might even help you clean up those icicles after Christmas."

"Really? You know I only did it because I thought it would be funny, right?"

"Of course, but you have to understand that Mom's relationship with that Hoover is a bond you can't break. She loves that thing."

I gently carried the baby to the bassinet, walking heel to toe—just like in marching band—to keep my upper body as still as possible. Slowly, I released the baby from my chest and lowered her to the waiting surface. Then I quickly covered her with a blanket in the hopes she wouldn't miss my body heat too quickly.

When I turned around, Holly studied me with her head cocked to one side. "You know, you never did tell me why you and Corey didn't have children?"

"Sure I did."

"No, you didn't. You just kept asking why I was asking."

The woman could not take a hint.

I held out one finger for her to hold that thought and ran to the bathroom, hoping she would forget her question while I was gone.

"So?" she asked as I sat back down in the recliner.

At this point she was going to be like a dog with a bone. If that woman didn't get her period or have a positive pregnancy test soon, I was going to lose my mind. Might as well get it over with. "We didn't have children because we couldn't."

"Couldn't?"

A normal person would understand that anything beyond my original answer would fall under the category of insensitive prying. My sister, of course, was no normal person. Then again, did I have any reason to keep such information from her since Corey had already left me for Marilyn Monroe just as he'd always promised he would? I dearly hoped the two of them were attending harp practice together in the clouds and that she would sing a breathy version of "Happy Birthday" to him next month.

"Look, you know we met in anthropology class and started dating. I thought everything was going great until one day he shoved a letter under my dorm room door telling me to go find another man, a better man. That day lives on as one of the worst in my life. In some ways, reading his letter was even worse than finding out the cancer had come back because I didn't know why. I hadn't expected it in the least."

Maybe that's why I still haven't opened the letter he gave me right before he died. I didn't exactly have the best track record with letters from Corey.

"Well, don't stop there," Holly said.

"First, I sat down on my bed in shock. Then I cried. Then my roommate went out for ice cream and rum, which turned out to be a lethal combination. Once I'd tossed all of my stomach contents at about two in the morning, I'd made enough room for anger. I sneaked out of the dorm and down the street to the off-campus apartment where Corey lived. I marched up those stairs, pausing only once to calm my stomach. I pounded on his door, not even caring if the neighbors heard me. Then he answered the door looking as bad as I felt. All of my anger dissipated."

Just the sight of his red eyes and hangdog expression had made me want to burrow into his arms and never let go. I had to remind myself I was angry.

"What are you doing here?" he had asked, a slight quiver in his lips giving him away.

"We need to talk about this letter you shoved under my door like a freakin' coward."

He wouldn't meet my eyes, but he did step aside so I could enter the apartment. I paced in front of the futon, searching my pounding head for where to start. "Your roommate here?"

"He went camping."

"Good. Because I may have to yell at you."

He went to cram his hands in his pockets only to realize he wasn't wearing pants, only boxers. "That's fair."

"What are you thinking? Am I crazy here? I thought that you and I had something special. I was half expecting a ring, not a Dear Jane letter."

We stood in the middle of the floor staring at each other like fighters facing off.

He hedged. "Ivy, there are some things you don't understand. It's complicated."

We circled each other. "Try me."

When he wouldn't meet my eyes, I told myself he'd found another woman, but somewhere in the back of my mind, I had always known it had something to do with his childhood bout of cancer. I foolishly thought I could handle anything related to the cancer as long as it wasn't another woman.

Finally, he mumbled, "I can't give you children."

"That's it?"

His flashing eyes met mine then, that little muscle on the side of his jaw contracting. "What do you mean by 'that's it'?"

"I mean that's the stupidest reason ever to dump me. I love you, and I want to be with you. I'm not even sure I want children."

"But *I* want children."

"Then we can adopt."

"But you said . . ."

"I'd like for the world to have another piece of you, but if that can't be, then we'll have to make sure we raise a child with your values and your sense of humor. But not your housekeeping skills."

"You're saying this like it's a foregone conclusion."

"Oh, fine." I got down on one knee and looked up at the man who was normally three inches taller than me. "Corey Renfroe, will you marry me?"

He said yes, and . . .

We finally had sex, very good sex. Like break up and make up and we're going to get married sex.

"Hey, where did you go just now as you stopped telling the story, and why are you blushing?" my sister asked, bringing me back to the dim living room.

I cleared my throat. "Just remembering some things."

"Uh-huh."

"Did he say yes?" she persisted.

"You know he did."

"Then what happened?"

"Look, I'm not telling you every last little detail."

She shrugged and went to the kitchen, bringing back a glass of water for me even though I hadn't asked for one.

"There's one thing I don't understand."

"One thing?"

"Yeah, with such a dreamy love story like that, why'd you quit writing?"

Oh, that.

I thought of the manuscript spread across the table. "At first I was too busy and too tired—both physically and emotionally—but then I couldn't make the words come. I'd forgotten how to make a love progress. No matter what obstacles I threw at my couple, I couldn't shake the feeling that those stumbling blocks were mundane—especially those inner conflicts that kept them from running to their one true love when I could no longer run to mine."

"And now?"

I gestured toward the dining room. "I'm trying. I guess."

"Do or do not—"

"Don't Yoda me. I had a book out," I said, studying Zuzu rather than meeting my sister's steely gaze. "Achievement unlocked and all that."

"Ivy?"

"Mm-hmm?" I silently willed the baby to wake up so I wouldn't have to answer her next question, but Zuzu slept on.

"You've been writing stories since elementary school. It's all you ever wanted to do. Why did you quit?"

I sighed and closed my eyes. "Believe it or not, I've tried over the years. I didn't want to tell anyone, but I tried. I tried typing on the laptop until it died. I tried writing with pen and paper. Once, I even invested in this dictation software."

"What happened?"

"The way I record a story doesn't matter because I don't have any more stories to tell."

"That's insane."

"No, I'm a romance writer. Pretty sure a part of me has wanted to be a romance writer ever since reading *Pride and Prejudice* in eighth grade, but now I can't write a happily ever after to save my soul. Writing someone else's love story reminds me of how mine didn't end properly."

My sister stared through me. "Write something else, then. Write something with an unhappy ending."

I laughed, but the sound held no humor. Movement from the bassinet caught my eye. Zuzu had jumped in her sleep, so I lowered my voice. "I don't know how to write anything else. I don't *want* to write anything else."

"Well, maybe," Holly said as she stood and took her usual perch on the elliptical. "Maybe you need to write a happy ending before you can find one."

I flopped back in the recliner. "What if we each only get one chance at a happy ending in this life?"

"That's ridiculous. Liz Taylor had seven husbands."

I sighed. "That doesn't mean she had seven happy marriages—"

"Eight, if you count the second marriage to Richard Burton," Holly said breathlessly as she pushed herself on the elliptical.

Yet another reason I wanted to throw things at my sister. "That's even worse. Besides, who would want seven husbands?"

I sat in silence, Holly's legs churned as she chased some demon on her exercise equipment. Finally, she spoke up again. "Just finish the one on the table. It's pretty good, but I kinda want to know what happens to the duke and the widow."

"What the heck? Why are you reading my manuscript?"

Holly shrugged, almost losing her grip on one of the poles as she did. "It was on the table, and I was bored."

"Nosy heifer."

She ignored me, increasing her speed.

"Seriously, should you be exercising this late at night?"

"It's fine. I'm conditioned."

"What about if you're pregnant?"

"Test's still negative."

If she could be blunt and in my business, then I could return the favor. "You're not throwing up again, are you?"

She looked straight ahead and traveled even faster. "No, I am not throwing up. I had a weak moment earlier today and ate half a box of chocolate-covered Oreos. Fixing that now."

I walked over and placed a hand on one of the poles where her hand rested. "Holly. Maybe if you let yourself have one chocolate-covered Oreo from time to time, you wouldn't eat half a box and then feel like you needed to do . . . this."

She stopped and looked down at me. "I didn't ask for your advice. Besides, maybe if you would write something, anything, then you'd have a career beyond the Dollar General."

A physical slap couldn't have hurt worse.

"Okay. Fine. Exercise away." I grabbed my purse. "Mind keeping an eye on Zuzu for a minute?"

"Not at all. Go blacken those lungs while I work on strengthening mine."

By the time I got outside my hands shook so badly that I almost couldn't light my cigarette.

And to think I'd bothered to tell her something personal about me and Corey in a weak moment.

After several clicks I managed to coax flame from the cheap Bic lighter. A cold front had moved through, and I could see my breath before I even took my first drag. But two puffs in, and I felt like I could handle my sister again.

You shouldn't have tried to tell her what to do. You know that.

Old habits die hard, and she was my younger sister even if less than a year separated us.

When I came through the back door, there was Mom reaching under the sink for the Jack Daniel's. She opened her mouth to comment on my smoking, then looked at her whiskey and shut that same mouth.

"Aren't we quite the family?" I asked, the whirr from the living room telling me Holly was still on the elliptical.

"You know we are," she said as she downed the shot.

Chapter 24
Gabe

When I got up the next morning, I didn't know how things would go. After all, Dad had bared his soul to me. Did he have any other stories of my mother to tell me? I descended the stairs cautiously and found him in the kitchen. When I didn't see him, I went straight for the barn where Julian had already started getting the goats up.

We worked in companionable silence, and by the time I got back to the house, Dad had hobbled to the kitchen where he sat at the table with a cigarette in one hand and a coffee mug in the other. "We're out of honey buns."

From him, such pronouncements always came with such gravitas you almost expected cable news outlets to show up and declare it breaking news: Today in rural West Tennessee a local goat farmer proclaimed, "We're out of honey buns." Let's go to our panel of pundits to get their take on this dire situation.

"Hit me with some of that," he added, gesturing toward the coffee pot.

I almost regretted that Dad had interrupted my inner monologue in which people on camera argued over the merits and demerits of the honey bun, but I refilled his cup anyway. Once I'd fixed a bowl of cereal, I sat down across from the old man.

"Since we're out of honey buns, why don't you take me to get a sausage biscuit over at the McDonald's?"

I'd just poured milk over my cereal, that first spoonful halfway to my mouth. It was on the tip of my tongue to say McDonald's was the last place I wanted to go, but going for breakfast reminded me of our trip to Burger Paradise so long ago. I put my almost full bowl of cereal in the sink.

Just because he was doing the asking didn't mean I couldn't have a little fun, though. "Want to go in the Jaguar?"

"Hell, no. I can't get in and out of that thing, and it rides rougher than a cob."

"I guess I'll go bring your truck around, then," I said, trying hard not to smile and give away the fact I'd never intended to take the Jag. The sports car had been lounging in the garage the whole time I'd been home. I was thinking about trading her in for a truck or a Jeep or something more practical.

I'd hardly taken two steps outside when my phone rang. I immediately recognized the number as that of the law firm that was handling my case. Hopefully, my lawyer had an update for me because the whole thing was dragging out far longer that it should.

"Why, hello, Katherine."

"Good morning, Gabriel."

Katherine, like my ex-wife, was sleek and beautiful. I had hired her, however, because she was an exceptional lawyer. She always called me Gabriel, which made me want to call her Katie for some perverse reason.

"Do you have any news for me?" I could hear her shuffling papers on the other end of the line. It wasn't like Katherine to beat around the bush.

"The insurance company is probably going to settle."

To settle? But the whole claim was utterly ridiculous. Stunned, I sat on an upside down five-gallon bucket that had collected water overnight, soaking my ass in the process. As I hopped back up, I said, "But I didn't do anything wrong."

"I know, Gabriel, but the insurance company may not want to chance a trial."

"It was meningococcal meningitis! By the time the child got to us, it was too late. Surely anyone can see that. It's sad, and I feel for them, but there was nothing we could do."

"And you may be right, but there's nothing *I* can do to ensure a jury would see things your way. There's no guarantee that you would win in court, and if you decide to go to trial against the wishes of your insurance company, then you'll be on the hook for a million or more. So I want you to think hard before you—"

"A settlement would be a black mark on my record. I should be able to defend myself."

"Gabriel, listen to me. If there's a settlement, it would include a stipulation that there was no wrongdoing on your part."

I sighed. "That stipulation isn't worth the paper that it's printed on, and we both know it."

She said nothing because she knew I was right.

"But it's not over yet, right?" I was grasping, and we both knew it.

"No. Not yet, but you need to prepare yourself for the idea of a settlement."

We said our goodbyes, but I wasn't about to consider settling. Easy for the lawyers and the insurance companies, they got to duke this out and play by their own asinine rules. When I'd decided to go to medical school, I hadn't put much thought into cases like these. I foolishly thought doctors who did the right thing wouldn't be sued.

I should've known better. People like the Burtons were wealthy enough to think they could buy their way out of any problem, but sometimes a solution couldn't be bought. Bacteria didn't discriminate between rich and poor.

I thought back to Abigail, the Burtons' middle daughter. I'd been taking care of her since she was a newborn, and she was a pistol. The nurses used to warn each other when she was led back to an examination room. She'd been known to take cabinet doors off their hinges or try to eat a latex glove or spin around on my chair until she barfed. It was almost as though she weren't supervised, which, I thought, had been the case since her mother bought that first Blackberry.

Probably, the Burtons were suing me out of some form of guilt. They hadn't thought anything would happen to one of *their* kids, and they'd been distracted by work and sports practices and music lessons and all of the things that parents rushed around to do. Abigail's mother admitted to me that day that she hadn't take her daughter seriously when she first told her about chills and a bad headache. It took throwing up to get her mother's attention. Unfortunately, that particular kind of meningitis could go from first symptom to death in a few hours, and that is exactly what happened.

They'd latched on to how a harried nurse had put the wrong file outside the wrong door, delaying their daughter's treatment by maybe five minutes. Those five minutes wouldn't have made a difference, but they didn't want to believe that—especially not the mother who'd brushed off Abigail's complaints.

Dammit, I had loved that little girl, too. She'd been one of my first newborns, and I'd foolishly thought I might one day get to hold her first baby. She told me she was going to be a doctor just like me and the cartoon character on the Disney Channel. I'd let her practice with my stethoscope that day at her five-year-old checkup. As she got older I'd ask about her math and science grades. She always had all As in those, but she hated English with a passion.

Why does life have to sometimes be so shitty?

It is what it is.

Aunt Vi's mantra came back to me, but it didn't satisfy me. It never did. I'd become a doctor so I could solve problems, and it was disheartening to know some problems couldn't be solved, no matter how much education and experience I had.

The one problem I could solve was changing my pants and taking my father into town for a breakfast at McDonald's.

After enduring Dad's laughter at the wet spot on my pants, I changed, and we went for what I'd assumed would be an uneventful trip to McDonald's.

I didn't count on running into Dr. Malcolm.

"Hey, Doc, how's the little girl I sent you?" I asked as I walked over to where the good doctor stood in line.

"She has a follow-up in a couple of days, and I told the mother to call me if the wound didn't improve." His clipped tone suggested he didn't want to talk to me.

Unfortunately for him, I didn't always take a hint. "Thanks for your help. I couldn't have—"

"You're not welcome," he said, his eyes glued to the menu.

"What?"

He made me wait while he ordered his Egg McMuffin and coffee. Once he'd received his order he sat down in a booth across the restaurant from Dad. I followed the doctor and slid into the seat across from him despite his scowl. "What are you talking about? The little girl was in danger of sepsis."

Dr. Malcolm put down his sandwich and stared through me. "Either fish or cut bait, boy. I can use all the help I can get, but I don't need people coming in and questioning me because they've seen you."

"That wasn't my intention. What could Olivia have possibly questioned you on?"

"When I tried to give her the generic form of Silvadene, she insisted on having exactly what you said. Now I may not be young and handsome, but I am still the only practicing doctor around here, so either come be a part of the solution or, at the very least, quit causing problems."

I didn't even think to tell her the Silvadene might come as a generic. "I was trying to help."

He put his sandwich down again. "Yeah, you'll see what kind of help you've done. That girl will tell people about you, and someone's going to show up at your door with a problem you can't fix. You mark my words."

I swallowed hard. What would I do if a farmer with a bloody arm dangling only by a sinew showed up on my front porch? Or if someone called me to a field where someone lay under a piece of farm equipment? People didn't necessarily understand that doctors were limited in which patients they could see. Sure, there were emergency situations, but I was certified in pediatrics. Others might not understand or respect that distinction, especially since I hadn't spelled it out for Olivia.

"Is the need that great?"

Dr. Malcolm scoffed and almost choked on his Egg McMuffin. "Come stick with me for a day and tell me what you think."

"All right. I will."

He stared at me as if he hadn't believed I would actually take him up on his offer.

"If you'll tell me where I can find Taylor so I can check on her."

He gave me a lecture about HIPAA—something I already knew plenty about—then segued into how in his day people could come in, see him, pay a reasonable amount and leave. I didn't want to talk about insurance or HIPAA or bureaucracy. In the corner of my eye, I saw Dad shifting in his seat. I hadn't even bought our breakfast yet.

I turned to Dr. Malcolm. "I'll be there on Monday morning, how about that?"

Chapter 25
Ivy

While Zuzu took her morning nap, I read through the old copy of *Her Mad Vicar* scribbling in the margins and making notes about how the story should end. Reading through the pages of my manuscript, I felt a hundred years old. I wasn't the same woman who'd written this story about a Regency widow hiding in the country. The hero thinks she poisoned her husband and is pretending to be a vicar to gain her trust and get to the bottom of things. To make matters worse, I'd decided to make her a virgin widow.

Because that didn't sound ridiculous at all.

I banged my head against the dining room table.

The whole story was stupid. I'd never intended for it to be a serious story, more of a madcap semi-mystery with a marriage of convenience thrown in a third of the way through after the vicar got caught being a little frisky with the widow and then had to reveal his true identity and marry her. Only he still thought she might have poisoned her first husband—especially when he discovers she's a virgin because, come on, her husband had been a mean septuagenarian and the widow had been only eighteen when she'd married him.

Oh, the intrigue!

Oh, the silliness.

You are too cynical for your own good.

The idea of writing a trilogy about widows had come to me one day when Mom was talking about her book club, a group of widows who'd named themselves after a certain type of lingerie. The publisher had even labeled my books as the Merry Widows Series, which had been an interesting brand and a fun nod to Mom's book club.

At the time, I'd never dreamed I would be a widow one day myself.

And the minute I became a widow the joke wasn't all that funny.

Maybe if I finally joined her book club, I'd relearn the merry part.

I should probably do some research on Regency lingerie and when the term *Merry Widow* originated. . . .

Or I could be procrastinating.

Sit down and read the pages. All you have to do is read the pages.

And so I did. I sat at the table and marked through the rest of the manuscript until Zuzu demanded that I feed her and change her and supervise some tummy time. She seemed a little fussier than usual, but her slightly runny nose had quit a day or two before. Thank goodness it had because neither she nor I were a fan of the suction device.

She perked up when we read a cloth book about a lost hippo. Spoiler alert: The hippo wasn't lost long since the book was only six pages. Finally, we rattled plastic keys.

"Shake it, shake it," I was saying when Mom came into the room. She did a little hip shimmy.

"Mom. I was talking to Zuzu, and I meant the keys."

"Are you saying you're not ready for this jelly?"

My mom, ladies and gentlemen. So hip and with it—or she would've been ten years ago or so when that song actually came out. "I am never ready for that jelly. However, a peanut butter and jelly would be divine since Holly is running late, and I need to be out the door in ten."

"Fine," she said with an overly dramatic sigh. "I'll make us some sandwiches even though you do it so much better than I do."

"Oh, yes. I am nationally recognized for my PBJ skills." The *you make it so much better than I do* trick worked for years on things such as browning ground beef, making sandwiches, and capping strawberries. I was in college before I realized what my sneaky mother had been up to.

"I see you're working on your book," Mom said casually.

"Yes. I am going to *try* to turn it in on time."

"Why don't you come to the book club on Saturday? We're talking about *Outlander*, and I know you read it. Wendy heard they're going to make a television show about it."

"Mom. Weren't we just talking about the book that's due in a little over two weeks?"

She shrugged. "I thought you might need to watch some widows in their natural habitat for research purposes."

Had the woman read my mind about procrastinating earlier? "Maybe."

Mom stopped what she was doing, and a plate crashed to the floor. "Did you just say that you would consider going to the Merry Widows book club? I want to make sure my ears were not deceiving me."

"Don't get too excited. It's a gut reaction to anything involving Jamie Fraser. If you're going to make a big deal out if it, I won't go." I turned to Zuzu and said in a cutesy voice, "No, I most certainly will not."

She fussed in response, which was how I felt about the whole idea, but I was going to finish up the book for Datya. Maybe I needed to remember the reason I wrote: readers. Mom and her book club had been so supportive when my one and only published book, *His Wanton Widow*, came out.

I changed my charge, fed her, changed her again and was eating a PBJ with my left hand while holding Zuzu against my body with my right when my sister came in.

"You're late," I said. She was supposed to watch Zuzu for me this afternoon and evening while I worked my shift and then played Mary for the penultimate time.

"That is no way to treat a lady who has come bearing gifts." Holly plopped down in the chair at the end of the table. She looked ridiculous in her Santa hat, but she put a Walmart sack on the table beside my plate. "Please take note of the very fancy wrapping job I did."

I nodded because my mouth was full of sandwich. "Outstanding. Want a baby?"

She took Zuzu, and I reached into the sack and brought out . . . a baby carrier, one of those that looked like a huge pashmina shawl that had been wrapped around you several times. "Thank you, Holly!"

"Sorry, I didn't get here soon enough for you to try it on— Oh, you're almost done reading through your book!"

I closed my eyes and reached for the manuscript pages I had stacked at the end of the dining room table. "Yes, but it sucks. Please don't touch anything because I have all of those pages where I need them."

Mom cleared her throat to remind me that she, like Corey's mother, did not care for certain words that rhymed with *duck*.

"It stinks." *Skunk balls.* "It is not good. It reeks."

Holly waved away my concerns. "But now you can fix those things and write the ending."

"Easier said than done," I grumbled.

"Whatever, go be a retail goddess," Holly said.

I considered gathering up my manuscript pages because I did *not* need her to take screenshots and post pages online for people to get their jollies from my unpolished words.

No, that wasn't fair. Holly and I might have our differences, but the one thing she'd never disparaged was my writing. My manuscript would be safe there on the end of the table.

Gathering my purse and name tag I headed for the door, but halfway there I stopped and turned to my sister. "Mom has that appointment this afternoon. Are you sure you can handle this?"

Holly looked up from where she had Zuzu cradled in her arms. "She's practically asleep. It's all good. I've got this."

Chapter 26
Gabe

I was still thinking about what Dr. Malcolm said while I finished the rest of the morning chores. Normally, I would've fed everyone first, but the call from my lawyer and the great honey bun shortage had derailed my train of thought. Dad had ambled out with his walker to tell me I needed to brush down the donkeys before taking them to the Nativity scene, too.

"Okay, Dawn," I said as I turned from one donkey to another with my brush. I knew which was which now because Dawn had a blaze, but Donna did not. "Now, it's your turn."

As I brushed the jenny down, she made a noise that made me wonder if brushing a donkey was something like a massage for people. She and her sister rubbed noses when I was done, and I gave them each a baby carrot. Julian had told me not to feed them too much because donkeys were susceptible to gaining too much weight. Now that I'd passed forty I could sympathize. Matter of fact, I needed to start running again.

As I thought it, the goat with a purple chain, Kathy, went tearing out across the backyard, the plastic links clinking as she ran. I made sure the donkeys were securely in their paddock before running after the goat. Fortunately for me, she got distracted by grape vines left over from Dad's brief flirtation with winemaking.

"I'm going to put a bell on you," I said as I tried to shoo her back into the pasture. "How did you get out?"

The gate creaked, and I looked over in time to see Elizabeth nudging her way out. I'd left the padlock off the gate last time.

Julian drove up as I was looking from the goat chomping on the grape vines to the one at the gate.

"Need a hand?"

"Yeah, I forgot to put the padlock on."

I waited for him to say something about what a city boy I was, but he didn't. Instead he said, "I'll get both of them back up."

He walked away from where Kathy still munched on grape leaves hanging from the ancient arbor that leaned precariously to one side. "Where are you going?"

"You'll see."

He came back with a bucket of grain feed, shaking the feed bucket and singing, "You know Kathy and Betty and Donna and Teresa" to the tune of the Rudolph intro. Elizabeth darted back inside, and Kathy came running. I opened the gate, and he tossed the grain inside where both goats chowed down while I secured the padlock properly. They were soon joined by other goats, the ewe, donkeys, llama, and alpaca.

"Don't you think you're rewarding them for getting out?" I asked.

"Naw, I'm rewarding them for coming when I call them."

If only such tricks worked on people.

"Well, thank you."

He grunted something that sounded like "you're welcome" and I realized, between that and his "it was the least I could do" that my brother wasn't good at accepting thanks.

"What brings you back over here?" I asked.

"They didn't need me at the dealership, so I thought I'd come over and see if you wanted to get a beer."

"What's the occasion?"

He kicked the dirt. "Bonding. This morning before she left for work, Romy said we should bond, but she didn't say how. I figured beer was as good a way as any."

I couldn't argue with his logic. At the rate things were going, though, I was in danger of falling into a Hallmark movie. They could call it *The Prodigal Son*. The description would read, "Shocking secrets are revealed and manly men bond when Gabe finally finds out the truth about his mother. And father. And secret sibling."

One touching scene would be me, getting a beer with my . . . brother.

"It's on me," Julian said. "I reckon that's the least I could do."

There were those words again.

"You talked me into it," I said, understanding the offer was a truce, an understanding we were both trying to be brotherly even if it was awkward. Beer would help with that—or make it worse. In my experience alcohol either eased the awkwardness or exacerbated it.

"Wait. What about the Nativity?"

Julian scoffed. "I don't know about you, but I'm only planning on one beer. I think I can do that and still make it to the Nativity. Or are fancy doctors like you too lightweight for even one beer?"

It could've been an insult, but I knew he was teasing this time. I thought about regaling him with stories of hospital cocktail parties and exactly how much liquor a few of my coworkers could hold, but I decided not to. "One'll do. Let's go."

"I'm driving," he said.

"Fine by me," I said with a shrug. We'd both been tromping around the barn. Better his floor mats than mine.

Chapter 27
Ivy

"You're late."

Two words one did not want to hear from Mavis. "I'm sorry. Holly was running late so I'm running late."

Mavis took me by the shoulders. "Look, it's not that I don't want to cut you some slack, it's that I can't. All of your times from clocking in and out, all of the absences—it goes straight to corporate. Human Resources has flagged you because they see *everything*. You understand?"

I swallowed hard. I'd been doing so well since Mavis and I had had the one more strike and you're out discussion. If I'd known I was going to become the guardian of the world's cutest baby, maybe I would've been more conscientious about coming into work on time from the very beginning.

Then again, probably not. My husband had died and I had more bills to pay than I could process. Back then I hadn't wanted to do anything but burrow under my covers and wait for it all to be over.

"I understand, Mavis," I said as I put on my smock.

"Why do you want to take care of a strange baby anyway?" Mavis asked as we walked toward the registers. She didn't add the part about how I had a hard enough time taking care of myself, but her accusation hung heavy in air between us nonetheless.

"Someone has to do it."

"Yeah, and that someone doesn't have to be you."

I paused. "I'm pretty sure this is temporary, but sometimes I feel as though this were meant to be, you know?"

Mavis rolled her eyes. "You happened to be the person who looked in that manger. That's it."

"But I also happened to be on the list to be a foster parent and I happened to mention that to the police officer, my mouth moving before my brain caught on. That's a lot of happening. You can call it serendipity or the Holy Spirit or fate, but I think I was meant to take care of this baby. At least for a little while."

It was on the tip of my tongue to tell her about how I'd been thinking about my husband and looking for a sign. Mavis was too practical to believe in such things.

"Mm-hmm. You are also *meant* to take the first shift at the registers. I'll send Lorraine to spell you in an hour and a half for your first break."

The first half of my day flew by until my lunch, mainly because the line of people was steady without being long enough for me to have to call for backup. They asked about my mama and my sister and the baby they'd heard was staying with us, but they never asked about me. Corey's death was too long gone for anyone to express condolences or ask how I was doing. No one asked about my book anymore, which they used to do when it first came out.

I was stagnating here in the Dollar General. How many years had I wasted?

Now, Ivy. The ol' DG has been very good to you.

My grief counselor used to love to tell me not to be so hard on myself, to think about how I would feel if someone else talked about me the way I talked about myself. I'd stopped going to that counselor the first chance I got, so it was kinda funny that I remembered anything she said.

She'd called me a few times after that, but I let her go to voicemail. Whenever I saw her, she wanted to dredge everything up to the surface, and I wanted it all to lie there undisturbed. I swear she got some kind of perverse joy from watching me cry. Either that, or she had a ton of stock in Kleenex.

Out of the corner of my eye I saw a redheaded woman sneaking glances at me from behind the display of Christmas tree–scented candles. She kept staring at me as though she knew me, but I couldn't place her. Mystery shopper, maybe?

But she looked so sad, her eyes hollowed and her collarbones showing. Lorraine had taken the register, so I approached her with a smile. "Can I help you?"

"Do you have any more of these, uh, Christmas socks?"

She held up the last pair of socks with the Christmas lights pattern. I really needed to change that end cap display. "Um, I think that's the last pair."

"Could you go check in the back?"

Ah. She probably was a mystery shopper. I pasted on a brighter smile. "I'll be glad to."

I looked through the new shipment, but there were no new socks. I knew this, but I wanted to do my due diligence in the name of customer service. Only when I returned, she was gone.

"That's odd."

"What's odd?" asked Mavis, her hands on her hips. "Other than the fact that you need to take your lunch or you're going to throw the whole schedule out of whack."

"I'm going, but there was a jumpy lady who asked me about socks. I think she was a mystery shopper, but she disappeared before I could tell her we didn't have any more."

"As long as you did your part. Now scoot."

I hustled to the back so I wouldn't throw off the schedule even though we all knew that Lorraine would wreck the whole thing, causing one or both of us to miss our breaks. I'd just clocked out for lunch and was trying to decide if I wanted to walk to the Mc-Donald's or drive to Burger Paradise when Mavis called for me over the loud speaker. "Ivy Long, come to the front, please. Ivy Long to the front."

That couldn't be good. Mavis knew I was headed to lunch.

Not sure what to do, I walked to the door, then to my locker, and back to the door before I decided I would keep my purse with me. That way I could leave if I needed to, but I'd have to come back here to clock in again anyway if I still had to work. As I walked to the front I scanned the store for the mystery woman, but I didn't see her.

Instead I saw a black woman in a smart navy pantsuit. She wore a colorful scarf and smelled of the same Lancôme perfume that my mother wore, the one whose name meant "life is beautiful." I wondered if she wore it because she liked the scent or needed the reminder. She extended her hand with a smile. "Ivy Long?"

I nodded.

"I'm Yolanda Gibbons. Is there a place we could talk about your foster care situation?"

"Sure. Break room? Or McDonald's maybe?"

She chose the latter, and we walked over to the McDonald's, easily finding a quiet corner since the restaurant wasn't quite to the supper push yet.

Yolanda and I reviewed all of the important parts of being a foster parent. She informed me that she would make a home visit soon but that she'd been in town that day to go to court and had wanted to meet up with me, first. We looked over paperwork and reviewed procedures until my eyes glazed over and then she gave me a hard look.

"Ivy, I need to know if you are serious about adopting this child."

"But I thought . . ."

"You thought what?"

"I thought this would probably be a temporary placement since Corey had died, and—"

She pinned me to my booth with her look. "You are on the foster to adopt list. As you well know, nothing is ever certain, but often the parent doesn't come back in these cases. If your baby girl was born anywhere in this area, we should be able to find her, but I haven't found anything in TFACTS yet. The parent's note left no indication of an intended caregiver. The child is well past Safe Haven and wasn't even left in an official place. We had the probable cause hearing earlier today and the deprivation hearing is in less than two weeks."

"Okay," I said, not sure how to translate all of this to English. I wracked my brain to remember what had happened with Byron, only to discover my mind had packed away almost all of my memories of Byron—probably because those later memories had been so painful.

"Are you in? Are you prepared to take care of this girl for the long haul?"

"Yes." The word left my lips even as I was still thinking about the implications of what I was doing. For heaven's sake, I hadn't planned on this. I had been so sure that Zuzu would go to an intact couple, not a broken widow.

"Look, the court calendar looks light leading up to Christmas, so I don't expect any delays with the deprivation hearing unless one of the appointed attorneys requests a continuance. Also, the judge who's presiding has *no mercy* when it comes to neglected children. I'm going to request a finding for non-reunification. Whoever the court appoints may ask for that continuance, but we will follow procedures and get there when we get there."

I remembered this part. Even though Zuzu had been abandoned, we had to show due diligence in notifying the parent before terminating parental rights. That's how I'd lost Byron. His mother had shown up before the termination of her rights and then we'd gone into a reunification plan, and I'd sat through countless supervised visitations before I had to kiss him and let him go.

"Why are you crying? This is good news. Unless you don't want this baby. If you don't, I need to know *right now* because I am not going to have that child in the middle of a game of ping-pong."

I told her the short version of my experience with Byron.

She patted my hand. "Oh, honey. You know I can't promise you the same thing won't happen again, but I think it's unlikely."

I nodded.

"Now," she said, serious once again. "Let's talk about all the things that need to be done right now." She asked about day-to-day care and then talked about what needed to happen in the home, my job, all sorts of things. The sheer number of things I had to do increased to daunting proportions, but I'd been through home visits before. For the past few years it had been the annual visit, but now I needed to gear up for more frequent visits.

"Oh, and I'd suggest that you quit smoking."

"What? How'd you—"

"One or two cigarettes a day, is it?"

"Yes," I said, studying Yolanda. Did she have telepathy?

"We know our own. I haven't had a cigarette in six years, eleven months and"—she paused to mentally count—"thirteen days."

"Wow. You know it to the day?"

"Yes. So, if I can do it, you can, too. You need to go cold turkey. Just quit."

I swallowed hard. The thought of quitting made me want a cigarette right then and there in the middle of the day.

Yolanda continued, "Here's my card in case you need anything, anything at all."

"Thank you," I said.

She put a hand on my arm. "Somehow you got yourself bumped to the top of the line like a bona fide Christmas miracle. Don't squander it."

Chapter 28
Gabe

As we pulled up to The Fountain, I noticed that it had a new banner outside that read, "Under New Management."

"What happened to Bill?"

"He retired and moved to Florida. Claimed he was going to open a strip club, but I think he was yanking my chain." Julian parked the truck and he walked across the parking lot, gravel crunching under our feet.

"Who the heck is running the place, then?"

"The Gates brothers," Julian said with a smile. "Although I think Greg is more of a silent partner."

I stopped outside the door. I hadn't been inside The Fountain since a couple of summers back. The Gates brothers had gotten into a fight and almost dismantled the place, so I wasn't sure if I was walking into a cinder block country tavern or a war zone.

What the hell?

I stepped inside, and the place still smelled like the old country store it had been for who knew how long before. Same old counter, same old trough full of ice and beer, same upright on risers, and the same pool table to the back. I half expected to see Bill behind the counter, but it was Pete, complete with his chipped-tooth grin.

"What'll ya have?"

"I'll have a Bud Light, but I bet City Boy here wants something fancy."

"I swear I'm going to hit you upside the head with my empty beer bottle, *Bubba*, if you call me that one more time." I turned to Pete. "A Bud Light would be fine."

"Whoa, I didn't mean to hurt your feelings like that," Julian said as we took a seat at one of the tables in front of the risers. Almost no one was there at that time of day so we could sit anywhere we wanted.

"You didn't hurt my feelings," I said. "I'm just sick of your 'City Boy' nonsense. So I forgot to put the padlock on? Big deal. I've also milked goats and brushed donkeys and mucked stables. Most of my city is gone."

"I didn't say anything about the padlock."

"You thought it."

"Yeah, and I also thought about the fact you wouldn't know goats are escape artists." He drank down a quarter of his beer. "Look, I guess I'm nervous because you've got all of this education and polish, and I didn't think about how The Fountain doesn't have anything fancy."

I snorted. "I don't want anything fancy. I have a fancy car and had a fancy woman. They were equally unreliable. I gave up on developing a taste for caviar, and I couldn't begin to tell anyone the difference between a twelve-dollar bottle of wine and a hundred-dollar bottle. Fancy is overrated."

"Now you sound like Romy," he said with a smile.

"Oh?"

"Yeah, she went off to Vanderbilt and got this fancy degree. Next thing I know, she's planting a garden and singing along with Miranda Lambert."

"Well, I'm not singing anytime soon."

Julian raised his beer. "Well, here's to brotherhood. And not being fancy."

I clinked my longneck against his.

Brother.

All those years of wanting a brother. Now I had one. Pretty sure

I needed to be more careful in what I wished for in the future, but I did have a brother.

"So," Julian said.

"So."

We each shifted in our seats and nursed our beers. We were still searching for a topic of discussion when Holly Long came flying through the door, letting the screen door slap behind her. She stopped in the doorway, blinking her eyes to adjust to the darker lights.

And she had the baby carrier in the crook of one elbow and the diaper bag slung over her other shoulder.

"Oh, thank goodness! Gabe, I need you to take the baby."

"Me?"

"Yes, I saw Julian's truck and was going to see if he and Romy could take her for a few hours—"

Julian spewed his beer at the mention of his name, but Holly pressed on. "But seeing you is even better, since you're a doctor and all that. One of the girls got sick and can't come in to teach her spin classes. Mama's at the eye doctor. Gotta go, thanks!"

Before I could remind her that Ivy and I weren't currently on the best of terms, she had transferred baby and diaper bag to me and was halfway to the door. First she threw me under the bus with the mistletoe and now this?

Julian chuckled.

"What?"

"Just remembering that line from *Sweet Home Alabama* about having a baby in a bar," he muttered. "Romy's gonna laugh when I tell her this story."

The whole world had gone mad. Based on the purple of Zuzu's face and the deep concentration of her eyes and brow, I could guess she was working on a little project of her own. Sure. A dirty diaper in a bar that didn't have an official restroom, much less a changing table—that seemed to square perfectly with the events of the past few days.

"I can't escape this baby," I said, thinking out loud more than anything.

"Maybe you're not meant to," Julian said.

Zuzu chose that moment to unload in response.

"Oh, dude," Julian said, then he sighed and held out his arms. "Hand me the baby."

"Where in the blue blazes are you going to change her?"

"My tailgate, of course. They're practically meant for it."

I didn't think his statement was factually accurate, but I was getting out of changing a truly disgusting diaper, so I followed him outside to see how his tailgate theory would work. He lowered the tailgate with one hand and then put the car seat up top, balancing it with one hand while he laid out supplies with the other.

I had to figure this strategy wouldn't work well with people who didn't keep their cars clean, but Julian's truck bed gleamed in the chilly winter sunshine.

"There, there. That was some hard work, wasn't it?" he said as he lifted the baby and laid her down on the handy pad that had come with the diaper bag. I kept a hand on the baby while he changed the diaper with a deftness that told me Romy hadn't been unduly burdened when Portia was a baby.

"And there you go! Now you sit here with the baby," he said as he wrapped her in a warm blanket. "I'll find a place to put this and wash my hands."

"Wait right there."

We turned to see a short black woman leaning over the driver's side door of a sedan.

"Yes?"

She looked at The Fountain and back at us and hesitated for a brief second but then grimly set her mouth and narrowed her eyes to solider on. "I just saw Holly Long leave. Is that the Jane Doe who was found at the Nativity scene?"

I swallowed hard, hoping that my answer wouldn't get Ivy into some kind of trouble. Lying would be even worse. "Yes. Who's asking?"

"Gibbons, Yolanda Gibbons. That sweet thing's case manager."

In another life I might have laughed at a social worker who introduced herself in the style of James Bond, but Yolanda didn't appear to have a sense of humor.

The social worker stepped toward us, slamming the door as she did so. "Why do you have this child?"

"I'm babysitting."

She crossed her arms over her chest. "Are you on the paperwork?"

"Kinda," I said with my most charming grin.

"What does that mean?" She was not amused by me.

"I'm the physician who traveled with Zuzu to the hospital. I'm on the paperwork, but I don't know if my background check has gone through yet."

"Does Ms. Long know that her charge is in your custody?"

I hedged, searching for an answer that was true but wouldn't get Ivy in trouble. "I believe she's at work."

"Mm-hmm."

"Her sister then got called into work, too."

"Mm-hmm. And you thought a bar was a good place to babysit?"

My eyes widened. I hadn't thought about how the whole thing looked. "No, ma'am. Holly came by while Julian and I were having *one* celebratory beer, which I put down the minute I took the child."

"Mm-hmm."

"The minute we got the baby we were going to be on our way, but we needed to change poor Zuzu first."

Julian held out the diaper, which was probably also not helpful but definitely a testament to our need to change the baby before leaving.

"Mm-hmm."

"Look, I know how this looks, Ms. Gibbons, but I can assure you that Ivy is doing a fantastic job with Zuzu. I give you my word as a pediatrician."

Blessedly the baby chose that moment to smile.

"Your name?"

"Dr. Gabriel Ledbetter."

She tapped her chin with one finger. "Ledbetter. Where have I heard that name before? Oh, yes. You were just in the news because the Burton family is suing you over their daughter's death."

Julian's head jerked toward me.

I took two deep breaths and ignored his curious gaze. This was why I wanted to go to court and defend myself. People would hear the news and think the worst of me.

"With all due respect, I am against the settlement. Abigail Burton contracted a very severe form of meningitis. We did everything we possibly could, but we lost her. Haven't you lost a kid or two no matter how hard you tried?"

Her expression softened. "Listen, Dr. Ledbetter. If I looked hard enough, I'm pretty sure I could come up with a reason to take that child back into protective services. As it is, Ms. Long and I are going to have a conversation about appropriate childcare situations."

I nodded, and we stared at each other for a minute. As someone who sometimes had to make quick decisions based on intuition, I recognized she was doing the same. I exhaled with relief that Julian and I had passed muster.

She *had* lost a child under her care, too. That much I could tell. The way social workers today were overburdened, it didn't surprise me. It probably took superhuman strength to see the needs of all of the children on her caseload. She understood my situation, too. Sometimes, your best simply wasn't good enough.

"I'll be sure to take Zuzu to the drive-through Nativity where Ivy is going to be tonight. She should be off from work soon."

At least I hoped she would.

"That's good to know," Ms. Gibbons said. I wondered if I'd made a tactical error by telling her where we were going to be.

"Thank you," I said.

Yolanda Gibbons returned to her car, and Julian left to finally take care of the diaper.

Zuzu and I sat on the tailgate for a second. A chilly breeze blew, so I tucked her blanket around her more tightly. She cooed as the breeze picked up a few strands of her fine hair.

"You didn't mind the bar that much, did you?"

She babbled, and I gave in to the urge to kiss her head while no one was looking.

Chapter 29
Ivy

When Gabriel showed up with Zuzu, I was confused. Then frightened. Then downright angry. I met him out in the parking lot still wearing my smock and name tag and everything. "Is she okay?"

"She's fine," he said. "Your sister had to teach a spin class and your mom was at the eye doctor or something."

"What?" I forced myself to look into his eyes because whatever had happened with Zuzu was more important than any history between us.

Gabe shrugged. "Holly came into The Fountain with Zuzu and—"

"She did what?"

"—told us she needed to go to work. She saw Julian's truck and thought Romy might be able to help, but handed Zuzu over to me instead."

"She didn't."

"She did, and I'm afraid there's more. You might want to be sitting down for this one."

"What did she do with my baby?" I said through gritted teeth. I could already feel a certain tenseness that meant I would end up clenching my jaw during the night.

"Well, like I said, Julian took me to The Fountain to get a celebratory beer and—"

I buried my face in my hands. This was so Holly.

"Before we could leave, a social worker named Yolanda Gibbons showed up out of nowhere—"

Oh, dear God, no.

Within an hour of meeting with my case manager, she'd already spotted my child at a tavern. Sororicide was generally frowned upon, but surely a jury of my peers wouldn't convict me.

"And lectured me on having a baby in a bar—"

"To be fair we were changing her diaper on a tailgate at the time," Julian piped up.

"You changed my baby on a tailgate?"

Gabe shot him a look that suggested he wasn't helping. "I had to admit that I wasn't completely official since they hadn't run my background check yet."

I couldn't even make it a week without messing something up?

"So, if you don't mind, Gabe and I need to go get the animals," Julian said.

"Only if you're fine," Gabe said through clenched teeth.

Oh, what did he care whether I was fine or not? "I'm fine."

He hesitated.

"Go on," I snapped. I was angrier with Holly, but Gabe seemed to always be in the thick of things, too.

Yeah, because you keep dragging him into them.

I took the car seat and looked over Zuzu, knowing that she was absolutely okay but needing to check her over carefully nonetheless. When I walked into the Dollar General, Mavis lifted an eyebrow from where she was covering my spot at the register. "Clocking out early?"

"Yes, please."

She eyed the long line of customers and sighed. "Send Lorraine on up."

Lorraine couldn't make change for anything, but I would willingly make up the difference in her till if I could only sit in the back with Zuzu for a few minutes. Even though she was sleeping, I took her from the car seat and held her to me, feeling her warmth, smelling her hair, hearing her coo.

My love for a little girl I'd only met a couple of days before was beyond irrational, but the surge of emotion reinforced my earlier crazy decision to adopt. Her shock of fine blond hair reminded me of Corey, and remembering my late husband wasn't as painful when I thought of how much he would get a kick out of the situation.

Whatever Yolanda Gibbons told me to do, I would do it if it meant keeping Zuzu. I'd quit smoking. I'd get a better job. I'd hire a nanny who'd passed a hundred background checks and wouldn't leave me in the lurch to take a damn spin class.

When I saw Yolanda's name flash on my phone screen, I took a deep breath. At least I was prepared for what she had to say.

Since I'd already fed and changed her, Zuzu did pretty well while Gabe and I played Joseph and Mary. She fussed off and on, but she liked the way the headlights from the cars would flash on the ceiling of the stable. It was like an intricate mobile—an intricate mobile that kept her entertained until about fifteen minutes before we closed.

"I'm tired of all this, too," I murmured. My instinct was to rock the manger like a cradle, but the shop boys over at Yessum County High hadn't had real babies in mind when they built it, so it didn't have any give. Daring Miss Idabell to fire me, I picked up the baby. Gabe moved in closer and looked at her, too. We had to look like a Christmas card scene to the people driving through.

"One more night," I said to myself almost as much as the baby. Starting next Monday, there would be a new Mary and Joseph in town.

"I'm guessing you got an earful from Ms. Gibbons earlier?" Gabe asked.

"Yeah. At times I had to hold the phone away from my ear a bit so I didn't permanently damage my eardrum."

"Sorry about that."

"Oh, the blame lands squarely on my sister," I said. "And me for trusting her."

We sat in silence as the cars curved around the scene.

"Weren't you supposed to bring some wine? I swear I remember your saying that you would bring some wine," he said.

"I didn't have time to drive all the way to Jefferson to get it."

Not that I want *to bring you any wine.*

"I keep forgetting that Ellery is a dry town," he said.

The llama behind me spit at that. I had to agree.

"Man, there are a few things I miss about Memphis."

"Just a few?"

"Yeah, only a few," he said with a wonder that suggested he'd surprised himself.

I was so aware of his presence I could almost feel his body heat radiating toward me. Of course, it was a little nippy that night, so it was simple biology rather than any sort of attraction. My traitorous body wanted to lean into him, but I couldn't. Heck, I wouldn't. Not after he'd embarrassed me.

I shivered a little at his breath on the nape of my neck as he reached over my shoulder to tuck Zuzu's hand back into the blanket.

"Sorry, I didn't mean to crowd you," he murmured.

He'd seen me shiver. Oh, Lord. He had *seen* me shiver. I sucked in a deep breath, glad he couldn't see my pink cheeks. "You didn't crowd me."

Zuzu squirmed and fussed, and I put a hand to her forehead. She felt a little warm. Surely, I wasn't overheating the baby. Mom had warned me about that, telling me about the time she put Holly and me in all sorts of layers to brave subzero temperatures only to have the two of us start hacking up a lung once we'd been in the well-heated mall for a while.

That was a Christmas shopping trip cut short, and I think she still held a grudge.

Come to think of it, I only had a few more days to finish the shopping that I hadn't even started. Fortunately for me, I didn't have that many people to buy for.

Or was that unfortunately?

"What are you thinking about that has you frowning all of a

sudden?" Gabe asked, jarring me back into the rough-hewn stable with its sound of carols and cars.

"Just thinking about how my Christmas shopping list isn't that long. Maybe I am a hermit. That's what Holly says."

Not that Holly would be opining on such things in the future because I planned to incapacitate her for the stunt she'd pulled this afternoon.

"Funny, I don't, either," Gabe said.

"You're not a hermit."

"No, but my ex-wife did accuse me of being married to my job."

Again, I was glad that he sat behind me, so he couldn't see my surprise because of course he'd been married. I'd been married, hadn't I? And he had to be bored to even broach the subject. Curiosity got the better of me. "Were you?"

"Probably," he admitted.

"Do you miss her?" While I was prying, I might as well get my money's worth.

"The wife or the job?"

"Very funny. The wife."

"No. Not really. Sometimes I miss the idea of her, but I don't miss her. I'm sure she's happier with her orthopedist, too."

He didn't ask me about Corey, and I was grateful. At this point, I missed the idea of him, too. For the first year, the grief had come and gone—but mostly come—in violent stabs of pain. Then I went through a year of utter numbness. I went to work, I came home, and I slept. Sometimes I ate. Often I didn't. Year three I ate too much, but the pain was down to a dull ache, and I could forget about the shitty hand love and life had dealt me for a few hours at a time. Now, I thought of my husband fondly, figuring he was goofing off on a celestial golf course with Bob Hope or learning to cook with Julia Child.

I still missed him, but, somehow or the other, I'd finally stumbled into acceptance.

So, it's probably time to open that envelope and finally let him go.

* * *

By the time we got back to the house, I was pretty sure Zuzu had a fever rather than any kind of overheating. I'd stripped her to her diaper, but she was still burning up. I didn't even have time to properly chew out my sister, but I told her to pencil me in for tomorrow because I had plenty of words I needed to say to her.

"Zuzu, baby, what is it?" I cooed as I bounced her down the long hall and back to the living room. "What's the matter? How can I make it better?"

But she fussed on.

Sometimes those fusses escalated to all-out wails. Both frayed my nerves. I wasn't even her real mother. I didn't have that mother's intuition thing going on. Should I take her to the emergency room? Had I hurt her by taking her to the Nativity with me? Had she caught some kind of disease at The Fountain?

"Ivy, darling. Sometimes babies just cry," Mom said.

"Feel her forehead, Mom. She's hot."

"Maybe a little. Do you have a thermometer?"

The one I'd bought so long ago for Byron was dead—the battery had corroded—but Mom thought she had a couple of the old mercury ones she'd used on us. After a few minutes of her rummaging around in the bathroom drawers, she cried, "A-ha!"

Soon—once the thermometer had been properly sanitized—Zuzu suffered the indignities of a rectal temperature reading with me trying to hold her still so the thermometer would stay in long enough to get a reading. I couldn't blame her for howling at that. Then Mom couldn't read the thermometer, so I had to get the diaper back on the squirming child and pass her to Mom while I held the ancient mercury thermometer up to the light to read it.

One hundred degrees on the money.

So then I Googled fevers and babies because I couldn't remember. All of the information said one hundred one or higher but one hundred point four for babies under three months, but we didn't know how old Zuzu was for sure, and what if I hadn't read the thermometer correctly? I picked up the diaper I'd recently changed. Was it heavy enough? She had peed, but had she peed enough? Had I dehydrated the child by wrapping her in too many blankets while we were outside?

My mom laid a hand on my arm. "Ivy, stop."

"Mom, how did you do this?"

She closed her eyes and sighed with a knowing smile. "Well, I don't know that I always did the right thing, but you're still here, aren't you? Besides, I was a nurse and young and stupid enough to think I knew everything."

"But you worked in anesthesia!"

"And don't think I haven't considered about ten ways to help this child sleep, *but* that's not in her best interest or ours."

"What do I do?"

"You pace with her until the sun comes up, and then you call a doctor. Then you pace some more until the appointment because, believe me, you don't want to take her to the emergency room unless you absolutely have to. No telling who or what is in the emergency room at this time of night."

Pace until I could call a doctor.

I *could* call a doctor right now.

Which is not to say he would take my calls.

"So I should give up on getting any sleep at this point, right?" Holly yelled over the baby's wailing as she plopped down in the recliner.

Yes, Holly. Because it's all about you.

"You be glad the baby's yelling so I can't yell at you."

Mom squeezed my shoulder. "I'm sorry I don't have better answers, but this too shall pass. Welcome to motherhood."

She trudged to the kitchen, and I soon heard water boiling in the kettle. Zuzu's wails had reached an entirely new decibel, so I decided to pace the hallway again to see if that would calm her down at least a little bit.

You don't need to call him.

Mom says it's fine.

But he once said I could call him anytime.

Yeah, do you think that offer still holds? Besides, do you want him to laugh at you if this is something simple?

And you'll have to face him again—in this house.

My eyes traveled to the mistletoe that still hung in the doorway between living room and dining room.

I'd do it, if it meant I'd know for sure there was nothing seriously wrong with Zuzu.

I marched down the hall with purpose and handed the crying baby to my sister. "You walk with the baby while I make this phone call. And don't you dare take her to The Fountain, either."

"Never going to live that down, am I?"

"Nope," I said as I scrolled through my contacts. I had to call twice, but he finally picked up.

Chapter 30
Gabe

My phone wouldn't stop ringing. I was supposed to be on sabbatical. Doctors on sabbatical got to sleep until it was time to milk the goats, dammit.

I rolled over and looked at the phone.

Three in the morning?

I answered with a "Yeah."

"The baby won't stop crying."

"Babies do that," I said as my foggy brain tried to put that voice with a name. I pulled the phone away from my ear to see who was calling, but either I'd been too lazy to put the name with the number or the person calling me was someone I'd never called before.

Baby.

Crying.

Ivy.

Zuzu!

I sat up, suddenly alert. "Is she peeing and pooping and eating?"

"Yes, yes, and kinda."

"Fever?"

"Just over a hundred."

I ran through all sorts of possibilities, some mild and some catastrophic. "I'll be there in a minute."

"Gabe?"

She sounded as though she were on the verge of tears.

"Ivy, calm down. It's probably an ear infection or maybe she's teething early. You need to be calm because the baby can pick up on your emotions," I said as I jumped into pants and rammed my feet into my shoes without bothering to untie them.

"Holly's holding her, so there's no telling what new germs she's picking up."

Humor. That was good.

The little hiccupping sound that suggest she'd been crying? That was bad.

"I'm hanging up now, but it's okay, and I will be there in a minute."

I disconnected the call before she could say anything else and pulled a shirt on.

Backward.

I shoved the phone into my back pocket and turned the shirt around before grabbing my official satchel, the one that had been collecting dust up until the point Olivia showed up with her baby and those darned chickens.

I almost tripped on the bottom stair and made a note that the carpet was coming up. A few steps into the living room, and there Dad was, sleeping in his chair. I woke him up. "Going over to the Longs to check on the baby."

"What'dya wake me up for?"

"Because you told me to."

"Oh. Yeah. Thank you."

And, just like that, he was asleep again.

When I got to the Long residence, Mrs. Long calmly sipped her tea despite the fact little Zuzu was wailing like a banshee. It didn't take long to discover the problem.

"Double ear infection."

"What can we do?"

"Not a lot until tomorrow when you can get some antibiotics."

"What about a twenty-four-hour pharmacy?"

I hedged. The ear infection was uncomfortable, but Ivy didn't need to get into the habit of thinking such illnesses could be solved so quickly. "I guess there's one in Jefferson? Do you have any acetaminophen?"

"I think so," she said, rushing for the diaper bag. She tossed out diapers and a travel box of wipes, then a cloth book, before emerging with the medicine in question.

"Okay, so we'll give her a little of this for now."

I asked her about Zuzu's weight, and I already knew we had no idea about possibility of allergies. My hand hovered over the pad. This would be my second prescription in a week. I *could* write these out all the livelong day, but the precedent was sending me down a slippery slope. I jotted out the prescription and held out the sheet of paper to Ivy. "You can go in the morning and pick up the prescription along with some probiotics to hopefully stave off an upset stomach."

"Or I can send Holly right now?"

"Say what?" interjected her sister, who was laying across the recliner horizontally in cartoon pony pajamas.

Ivy turned to level a frightening glare on her sister. "After the stunt you pulled, you owe me."

Waving off her sister's anger, Holly stumbled down the hallway, saying, "Fine. Whatever. I'm getting clothes and going." Through a yawn.

Ivy bounced Zuzu and turned back to me. "But how did this happen?"

Oh, new mothers.

"Has she had any cold symptoms?"

"Maybe a little bit of a runny nose a day or two ago."

I shrugged. "Someone gave her a cold. The cold went to her ears. I will say this: She's a tough cookie not to cry before now."

Ivy cradled the back of Zuzu's head and kissed the front. "Maybe she was fussing, and I missed it. Do you think she got anything in The Fountain?"

She looked down the hallway after Holly with a gaze that would've converted any mere mortal to stone.

"No, Ivy," I said gently. "She had the cold before Holly took her to The Fountain. It's okay. This is all a normal part of motherhood. Now hand the baby to either me or your mother and get a little bit of a rest."

"Whoa. What if Holly would like to get back to her little bit of rest?"

Mrs. Long snatched the prescription and Holly's keys. "Then go back to bed, and I'll go. I drink caffeine, unlike you," she said as she headed for the door, slamming it behind her.

"Oh, I didn't mean for Mom to do that," Holly said, clearly feeling guilty. "Hand me the baby."

She took the child and started pacing up and down the hall. "Aunt Holly is going to teach you how to avoid these ear infections because you, young lady, are crying like a Valkyrie in one of Kresley Cole's books."

What Holly said made no sense to me, but the baby stopped fussing and looked up at her as if she were imparting vital information. Ivy, meanwhile, had lay back in the recliner with her eyes closed. I needed to plan my escape, but Ivy and I had unfinished business. If she could trust me with Zuzu, then we could talk about what happened earlier.

Meanwhile, Holly talked to Zuzu as they walked up and down the hallway. "I would read one of her books to you, but they have too much sexy times for tender, young ears, especially tender, young ears that are infected. But when you're older, Aunt Holly will make sure to sneak you only the best romance novels. But not one of your mother's. Because that would be weird."

"I can hear you, you know," Ivy said without opening her eyes.

But she smiled and sat up to watch her sister parade up and down the long hallway, carrying Zuzu in a colic hold. Again I saw her as I had the evening the sun shone behind her, giving her an honest-to-goodness halo. I clenched my fists at my side because I wanted to run my fingers through her glossy hair. Or maybe pull her underneath the mistletoe for that mulligan.

I searched for a question to distract me. "You write romance novels?"

She flinched, and I wondered if I'd asked the wrong question. With a sigh, she pulled herself to an upright position, glancing for a second at an ancient laptop and a stack of papers on the corner of the dining room table in the next room. "I used to."

"That's pretty cool."

"Not as cool as being a doctor."

"I don't know about that," I said. "Maybe your work does a different kind of healing."

She cleared her throat and finally met my gaze, her cheeks pink. "Thank you for this, by the way."

"For what?"

"For making a house call in the dead of night for a paranoid woman."

"The last woman I assisted brought me chickens. Now I'm making house calls. Maybe this really is the nineteenth century."

Ivy frowned. "I can't pay you in chickens."

"That's okay," I said as I picked up my bag. I had a better idea than chickens. "I don't want to have to build a bigger coop."

And I was rambling because I didn't want to leave yet and didn't know quite how to take the next step toward that mistletoe mulligan I wanted.

Inspiration struck when I spotted the prescription pad I'd forgotten to pack. I took three steps into the kitchen, then turned back. "Think you could hand me my notepad? I left it on the coffee table."

"Oh, sure," she said. I timed it so she would enter the dining room just as I got to the mistletoe.

Chapter 31
Ivy

I reached for Gabe's pad and then headed for the kitchen, running straight into his hard chest. I looked up and my face drained of all color, which quickly flooded back. Of all of the places for me to be, I was under that damn parasitic plant that had contributed to my earlier humiliation.

I couldn't catch my breath enough to say excuse me, but then Gabe placed his index finger under my chin, gently lifting, so my eyes looked into his. I couldn't read the expression behind his light gray eyes.

"Can we pretend this is the first time we've ever met underneath the mistletoe?"

I swallowed hard and nodded yes.

His head dipped toward mine, but I didn't dare close my eyes this time, at least not until his lips touched mine. Attraction, a long-forgotten sensation, swirled through me, and I forgot to breathe.

Gabe's hand splayed across my lower back to steady me, and I wanted to weep. Support. My God, how I'd needed support, both literally and figuratively.

"That's what I should've done the first time," he said softly before turning toward the back door.

"Do you have to go?" I asked, immediately regretting how needy I sounded.

"Don't you want me to?"

I swallowed hard. "No."

"Maybe I need to stay a little longer to see if the Tylenol kicks in," he finally said, his eyes twinkling.

"Absolutely, I think you should. We need to think about the baby."

Holly appeared, and I wondered how much of the kiss she had seen. "Yes, we do need to think about the baby. We also need to think about Aunt Holly's sore arms."

I took the still-fussing Zuzu and began pacing up and down the hall until Gabe took a turn.

I wanted to tell him a hundred things, but I didn't know how to put them into words so I focused on Zuzu.

Chapter 32
Gabe

By six forty-five in the morning, Zuzu had finally cried herself back to sleep after her first dose of antibiotics. Ivy laid her gently down in the bassinet and surveyed the living room where her sister and mother had both already fallen asleep. She looked at me and whispered, "Are you sleepy?"

"Not really."

"Wanna go outside for some fresh air?"

I nodded, hoping to explore what we'd started earlier. I could only hope our kiss had left her pulse racing, too.

She grabbed the baby monitor and the pink thermal blanket from the back of the sofa, and I followed her outside to the back stoop. She started to light a cigarette, but then she looked at the cigarette and shoved it back into its pack. "Can you just take these?"

I took the pack. "Finally decided to quit?

"Yeah. Yolanda suggested I go cold turkey."

"It is better for both you and Zuzu," I agreed.

She looked at me, opening her mouth to say something and then closing it before unfolding the blanket. "I thought I had two. I guess we'll have to share."

We sat down together, the brick steps cool under our pants. For a few minutes we tried to stay under the blanket while keeping at least two inches between us. Finally, I sighed and said, "Come on, Ivy. We've already acted out a virgin birth and kissed under the mistletoe. I think we can huddle a little closer."

Mistake. She smelled of baby shampoo and soap with only the faintest tinge of tobacco, a far cry from the loud perfumes Brittany had always preferred. Now we sat shoulder against shoulder and thigh to thigh under the same blanket. Maybe being alone with her wasn't a good idea.

Or maybe it was the best idea.

I didn't know how to get us back to where we'd been after our kiss, so I said, "Bet you're thinking twice about taking in an infant after tonight, huh?"

"Nah. I wasn't ready for tonight, but I made it through, thanks to you."

"Oh, you didn't need me," I said.

She almost grabbed my hand but put her palm on her own knee instead. "No, I did. I've read and studied, but this was a baptism by fire. Byron was older."

"Parenthood is always baptism by fire—at least that's my going theory."

We sat in silence for a while. Ivy started to say something twice but then didn't. She fidgeted, and I was afraid she'd go back inside before I could figure out how to kiss her again. "So, about these books you write. . . ."

She laughed out loud, clearly not expecting that question. "You don't want to hear about them. They're probably not your cup of tea."

"You'd be surprised. I used to sneak Aunt Vi's books from time to time. I remember some book called *Savage Thunder*. It was, uh, very educational."

"Isn't that the one where—"

"Two characters have sex while riding a horse? Yes, yes, it is."

She laughed again, and I wanted to make her laugh at least ten times every day just to hear the sound. It wasn't a polished, practiced laugh like that of my first wife, actually more of a bark, but her joy was infectious.

"It was quite educational when Aunt Vi then sat me down and had an expansive talk on the birds and the bees, followed by a point-by-point analysis of everything that happened in the book that I should not do."

"Point by point?"

"Point by point."

"So, no sex while riding a horse for you?"

"That was one of the points. She gave me an extensive lecture on consent and not having sex with any lady who was in less than enthusiastic agreement."

I couldn't help but wonder what Ivy's enthusiastic agreement might look like.

Ivy nodded. "She's a good woman, your aunt Vi."

"That she was," I said.

We sat in silence because I hoped she might make a move on me. Finally, I said, "I could use a story. Tell me a little bit of yours."

She burrowed into the blanket. "I used to write Regency romances, so sex in a coach, I guess?"

"That sounds more comfortable."

"I'm thinking it had to be," she said with a giggle that faded as she added, "It was fun to write anyway."

"Was?"

"Well, it's hard to write about happily ever after when your husband dies."

Ah. Maybe our kiss didn't mean as much to her as it had to me.

If that's the case, why'd she ask you to stay? Why'd she invite you out here?

"But you're writing again?" I asked as much to get away from my thoughts as out of curiosity.

"I'm trying. I'm writing all longhand because my laptop decided to give up the ghost while I've been on sabbatical."

My turn to laugh. "I'm on sabbatical now."

"Really?"

"Yeah. I needed a break." I started to tell her about Abigail Burton, but I hesitated. Would she be as willing to seek my help if I told her about that case? Would she think it was my fault, too?

Before I could stop myself, I told her about the teenager whose life had been cut short.

"Gabe, that's awful," she said when I finally finished telling my story. I had a hand on the step beside me, readying to stand and leave if she told me she didn't trust me. Instead, she grabbed my hand. "I can't believe they're putting you through all of this for an inexplicable tragedy."

I grabbed her hand and squeezed it, warmth from her fingers racing up my arms and warming me from the inside out.

She understands. At least one person understands.

"Sure you won't read me a bedtime story?"

"But the sun's coming up!"

Sure enough the horizon threatened to turn pink, and I still hadn't found the courage to kiss her again. I pushed a strand of hair behind her ear, my hand lingering longer than it had to. "But I told you a story."

She smiled. "Once upon a time there was a duke who pretended to be a vicar to catch a widow in a lie—"

"That sounds very mysterious."

She smiled. "Well, the widow wasn't a liar."

"I'm guessing she was beautiful, though."

Like you.

Ivy ducked her head as though she'd heard my thoughts. The dim glow from the east softened her features.

"Of course she was beautiful, and he was very handsome, but he had a bad reputation with the ladies. She, meanwhile, had a secret."

"Now I have to know her secret."

"She was still a virgin," Ivy whispered as if anyone were around to overhear.

For a second I wondered if Ivy were a virgin because, well, men do like the idea of going where no man has gone before. Gene Roddenberry made a whole show about it. I cleared my throat. "I'm guessing the vicar who was actually a duke decided to relieve her of such a burden?"

She laughed. "After they were caught in a compromising position and were forced to marry, he finally did but only after she asked him very nicely."

"Well, doesn't seem like there's much of a problem, then," I said as I shifted on the step.

She leaned forward and cupped her chin in her free hand. "But now she knows he's a duke instead of a vicar, and she's not happy that he lied to her. He, on the other hand, thinks she may have murdered her husband, and he's a little concerned for his safety."

"Sure."

"You're not taking his side, are you?"

The pink sky gave way to even more light behind her, and there was the halo behind her once again. I swallowed hard. "Never."

"Good. My last chance at turning in this book is January third, and I have to find a way to bring them back together, and they're being very stubborn about it."

"Well," I said, "if the sex is *really* good . . ."

She smacked my shoulder, but she laughed.

"I think it would help if you named this vicar-duke after me."

"You're only saying that because you want a character named after you."

I held up one finger. "Correction: I want a rich, handsome romantic *hero* named after me."

She studied me carefully. "I could do that. Gabriel wouldn't have been an unusual name. It does kind of roll off the tongue."

At the thought of tongues, I couldn't stand it any longer. "Ivy Long, I would like to kiss you again."

Chapter 33
Ivy

When words wouldn't come, I leaned forward and kissed him. At first, our lips met chastely, but then he nipped at my bottom lip. Soon our tongues entwined, my hands traveling over his bearded jawline and tunneling through his hair while his arms wrapped around me, drawing me closer. Parts of me that had gained cobwebs from disuse perked up when I caught a rush of cold air where Gabe's hand had gone under the hem of my shirt but then hesitated just below my breast.

I broke the kiss.

He withdrew his hands, the concern in his eyes that of a man who'd been well trained. "Too far?"

"Yes," I panted. "I mean, no, but yes for right now."

He started to apologize, but I cut him off with another kiss.

Then I ended the kiss because I had to know. "So you weren't repulsed by me the other day?"

"Oh, God, no. I was trying not to make you feel uncomfortable because of what happened in the hospital."

"I don't know why I did that," I said, my heart singing but my cheeks burning once again as I thought about backing out from under the mistletoe. "It's just the nurse had assumed we were married, and that made me think of Corey and . . ."

"You know, you're very cute when you blush, but I hate to see you do it so often," he said, this time taking my fingers and bringing the back of my hand up to his lips just as one of my historical heroes might have done.

"I'm out of practice with all of this."

"I know what you mean," he said. "But I've also heard that practice makes perfect."

We leaned toward each other for another kiss only to be interrupted by Zuzu's cries on the baby monitor.

Our eyes locked, and time stopped.

He's the one.

Ivy Long, you are sleep deprived. You haven't known Gabriel Ledbetter long enough to make such pronouncements.

He gathered our blanket, and I took the monitor. Once we were inside, I scooped up my girl, her sweaty hair clinging to her head and her mouth turned upside down in a grotesque frown. Gabe kissed my cheek. "I'll see you tonight."

"Why don't you stay for breakfast at least?" Mom asked through a yawn.

"I really should—"

"Bacon and eggs and biscuits with home-canned strawberry jam," Mom said.

I can't say no to that," he said, taking Zuzu so I could dispose of the diaper, wash my hands, and make a bottle. Just as he sat, though, he bolted back up. "I've got to milk the goats!"

"That can't wait?" asked Mom from the kitchen.

"Maybe a few more minutes," he said as he sat back down.

I held out my arms for Zuzu, but he took the bottle and fed her, so I went to help Mom with breakfast. All the better to escape Holly, who'd looked as though she were watching a ping-pong match as she looked from Gabe to Mom and back before she narrowed her eyes on me.

You know, you're pretty lucky to have all of these people who are willing to help you, Ivy.

Yeah, I was. Holly had taken turns walking the baby when my arms couldn't take any more. Who knew a person so small could eventually feel so heavy? Gabe had stayed over even though he clearly thought I was paranoid. Then he'd kissed me senseless.

I made the largest pot of coffee that the machine would allow, humming while I did so, and then made biscuits from scratch. Mom fried bacon and scrambled eggs. Gabe managed to coax most of a bottle down Zuzu. He said she probably wasn't eating much because it hurt to swallow. When I got the biscuits in the oven, I looked around the corner of the living room to see Gabe and Holly making faces at Zuzu. I started to call Mavis and tell her I needed to take a sick day. Mind you, I didn't have any sick days left for the year, but I couldn't leave a fussy baby with Mom, now could I?

Yeah. I'd wait to call her until after breakfast.

"Food's up," Mom called to everyone, and we assembled around the table. I had a hard time meeting Gabe's gaze for a different reason this morning, but I couldn't seem to look away from him, either.

"So, Gabe. Are you headed back to Memphis?" Mom asked

"That's the plan," he said as he used his biscuit to push the last of his eggs onto his fork. My heart paused for a second at the news, but I had no claim on Gabe Ledbetter, so I told it to keep beating.

"When do you think you're going back?"

"Mom," I said, hoping that my look conveyed the sentiment that she shouldn't be questioning the nice man who'd assisted us last night.

"Nah, it's fine. I'm on sabbatical and waiting for a few things to sort themselves out."

Now both Holly *and* Mom stopped eating to stare at him and then look at me.

"Gabe, don't mind them. They have no manners."

We ate in silence, the only sound that of silverware on plates. Finally, Gabe said, "When do I get to see your book?"

I blushed to the roots of my hair and held Zuzu a little closer with my left hand while I tried to get egg on my fork with my right. "Oh, about the fifth of never. It's out of print."

He held a hand to his chest. "You wound me. Don't you have a single copy here?"

"The basement in our house in Memphis flooded and ruined my author copies," I said through gritted teeth. The very thought of having Gabe read my first book—a love story that now felt so silly after all I'd been through—made me want to crawl under the bed. We had just kissed and now he was going to read my sex scenes?

Gabe added home-canned strawberry preserves to his biscuit. When he took a bite, he closed his eyes and made a sound that could've come from one of my romance heroes. Mom reached across the table and laid her hand on his. "Don't worry, Gabe. I can give you one."

"Mom!"

"Oh, Ivy, lighten up. You should be proud of your book."

"I am proud, but—"

"But what?" she asked, her glare more effective than the huge bright light in an interrogation room.

"But I'm not that same person anymore."

All conversation halted.

Great Ivy. Way to be a Debbie Downer.

Gabe cleared his throat and laid his silverware across his plate. "Well. That is the best breakfast I've had in a long time, but I should go take care of the goats now. Thanks."

"No, thank you. For everything," I said, standing up because I was at the end of the table and thus blocking him in.

"Least I could do." He stopped in front of me once he had his coat draped over one arm and his satchel in his other hand. It was like he wanted to say something to me, but he couldn't find the words.

"Oh, shoot! I forgot to go get a copy Ivy's book," Mom said. "I have about twenty, you know."

Mom ran to the back bedroom and returned with a copy of *His Wanton Widow*.

Gabe took the copy and slipped it into his satchel. "I'll see you this evening."

I had backed into the doorway, and he gave me a peck on the lips, then kissed Zuzu on top of her head. My cheeks warmed yet again. Blessedly, Holly waited for the door to close behind him before she said, "Well, well. My mistletoe may have been good for something after all."

"Maybe," I said, as I arranged Zuzu's floor toys for some tummy time.

"Say, Mom," I asked while I watched Zuzu, moving toys near her. "Why do you have so many copies of my book?"

"Oh, Ivy. I'm your mother. You're lucky I don't have a hundred."

Tears of joy pricked at my eyes, but I didn't let anyone see them.

Chapter 34
Gabe

When I came in from milking the goats, Dad was waiting for me in the kitchen. "Indulging in another one-night stand?"

"Sleeping on a couch to watch over a sick baby."

Dad took a drag and blew the smoke out through the side of his mouth before he finally spoke. "That doesn't sound anywhere near as much fun."

"It's not."

"Did ya milk the goats?"

"Of course," I said as I tromped upstairs for a shower.

"That's good. You develop an udder full of milk and you'll be mighty concerned about who milks you and when," he said. "Bet you'd want people to get up earlier to take care of you, I tell you that."

Dad was feeling frisky today.

"I'll keep that in mind," I yelled down.

After a quick shower, I took out Ivy's book. It had the requisite shirtless dude and gorgeous woman with a strategically unfastened dress. Ivy's picture in the back showed a bright-eyed woman with a mischievous smile, and her bio mentioned a happily ever after with her husband Corey but not much else. I flipped through a few pages, but I felt like a voyeur because I couldn't help but picture

Ivy as the heroine even though she'd described the character as a blond.

Instead, I opened my laptop to find out more. Then I remembered that Dad had no Wi-Fi. None. Nada. Zip. In the Year of Our Lord 2012, my dad still lacked any type of Internet access. I slipped the laptop into my satchel. Town, it was.

"Dad, I'm going into town for a while," I shouted as I reached the bottom step.

"Get some honey buns," he hollered back.

I took the Jaguar this time because I hadn't driven her in a few weeks, and I didn't want her to sit up. She'd need to be purring if I wanted to get the most out of a trade in. After Dad's pickup, the sports car felt claustrophobic. Why had I even bought the thing? Maybe I bought a Jaguar for the same reason I married Brittany: As a doctor it was what I was supposed to do. Like the Jag, Brittany was sleek and exciting. She looked the part of a young doctor's wife, a blond goddess who was imminently . . . suitable. One day I realized my wife and I almost never had deep conversations. When we did, our beliefs and tastes varied widely. She hated visiting Ellery; I grew tired of black tie charity events. She loved the Jag, but I preferred the Jeep. She'd talked me into trading in that Jeep, and now here I was with this little thing.

Heads turned as I rolled into the McDonald's parking lot, and I winced. No need to be so flashy in town. I often forgot that tiny Ellery didn't have as many fancy cars as Germantown or Collierville. I grunted as I unfolded myself to get out of the car—not having to contort myself to get into and out of a vehicle would be nice.

Since not having to contort myself to fit Brittany's idea of marriage had been a relief, I hoped not having to fold myself like an accordion to get into my car would be similarly liberating.

Once inside, I ordered a Happy Meal, thinking I could give the toy to Portia. Then I set up the laptop and went to work. Ivy Long had published one Regency Romance—the one her mother had handed me—back in early 2008. I did a search for "survived by his wife Ivy Long" and managed to find an obituary for a Corey

Renfroe. Interesting. She hadn't taken his name. Maybe because she knew she was going to publish a book?

Oh. He had died only two months after her book released.

In *His Wanton Widow*, she had written about a widow and then she had become one. My gut twisted at how awful that must have been, to not only endure her husband's death but then to be reminded of it every time she looked at her own book, her debut novel. The description was of a widow who never wanted to remarry, and the last line said it was book one in The Merry Widow Series and to be on the lookout for her next release, *Her Mad Vicar*.

That sounded a lot like the story she'd told me the night before.

A quick search showed that second book had never made it to the shelves, but I already knew that.

I studied the headshot of Ivy Long on her website. It was the same photo as the one in the back of her book, but having the portrait in color brought out the pink of her cheeks and the twinkle in her eyes. The website had a longer bio, too, and it mentioned that she'd worked as a substitute teacher, a bartender, and a telemarketer before realizing she was suited for only one thing: writing.

My widow wasn't wanton, but I wanted her to have that same smile as in her headshot. What could I do to help her that wouldn't qualify as sticking my nose where it didn't belong?

She'd mentioned having to write her books out longhand. How was she supposed to make a January deadline if she wrote everything out longhand?

In my mind I saw the laptop at the end of the Longs' dining room table. There was no way that dinosaur could be repaired. It had to have been ancient when she wrote her first book. Buying her a new computer would be over-the-top, but there was nothing stopping me from buying a new one for myself, now was there?

Maybe I'd go to Jefferson to look around the electronics stores. If I couldn't find what I wanted, there was always the Apple store in Memphis. At the very least, I could pick up a little surprise in Jefferson, something to help us celebrate our last night as Mary and Joseph.

Chapter 35
Ivy

My head pounded, my fingers tingled, and I dearly regretted giving my last pack of cigarettes to Gabe.

I'd gone through every purse I owned and checked all of the places I usually put my smokes.

Zuzu fussed, and I froze, ready to jump up and run back to the living room. Then she settled back into a fitful sleep.

Why was I doing this? I didn't want the baby to smell like smoke. I didn't want to waste money on the things. Forget about health reasons and the need to be the best foster parent I could be; I didn't have the time or money for cigarettes anymore.

Man, but how was I going to finish my book for Datya without coffee and cigarettes? Another night like the previous one, and I didn't see myself finishing that book at all. The good news was that I did indeed have two-thirds instead of a half and that I had finished reading through the old manuscript. The bad news? I still had no idea how I was going to put things back together for a happy ending once I wrote the worst moment of the story, the point at which all seemed lost.

I supposed I could hand in the Quasimodo of a manuscript as was, but my pride wouldn't allow me to eschew professionalism. Crazy premise? Sure. Typos and a missing ending? Oh, no.

Thinking about how the vicar/duke and his widow were going to overcome their black moment got me to thinking about Gabe, and I blushed all over again even though there was no one to see me.

My phone rang. At the sight of the Dollar General number, I blanched.

I had forgotten to call in sick.

"Hello, Mavis."

"Don't 'hello Mavis' me," she said. "Because one of my employees didn't show up for work on a Friday ten days before Christmas. And she doesn't appear to be in traction in the hospital or anything equally dire."

"I'm sorry. Zuzu was up all night, and I forgot. I won't be able to come in today."

Her silence spoke volumes, and she let me drink it in.

"Excuse me? Did I hear you say that you won't be able to come in today?"

"That's what you heard," I muttered.

She sighed. "Ivy, don't head down this path again. Remember what I told you about corporate. Things aren't always up to me."

I closed my eyes. I'd been so much better the past year. "This isn't the same! Zuzu has a double ear infection."

"Leave her with your mother."

"I can't do that," I said, thinking about Mom's lack of enthusiasm when it came to watching her pseudo-granddaughter.

"You're putting me in a bind. This place is crawling with people."

"I'm sorry, Mavis. Really I am."

"Sorry, sorry, always sorry," she muttered. "I guess you have to do what you have to do, but I won't turn down the help if you can drag your sorry self in here. Now find someone to watch that child this weekend. You close on Saturday and open on Sunday. Remember?"

"I remember."

She hung up on me before I got the last syllable out.

The back door slammed, waking up Zuzu, and I rushed to the

living room just in time to see Holly stomping through the dining room.

"I swear you are like a bull in a china shop," I whispered to her as I tried to coax the baby back to sleep.

She rolled her eyes.

"Can you watch Zuzu for me tonight? It's my last shift at the Nativity scene." I knew I should cancel on them if I hadn't gone in to work, but I had to see Gabriel. I needed to look into his eyes and see that our evening hadn't been a figment of my imagination. Besides I *could* take Zuzu with me if it were warm enough.

"If you're asking me for a favor, then I guess you're not mad at me anymore," Holly said.

"Oh, I'm still mad somewhere deep inside, but I don't have time for it right now."

She had the audacity to pump her fist. My sister—my *grown* sister—was such a child.

Zuzu and I went through a now familiar bottle and diaper routine complete with the added step of antibiotics. Once she was bouncing on my lap, apathetic if not completely happy, I turned to my sister.

"I'm also too tired to yell at you right now. I want to. I really want to, but I can't. Do you understand how you can't just take the baby to a bar because you have the opportunity for some time and a half?"

Her nostrils flared. "I will watch her tonight, but I did not ask for this responsibility. *You* gave it to me. It started with 'put up the play yard, Holly' and continued to 'walk the baby, Holly.' Now, she is adorable, and I feel for her situation, but my needs are just as important as your needs. If I hadn't taken over that class, then people would've been mad. Then those mad people might've left the gym. If we don't have enough members, then the gym closes and I don't have a job so it wasn't about time and a half."

I suppose I hadn't thought about it quite that way. The fact that Holly had thought the situation out so thoroughly surprised me. "Fine. But next time, think."

"Think? I left the baby with a pediatrician—how much more qualified can a babysitter get?"

Another surprisingly good point. "You didn't know he was in there. You saw Julian's truck."

She started pacing. "Yes, because I thought Romy might be able to help me out in a pinch."

"Holly, just help me out here."

"I have done nothing but help you out here. You could at least say thank you, you know."

She stared at me, willing me to admit she was right. Man, I hated it when she was right.

"You're right. Thank you for all of your help."

Her chin jerked in response. Wait. What if she had trouble with all of this because she herself was expecting? "Have you figured out if you're—"

"I have a doctor's appointment on Monday," she snapped.

Based on her tone of voice, her monthly visitor might arrive first. "You going to tell me why you're fit to be tied?"

"No."

"Does this have to do with your potential baby daddy?"

"I'm not telling you, Miss Goody Two-shoes."

So that would be a yes.

She probably wouldn't think I was such a Goody Two-shoes if she knew some of the thoughts I'd had about Gabe. My eyes automatically traveled to my purse in the corner. Corey's last letter lay tucked inside a pocket. In my mind I knew that he'd told me multiple times that he wanted me to go on and find someone new, but I still feared I'd open that letter and find disapproval.

Or maybe you're afraid to fall for anyone after what happened with him.

I looked at a sleeping Zuzu and thought of Byron.

"You're not going to leave me, are you, Zuzu?"

But, of course, she couldn't answer that question.

Chapter 36
Gabe

Julian and I surveyed the stable scene complete with llama, alpaca, sheep, two donkeys, rooster, cow, palomino, tripod beagle, three Wise Men, tiny shepherd with rabbit, and one angel. Mary was headed our way, and we made up Joseph and the remaining shepherd.

"We might have outdone ourselves," Julian said.

"Maybe."

"Well, let's get this over with," my brother said as he put on his head covering and headed for his spot between the cow and the llama.

He wasn't fooling me. He loved those animals, and he especially loved his wife and little girl. If Portia had asked him to put a whale in the Nativity scene, then he would've found a pod and lassoed an orca for her. Sure, he would've cussed and complained about it, but that little girl would've had her whale by hook or by crook.

Miss Idabell called for us to take our places, and I eased into my spot across from Ivy. "Brought you something."

"You didn't have to do that," she said, but her cheeks flushed.

"Well, I was thinking on possible miracles that our son might need to perform. So this is an integral part of our job as playing the parts of Mary and Joseph."

The corners of her mouth twitched. "Oh?"

"I thought I'd practice turning water into wine. Maybe the old man could teach the kid a thing or two."

I brought out two mini bottles of merlot and set them behind the manger where no one could see them but Ivy and me. Imagine wine in the middle of a Baptist Nativity. Elders somewhere spun in their graves like a pig on a spit. I needed to make sure Miss Idabell didn't see, because she was a teetotaler of the first order.

Finally, Ivy's eyes met mine for a brief moment before looking away again. "Look at that! I predict your skill will be in high demand."

"Yeah, but I'm going to teach the boy that it's not an everyday kind of miracle like, say, healing a leper. It's more of a special occasion miracle."

"So something like a wedding?"

"Exactly."

The cars started pulling forward, and we fell into silence for a few minutes. "You're something else, Gabe Ledbetter. It's been a pleasure being Mary to your Joseph."

"I can't think of a better Mary than you. You even managed to have an actual baby while we were doing this."

She laughed out loud, a rich and husky sound, and it was the best Christmas present I could've asked for.

"Oh, get a room," Romy said.

Ivy couldn't meet my gaze, but that just gave me more time to study her profile.

At the break, we sneaked our mini bottles to the back of the Dollar General to have a nip.

"I, uh, didn't bring glasses, so I suppose we'll have to drink straight from the bottle," I said.

"Well, I couldn't possibly do something so . . . uncouth."

For the briefest of seconds, I thought she was serious, but then she threw back the mini bottle and took such a generous slug that she coughed a little and had to wipe her mouth with the back of her hand.

"Be careful, now," I warned. "Red wine stains, and we have to turn these robes back in upon completion of our parts."

She giggled. "I can't believe I'm sneaking wine at the break. This is a bad time to mention I skipped supper, isn't it?"

"Chug it," I said.

"Oh, I don't think so." She handed me her bottle so she could fish around for the phone in her back pocket. "We have ten minutes."

"Then we'd better make them count." I returned her bottle, and we clinked the two of them together before sipping and looking everywhere but at each other.

"I can think of a better way to spend ten minutes," she said in a husky voice.

"Oh, really?" I said as I took her bottle and placed both of them on an electric meter box behind me.

She took two steps toward me, and I couldn't have pulled away from her if I'd wanted to. My lips were going to touch her lips, and that was all there was to it.

Her eyes fluttered shut, and my stomach roiled in anticipation as other sensations traveled south. I couldn't wait to kiss her again, but I also wanted to savor the moment. Then our lips met, and the world melted away as I lost myself in the feel of her lips with their taste of red wine and tobacco. I pulled her closer, and the spark of having her body up against mine had me considering ditching the Nativity altogether.

"What the heck are you two doing back here?"

We broke apart as though we'd scalded each other.

"Just, um, taking a break, Miss Idabell," said Ivy as she moved to block Miss Idabell's view of the meter box.

"Is that what the kids are calling it these days?" the older lady said. "Neck on your own time. Let's go."

Ivy walked away, but I grabbed her free hand, shocking myself with how much I enjoyed the simple pleasure of her fingers laced with mine. I could only imagine what it would be like to—

Gabriel, you've going to have to imagine that some other time.

"Ivy, think you'd be free sometime?"

She smiled, her eyes downcast. She had to be blushing, but I couldn't see for sure in the dark.

"I think I could make time for you."

"Do you now?"

She nodded as Miss Idabell called for us once again.

Chapter 37
Ivy

I wasn't sure I needed my car to get home.

I could've floated.

As I drove, I hummed, and my smile wouldn't fade because Gabriel Ledbetter had kissed me. Again. I hadn't felt those particular butterflies since college when I'd met Corey. Even so, either my memory was faulty, or kissing was better than I remembered. I had other urges, too, urges I'd tamped down for longer than I could remember.

You've been alone for a very long time.

Maybe not a *very* long time. I certainly hadn't taken things to Miss Havisham extremes.

You would have.

Quite possibly true. I might never have had the chance to get to know Gabe if it hadn't been for our parents conspiring to make us play biblical parts and then finding that little girl in the manger. Or even my sister pointing out the mistletoe.

Mistletoe!

Since my story about the vicar took place at Christmas, what better way for him to convince her to give him a second chance than to catch her under the mistletoe and remind her of the chemistry they had shared before she knew he was a duke and they'd been forced to marry for being caught in a compromising position because, well, of all that chemistry. I could start them on the road to their happily ever after using the same experience that had gotten me kissed.

Very meta, Ivy.

Then again, real life often creeped into my novels like that. No, I didn't have any dresses with an empire waistline, but something Mom said might strike me as the perfect piece of dialogue—adjusted for the period, of course—for my fictional mother to say. Back when Corey and I were first married, he had this riff on umbrellas that I managed to convert to a parasol joke. Then there was the time Holly broke Mom's gravy boat. While searching to see if gravy boats might be an anachronism, I fell down quite the rabbit hole to find out about these similarly shaped lady urinals called Bourdaloues. My editor wouldn't let me mention those in my book, though, for some odd reason.

Such a killjoy.

Now I could see my mad vicar again, feel him, hear him talk. I understood his motivations. More important, I understood what made my heroine tick, how she felt. I could write more authentically about a kiss because I'd just experienced one. Best of all, I could use mistletoe to straighten out the kinks and set my characters on the right path.

For the first time in forever, I bounded out of the car and shut the door, ready to tackle the problem of my abandoned manuscript.

With the aid of Tylenol, I managed to get in three one-hour shifts of work. First, I wrote the scene underneath the mistletoe. Then I backtracked to write the black moment. Finally, I sketched out the ending and the epilogue. Obviously, as the bard always said, "the course of true love never did run smooth," but the course of the writer always did run smoother with at least a hint of what was to come. Zuzu only woke up once, and I gave her extra cuddles for her stellar sleeping skills.

Now, I needed to find the thumb drive with the old manuscript and carve out time to go to the library to use their computer to type in changes and the ending. I hoped they had a corner computer for when I got to the love scene. . . .

Before I knew it, the early morning sun on the frost-covered grass brightened my legal pad. I had planned to go to bed when Mom got up and could take over watching Zuzu, but then she reminded me of my foolish promise two days before.

"But Ivy, you said you'd come with me to book club today. It's going to be a lovely potluck lunch, and I'm sure everyone will be delighted to see you."

"Mom, I've been up all night!"

"And whose fault is that?" she asked as she handed me a cup of coffee.

"Do you want me to finish the book or not?" I asked.

"I want you to write the book at a time when you are not working or attending this specific book club meeting," she said. "You've been promising them ever since your first book came out."

Well. That wasn't too much to ask what with all the extra time I had. Oh, wait, it *was* too much to ask along with a side of guilt trip. I'd taken in a sweet baby who still hadn't learned to sleep through the night. Even if she had known how to sleep from dusk to dawn, the ear infection guaranteed she'd wake up any time the acetaminophen wore off.

"Oh, Mom. When is the meeting?"

"Eleven o'clock."

Great. It would run until one at least. I'd still have time to go in for my close shift. "All right, all right, I'll go."

"Then I'll look after Zuzu so you can go to work"

I was halfway down the hall to a hot shower when I realized my mother had volunteered to watch Zuzu for me later.

Not for Holly.

For me.

Yesterday, Holly had—grudgingly—volunteered to take Zuzu so I could write.

I might actually pull this off.

Chapter 38
Gabe

"Know what? I might want me a Christmas tree."

I almost choked on my cereal. When I recovered, I tried to reason with him. "Dad, it's little over a week until Christmas."

"Well, I never did have a Christmas with my boy. Maybe I want to have at least one good Christmas before I die," he said as he lit another cigarette.

"Is there something you aren't telling me?"

"Naw. We just never know which day might be our last, do we? I got to thinking yesterday how a stroke took both your mother and your stepmother. I wonder what the odds are of that."

I wanted to get him to talk about something that wasn't so morbid, but morbid was his favorite topic. Aunt Vi used to have me pick up on the upstairs phone so I could converse with her and my father—not that I would've been able to get a word in edgewise. I swear, half of their phone conversations used to begin with "Did you hear who died the other day?"

Now those were some phone conversations I didn't want to relive. "Are you sure having a tree won't make you feel sad?"

I didn't want him to remember the sickly tree that he'd left up for so long as a memorial to my mom.

"Just get something other than a scraggly old pine. Hey! How 'bout you and Julian go get me a real tree."

Wait. What had just happened here? He'd clearly given this idea a lot of thought.

"A real tree?" I asked because I didn't want to broach the subject of Julian yet.

"Surely there's a fir or something on the back forty."

That had to be one of the most redneck things I'd ever heard. "All right, Dad. If you want a tree, then I will go get a tree."

"Get Julian to help you."

I opened my mouth to tell him that I could do it myself, but I realized he wanted to know his two sons could get along. He probably wanted all of us to be there when he decorated it, too.

"Do you still have decorations?"

He squinted his eyes and looking up at the ceiling as though expecting to use X-ray vision to scan the contents of the attic. "I don't think I do."

Fortunately, I knew someone who worked in an establishment that sold such accoutrements for decorating a Christmas tree, and she happened to be a woman I had kissed recently and desperately wanted to kiss again.

You know you're going back to Memphis.

So what if I was? Memphis was not even two hours away, hardly like moving to another country.

"Don't get any of those damned tinsel icicles," Dad said before going into a coughing fit.

"Okay."

"And don't go buying me any presents, either. You spend your money on you." He reached for his walker, and I wanted to help him, but he swatted my hand away.

"Where are you going, Dad?"

"If you must know, I'm going to the bathroom and then I'm going to watch some television with my eyes shut."

I frowned. He hadn't been out of the house in a long time. "You want to come with us to pick out a tree or any of the decorations?"

"Hell, no."

All right, then. I pulled out my phone to text Julian, who replied he'd be over in a minute. We took Dad's truck down the paths around the fields and pastures. Julian insisted on driving, and I didn't mind because I wasn't that used to roads that were nothing more than two faint dirt tracks for your tires.

"Did you bring a saw?" Julian asked.

"Yeah. I wasn't about to forget that," I said, chuckling at the memory of Chevy Chase's tree on the top of the station wagon complete with its dirt-covered roots hanging off the back.

"Good, I don't want to end up like that idiot in the movie."

I grinned. As different as my brother and I were, we had at least one thing in common.

About an hour later, my grin had completely disappeared. "Did he send us out here knowing how hard it would be to find a suitable tree?"

"Well, you probably know more about this land than I do, but he told me it had mostly been used for cotton before he converted it into a pasture, so there aren't a lot of trees. Most of what he's got are those big old pines along the edges."

We tromped through tall grass and came to the edge of the Ledbetter property as marked by a fence. And, of course, on the other side of that fence was a fir tree of the absolute perfect size and shape for Christmas festivities. "It's a shame that tree isn't on our side."

Julian looked at the tree and then at me and finally took in a panoramic view of the pasture we'd been traveling for the past hour. "I think we may have to borrow that tree."

"Borrow?" I asked as he hiked the fence and reached out a hand for the saw.

"Yeah, ol' Fraser won't mind. Look at all this brush. He doesn't even know it's back here. So we'll just borrow it."

"Why do I have the feeling you aren't going to bring it back?"

"I'm not—at least not exactly like it was, but Fraser's a cousin on my mama's side so this tree is basically family." He sawed all the way through the tree, then worked to hand it to me over the fence. As he grunted and sweated and panted, I wasn't quite sure what to do.

Once we'd hoisted the tree into the back of the pickup, it took up more space than I had anticipated. "Um, Julian?"

"Aw, we'll trim some off the end when we get there."

"Your ability to rationalize all of this is, well, scary." My hands were a little sticky from sap but, for the most part, I'd been able to avoid it. My shirt wasn't as lucky, but I didn't like it anyway.

"Funny, Romy says it's one of my finer qualities."

We rode back in silence to the house where it became readily apparent we would need to saw a good two feet off the end. Julian wanted to saw off the top. When I pointed out that it would look like a tree mesa and that we also needed a place for the angel, both he and Dad looked at me as if I needed to turn in my man card.

"Angel? The heck is that nonsense? We need a star," Dad said.

For a man who hadn't celebrated Christmas in a very long time, he certainly had oddly specific requests—especially with half of December gone.

"Make sure there aren't any tree rats in that thing before you bring it into the house," Dad said before he took up his walker.

"Tree rats?" I echoed.

"You know, squirrels," Julian said as he surveyed the best place to saw on the tree.

"I figured." I stood on one of the truck's tires and tried to hold the tree down while Julian sawed. The added pressure of holding the tree in place meant more sap. Gloves might be helpful.

"Oh, forget this," he said as he turned for the little toolshed a few feet away.

"Grab me some gloves," I shouted. At least I could be reasonably certain any squirrels were long gone between the movement of the truck and the vibrating of the tree from the saw.

Then Julian fired up the chainsaw.

"Don't you think that's overkill?"

"What?"

"Overkill!"

"Hell, no, it ain't a power drill!"

I waved my arms at him to just saw the tree and be done with it. He lopped off the end, and a roundish piece of fir fell to the ground. Then he took off a few of the lower branches so we'd have a place to anchor the tree into the stand.

Assuming there was a stand. Maybe I should've looked for that before we went on our journey.

I still didn't have gloves and didn't relish reaching inside for the trunk without them.

"So, this is a chainsaw," Julian started, his voice still loud from all of the noise a few minutes before.

"I know that," I said, brushing away thoughts of a Tennessee Chainsaw Massacre. "I was asking if you thought using a chainsaw to cut off a little hunk of tree was *overkill*."

"Oh, that," Julian said with a grin. "Probably. But it sure was fun."

We dragged the tree into the house, and Julian managed to get enough resin on himself to understand why gloves would've been helpful. Sure enough no one knew where the tree stand was, so I had to hold the tree up while Julian went to the attic to look for one. His cussing drifted down the hall along with enough non-cuss words that I pieced together his hand had stuck to the little trap door that led to the attic.

Finally, Julian emerged with an ancient cast-iron tree stand, and we grunted our way to getting the tree in place while Dad barked commands like "move it to the left," then "naw, to the right," followed by "can't you boys center anything?" When we finally had the tree secured, we stepped back to survey our handiwork, careful to keep our hands away from our bodies. As predicted, the tree looked a tad larger now that it wasn't in its natural habitat. The top hit the ceiling and bowed over sadly. The girth of the tree took up half the living room.

"We're going to have to take this thing outside and saw off some more aren't we?" Julian asked.

"Yep."

"But now I can't touch the chainsaw unless I want to go through life like that dude in *Army of Darkness*."

"Ain't nobody going into the army," Dad said. "Just put some WD-40 on to get the sap off."

Julian snorted, but we went for the tree and like idiots tried to go out with the top of the tree first, then got a lick of sense and turned it around to go out bottom first. At least Dad got his daily entertainment, laughing until he went into coughing fits. "If I'd known Christmas decorations were this much fun, I would've done this a long time ago."

"Glad he's having fun," I muttered once we got outside and headed for the shed for the WD-40 to take off the sap so we could saw off more of the tree, only to take it back inside and get more sap on us and come back to the WD-40.

"This better be worth it," I said as I prepared to spray Julian's hands. "Because I'm pretty sure I see mild dermatitis in our future."

"Mild what?"

"It's going to irritate our skin, so I hope it works."

"It'll work. It's like that guy in *My Big Fat Greek Wedding* who tells everyone to put some Windex on it."

"What?"

"Oh, sorry. It's a movie. There for a while I watched *a lot* of movies. Romy keeps telling me to keep my inner monologue more inner and—"

"I don't mind." Oddly enough I didn't.

"Well that's a good one. You should watch it."

"What year did it come out?"

"Sometime soon after 2000."

"Oh, I think I was finishing my residency then, so it's all a blur." I went to spray my own hands only to find my left hand stuck to the can. Julian pried it apart and we slathered on WD-40, then shuffled over to the work sink to lather up well with soap.

"You know, I think you had a good idea about those gloves," Julian said as we struggled to get the WD-40 and soap concoction off our skin.

"D'ya think?"

Thanks to a couple of pairs of work gloves, we finished getting the tree set up after another rousing round of "to the right" and "naw, to the left."

"Whew. I'm exhausted," I said.

"Exhausted?" Julian said. "You have to go get the decorations."

I groaned, but then I thought of Ivy and sat up straight. There were some perks to Christmas shopping after all.

Chapter 39
Ivy

The Merry Widows held their monthly book club in the Volunteer Room of the Yessum County Library. For the moment, the library was housed in a building that had once been Main Street's only grocery store. To enter we had to walk over an ancient black mat to get the old-fashioned grocery store doors to open.

"So weird," I said as I juggled Zuzu's carrier from one hand to another to avoid hitting the railing between in and out doors.

"And it lets in flies," librarian Wendy Cope said from where she stood behind the circulation desk. "That's why we're raising funds for a new and improved library—spread the word."

"Will do," I said. Mom was already halfway to the back of the library. I had to trot to catch up.

Once we got to the Volunteer Room, I took Zuzu from her seat and settled her into the sling that Holly had bought for me. She nestled perfectly against my chest, and I could move my hands. I had to admit my sister could be sweet when she wanted to be. Most of the Merry Widows were older than I was, and they sat on those hard folding chairs that had YCL spray painted on the back. More than one lady had brought a seat cushion with her.

Mrs. Morris, an elderly lady whose husband had died right after mine did, had wrapped herself in her afghan to guard against the chill of the high-ceilinged room. The county had done their best, but it was painfully obvious that we were in what had once been the stockroom section of the store. If I'd had any money, I would've gladly donated to the new library fund.

You might have some money once you finish this book.

Doubtful. I'd need my advance to help cover living expenses.

I told myself to shush and listen to Lark Adams. She was the local yoga instructor/resident hippie. Well, she wasn't much of a hippie, but the bar for rebellion was set pretty low in Ellery—she'd lived on a commune, partaken of free love and Eastern religions, and was an anti-war vegetarian so . . . close enough for most people. She wasn't even a widow per se because she hadn't married the father of her second child. He'd passed away, though, and the ladies in this group didn't quibble. Next to her sat her polar opposite, Caroline Anderson, dressed in a somber suit with her gray-streaked hair pulled back, looking every bit the funeral director she was.

Mavis was an infrequent member since her Saturday schedule often conflicted with their meeting.

I wonder if the Widows would consider meeting on a weeknight.

You are not a member. You are only here temporarily because you read Outlander *and you promised your mom in a moment of temporary insanity that you would come.*

The Merry Widows had once been a larger group, but one former member was now in assisted living, one had passed, and one had moved to Florida. My attendance that day brought the number to five. Mrs. Morris gestured to the chair beside her, and I took a seat.

Mrs. Morris didn't say anything, but she patted my knee, her old wedding band thunking against my kneecap.

Fortunately, Lark chose that moment to bring the book club to order. "Hello, everyone! I hope you enjoyed *Outlander*, and a warm welcome to Ivy. We've been hoping you might join us for a while. It'll be nice to get a writer's perspective on all of this."

"A writer?" Caroline said.

"Well, I have one published romance, but I finally started writing again."

"That's great!" Lark said. "I can definitely feel some positive energy flowing from you."

Caroline, meanwhile, sized me up with her head cocked to one side.

"So *Outlander*. What did we think?" Mom asked. Bless her for remembering we needed to move things along because I still had to go to work.

"I don't think it was right for her to marry Jamie knowing she was married back in the future," Mrs. Morris said.

"It's not like she had a choice!" Caroline surprised me with her vehemence.

We debated the legitimacy of Jamie and Claire's marriage for a while. Then we discussed the merits of time travel with four out of the five of us saying no thank you to time travel. As Mom put it, "Jamie Fraser is quite the man, but I do love my indoor plumbing."

Then we got into a rip-roaring debate over whether or not the novel should be considered a romance.

"She's committing idolatry the *whole* time!" Mrs. Morris shouted.

"I think you meant adultery," Mom said quietly.

"I don't care what you call it! It's wrong!"

Technically, she was right in that both of those things were wrong.

Caroline practically pinned me to the wall with her stare. "You're a romance author. What do you think?"

I opened my mouth but then closed it, wanting to choose my words carefully. I was only one woman and not able to speak for the entire genre. "I say yes, but with caveats."

"Oh, there's all kinds of caveating going on," Mrs. Morris muttered.

"I think you meant cavort—"

Mom shot me a warning look as Mrs. Morris snapped, "I know what I meant."

"As you were saying, Ivy?" Lark asked.

"Well, Jamie and Claire do fall in love and do end up together at the end of this book and—"

"Yes, but they don't *stay* together," Mom said angrily.

"Spoilers!" Lark and Caroline yelled at the same time.

"I'm just saying I don't think it's a romance if they're not even together at the beginning of the next book," Mom said.

"That's why I quit reading with the first one," Mrs. Morris snapped, then her cheeks turned pink as she realized she'd outed herself as having enjoyed the love story despite the idolatry and caveating. "Okay, I like Jamie Frasier and think she should leave that dud from the forties, all right?"

"Oh, so you *do* consider it a romance," Lark said.

"Come on, Mrs. Morris," I coaxed. "Jamie and Claire's story is even a common romance trope, the marriage of convenience. Let's say romance with a caveat or two."

Caroline nodded her head as though she approved of my answer, and I wondered what she was up to. She was up to something.

Meanwhile, Mrs. Morris was saying, "Oh, I told you there was caveating and fornicating and that spanking. I don't mean the sexy kind, either."

"I did have a problem with that," I said.

"But he more than makes up for that later, don't you think?" asked Lark.

I shrugged. "Romance with a caveat."

"And that's life," Mom said. "Romance with a caveat. Life doesn't always give you a happily ever after."

At the disgusted, cynical tone of my mother's speech, my temper flared. "Know what? I believe in happily ever after. There are all kinds of happily ever after, and I don't think they all require a romantic partner. It could be building up your own business or raising a child or, yes, finding love. Maybe, just maybe, some of us will be lucky enough to get a second romantic happily ever after. I don't think I'm ready to quit looking."

Mom dabbed at her eyes. I panted from the passion of my speech.

What are you doing?

But I wasn't done. No, I had books to write and fellas to kiss and children to raise.

"I wouldn't even say I've been cheated," Mrs. Morris said. "Fifty-nine happy years with my Leo. Mind you, the old coot was supposed to make it to the sixty-year mark with me, but you know how men are."

A couple of us snickered, but Lark cleared her throat. She preferred to avoid any kind of generalization. To change the subject, she launched into a discourse on her favorite part of the book: Claire's role as a healer with all of the botany and folk remedy references. When she started referencing Latin names, I zoned out. Apparently, Mom did, too, because the next thing she said had nothing to do with plants:

"Yeah, well, I liked the fact that the man was the virgin for a change."

"Mom!"

"What? We're all women here. We know how babies are made."

"That scene did steam up my windows," Caroline said, a dreamy smile on her usually dour face.

"I may have to get cable expressly to see that part of the new television show," Lark added.

All of the Merry Widows, myself included, took a moment to think fondly on Jamie's deflowering.

"Well," Mrs. Morris said, her wrinkled cheeks pink—and not from her haphazardly applied blush.

"And with that I think it's time for the punch and cookies portion of this meeting," Caroline responded.

"Or the cold shower portion," Mom muttered under her breath.

Zuzu fussed a little.

"I think it may also be formula time. What say you, little one?"

The other ladies made for the card table on one side of the room, and I took Zuzu over to a corner away from the food. I knew from experience that the library bathroom didn't have a changing table. No doubt that was yet another reason Wendy wanted a new facility.

I didn't realize Caroline had broken away from the others and was standing behind me until she made me jump out of my skin when she said, "I have a question for you, if I may."

"Shoot."

"Do you have any hints for a new romance author?"

I affixed Zuzu's new diaper and put her back into the car seat because I didn't feel like wrestling with the carrier before washing my hands. "Um, I don't recommend having a husband die on you. More recently, I've found it difficult—but not impossible—to write with a baby in the house."

"Well, I don't have to worry about either of those things at this point."

"Do you have a publisher? Are you doing it yourself?"

She shushed me. "I have an online publisher, and it comes out in three months. You're the first person I've told. I have them under a pen name because I don't want anyone to take the funeral home any less seriously."

"Congratulations! What a small world it is."

"I'll tell you more later," she said. I turned and saw Mom headed our way.

"What are two deviously planning over here?"

"Nothing," I said at the exact same time that Caroline said, "World domination."

We both laughed.

"Need me to take the baby so you can wash your hands and make that formula?" Mom asked.

Zuzu's cries were becoming more insistent, so I left Mom in charge of the car seat. She cooed over the child, and my heart squeezed in on itself. That was my mom with my child.

No, really. I had agreed to adopt her.

When I came back from washing my hands, Mom was already feeding the baby because Lark had mixed the formula for her. I leaned back and watched my mother fawn over a baby, a sight I'd often thought I'd never see. The Merry Widows had gathered around, making it look as though Zuzu had an entire court of ladies in waiting.

It was all so crazy. When I thought on the events of the past week, phrases like "God's plan" came to the mind for the first time since Corey passed. I'd quit going to church then. Sunday hours at the Dollar General made for a convenient excuse; people didn't have to know that I volunteered for those shifts. Other people wanted to go to church. I didn't. So why make them work on Sundays if I could do it for them? Mavis even trusted me to open so she had time to finish her church service before she came to work.

Now, that said, we needed to talk about this close shift on a Saturday night combined with an open the next day—that combo was brutal. I didn't see any writing in my future tonight.

Was Mavis right, though? Maybe I was making too much of all of this and I just happened to be the person who looked into the manger. But could there be any other explanation for how I'd found a baby and a handsome man at a Nativity scene, a place that represented the greatest miracle of all time? Since Zuzu had arrived, I'd started to see and feel life again instead of trudging through life in a daze. I had ideas to write. I had kissed a boy!

No, you kissed a man.

I did. I kissed a good man, a man who helped his father, paranoid mothers, and people who could only afford to pay him in chickens.

You need to remember that he works in Memphis and is probably headed back there.

Nothing tied me to Ellery. Even as I thought the sentence, I felt a stabbing sensation in my chest. My mom and my sister were in Ellery. Now that I'd finally gone to a Merry Widows Book Club meeting, I kinda wanted to attend again—not that I would be admitting it anytime soon. I'd just found another romance writer—Caroline—and I wanted to learn what she wrote. I might be able to have a critique partner again. My original partner had long since deserted me—deservedly so—because I didn't have the time or mental energy to help her with her work while I was also taking care of Corey. I also wasn't sending her anything to read for me. Now she was a *USA Today* best seller and I was . . . a cashier.

No. You are a writer. You have always been a writer. You will always be a writer.

"Ivy, don't you need to go?"

But for the next few hours you are going to be a cashier.

I drew my phone from my pocket and saw that I had ten minutes to get to the Dollar General, get situated, and clock in. "I gotta go." I looked around the room frantically. Mom had the bottle, but I'd lain the changing pad and the wipes box on the other side of the room. Then there was the baby carrier slung over a chair, and Zuzu's car seat was on the opposite end of the room and—

"Ivy, go to work," my mom said softy as she took the empty bottle from Zuzu and put the baby over her shoulder to burp her. "I might be rusty, but I think I can do this."

"We'll help her," Mrs. Morris said. "Not a one among us who hasn't raised a child."

"Go on," Mom said.

Was this the same woman who wanted no part of helping me with Zuzu? Hard to believe because she was laughing at the baby's big burp and kissing the child's forehead. I took in the tableau of the Merry Widows gathered around my orphaned charge—something that sounded far more ominous than it actually was—and I knew she was in good hands.

Chapter 40
Gabe

Once I had a new sap-free shirt and a shower I drove into town. This time I took the truck. That poor Jag's days were numbered, although I'd do my best to find her a good home.

As I pulled into the Dollar General parking lot, I glanced over at the makeshift stable. It felt so empty and forlorn even though I knew it would soon be full with a new cast of characters—except Julian, who would stay on to tend the menagerie. My eyes zeroed in on the empty manger.

Funny how I'd protested long and hard about playing Joseph only to cave when Dad said, "Look, son. I don't ask you for much."

It was true. He didn't.

I'd been doing all of the asking, and he'd been answering as best he could.

I took two steps toward the Dollar General, but I stopped. What if the kiss hadn't meant as much to her as it had to me? What if she'd changed her mind about making time for me? Should I even be doing this if I was going back to my practice? What if she wasn't even at work today?

The last of those questions was quickly answered because Ivy stood behind the register. She pushed a strand of hair behind her ear and laughed at something a customer said.

"Hey, don't block the doorway!"

I stepped to the side, and smiled when Ivy turned to see what the commotion was all about. I nodded to her and walked through the store looking for Christmas decorations. When I found the lone aisle, it had been sadly picked over. No lights left—but then most of the trees these days were prelit—and the only ornaments left were ugly glass orbs in orange and green. They did have plenty of postman ornaments and abstract shapes made out of cloth.

"I just want some balls," I muttered to myself.

"Oh?"

I turned and Ivy stood at the end of the aisle, grinning.

"Ornamental balls," I said.

Well, that made it worse.

She pretended to cough, but I knew she was hiding a snicker behind her fist.

"Look, you know what I mean."

"I know," she said. "You're probably going to have to try the Walmart in Jefferson, though, because we are completely out. A few kindergarten teachers came in and bought everything we had for some classroom crafts. They had ideas for each color."

I shuffled from one foot to another, feeling seventeen all over again. "Well, you know, I came in here for another reason, too."

"Why's that?"

All you have to do is ask her to dinner. That's it.

My mouth couldn't form the words, which was ridiculous because I had no trouble kissing her. In fact, I wanted to kiss her right then.

"Ivy, would you—"

"Ivy to register two, please. Ivy to register two."

"Go on," she said, leaning ever so slightly toward me.

"It can wait," I said. "So Walmart?"

"Oh, you didn't hear that from me," she said with a wink before heading back to her register.

I ran a hand through my hair in frustration. It shouldn't be this hard to ask a woman on a date.

Well, it has been a while.

She poked her head around the end cap. "I'm free on Monday night. Just in case you were wondering."

"How about the Burger Paradise at seven?"

"Done!"

Just like that she was gone, but my heart beat double time, and I couldn't wipe the grin off my face. Whistling "Deck the Halls," I walked out the door, destined for the madness of Walmart.

"What the hell is this?" asked Dad as he held up a string of LED lights shaped like little snowflakes.

"Lester. The baby," Romy said through gritted teeth.

"It's all they had left ten days before Christmas," I said, shuddering at the memory of Walmart. I wasn't exactly lying. It had been all they had left that I could reach. Buggy-to-buggy traffic, and everyone there had been anxious and on edge. I'd finished all of my Christmas shopping while in Jefferson because I wasn't venturing into town again until January. Maybe March.

Julian, Romy, Portia, and I had gathered to help Dad decorate the tree. As it turned out, we were doing the decorating, and he was supervising. Based on his unique technique, he wouldn't be writing any of those motivational leadership books anytime soon.

"I wanna hang the goat," Portia said.

I was rather proud of that find, even if Dad had only grunted in response to seeing it. I handed the ornament to my niece and she walked to the tree about to put the ornament on when she turned around and announced, "I need a hooker!"

Julian coughed. Romy didn't miss a beat. "It's a hook, baby doll, an ornament hook."

"But the goat needs a hooker!"

Even Dad laughed at that, his laughs turning into a coughing fit as sweet Portia tried to figure out why so many of the adults in her life were a few sandwiches short of a picnic. I couldn't help but smile myself, even though I knew that meant I had the mentality of a thirteen-year-old boy, too.

"What's that you need again, baby?" Julian asked. He was awfully close to losing the battle to keep a smile from his face.

"I need a hooker, Daddy!"

"A hook, Portia baby, a hook." Romy cut her eyes to Julian and hissed, "You're making things worse! Do you want her to say such things at the preschool?"

"Fine," Julian said. Then he added in a voice only Romy and I could hear, "But do hookers need goats? That's the question."

Romy smacked him on the arm, and he wrapped his arm around her waist, tickling her until she squealed.

"There go Mommy and Daddy," Portia said solemnly. "They like to wrestle."

"I think that's tickling," I said.

"I'm going to have a baby brother cuz they were wrestling."

"You told our daughter what?" Romy cried. She grabbed his ear and led him outside where we could hear the buzz of their argument, but none of the words.

"They do that a lot, too," Portia said.

I didn't quite know what to say to that. "Do they?"

"Yeah. That's a Come-to-Jesus Meeting. I heard Mommy say so."

I questioned whether or not Romy could ever tame my incorrigible half brother, but they calmly entered the house a few minutes later. He looked properly remorseful.

But she also looked thoroughly kissed.

What was it like to have a spat like that? For the most part, Brittany always did what I asked to my face but then whatever she wanted to do behind my back. She had this way of never making waves, but then I'd find the receipts for ridiculous shopping sprees she'd taken or my favorite recliner would just disappear while I was at work. Then there was the affair with the orthopedist. I hoped he had lost his favorite chair because it was "ratty" and was finding all sorts of receipts, too.

If Ivy and I ever got together, would we fight like Romy and Julian?

Out of the corner of my eye I caught Julian studying his wife with a hint of a smile, and it occurred to me that he might've instigated the whole argument just to get to the make-up kiss.

And to think I thought there'd never be anything for me to learn from my brother.

Dad let loose with a string of profanities, and we saw he'd managed to tangle the snowflake lights more than untangle them.

"I'll help, Grandaddy," Portia said. She walked right up to the old man and pushed his walker away, then climbed into his lap to help him untangle the lights. "See? It's not hard."

Dad kept one arm around her back, but he put his other hand on the armrest, content to let the little girl unravel the lights. "You have smaller fingers than I do," he said gruffly.

"My hands don't shake, either."

We all held our breath, afraid of how he might respond to the child's unrelenting honesty, but he kissed her head and said, "You're right, baby. They sure don't."

As I walked around the tree placing shatterproof balls, I sneaked glances at my father. He couldn't look away from his granddaughter. The man who didn't suffer fools listened patiently to her explanation of how he'd gone wrong with the lights only occasionally adding a soft, "Is that right?"

Finally, she finished and held out the string to her mother. "Okay, Mommy, put it on the tree!"

Romy studied the tree. "I don't think there's room on the tree for another string of lights. Besides, we're already putting the ornaments on."

Portia's lip poked out and she crossed her arms so forcefully that she caused Dad's leg to shake. "I did all that work for nothing!"

To hear a little child say something she'd obviously heard another adult say? Well, I had to hide behind the tree for a minute so I wouldn't hurt her or Romy's feelings with my smile.

"But you didn't do it for nothing," Dad said. "You had to show me how to do it, didn't you?"

She nodded, placated. Dad gave her another kiss on the forehead. "Why don't you go put some more ornaments on the tree while I think of a real good place to put these lights?"

She scooted down from his lap and proceeded to put half of the ornaments on the bottom fifth of the tree. Dad watched the whole thing with a smile on his face, and I realized he'd been bearing a burden, too. He'd felt guilty all these years for sending me away but also for wanting to keep me as a son even though he didn't have as much to offer materially as Aunt Vi and Aunt Lois did. Just to know that I had *wanted* to live with him instead had improved his self-worth.

I couldn't think too much about how he'd wanted to keep me but had given me up because he'd thought it would be better for me or my precocious niece would end up asking why Uncle Gabe had a couple of tears. I didn't think she'd accept dust as the culprit, either. The best Christmas present I could've ever received was to know that my father had wanted me. Aunt Vi and Aunt Lois had wanted me, too. I had been so very wanted.

As I walked to the kitchen to get a glass of water, Dad grabbed my arm. He looked up at me and said, "Thank you."

I nodded. Emotional dust was swirling, and I didn't trust myself to find the words.

Chapter 41
Ivy

No writing happened Saturday night because I came in late and knew I was headed out the door early the next morning. Both Mom and Holly were on Zuzu duty, but I'd told them I'd found a licensed daycare in town and would be trying them out on Monday.

Sunday was blessedly slow. I had no clue why the Dollar General even bothered to open at nine because everyone was either at church, pretending to be at church, or blatantly sleeping late. Even so, I enjoyed the quiet and being able to restock the shelves. I even caught myself singing along with the Christmas carols—all country versions, of course.

By the time four o'clock rolled around, I was glad to be headed home.

I'd hoped Gabe might call, but he didn't. When Holly got back from some of her personal training sessions, we all watched *Elf*. I called my sister a cotton-headed ninny-muggins, as one did. Then we all crowded around the blanket and cheered on Zuzu as she attempted to roll over.

"She's almost there," Mom said as I handed her a bottle for the baby. She'd specifically requested to feed the child.

"Isn't she a bit young for rolling over?" Holly asked.

I shrugged. "Well, I looked it up, and Professor Google says a baby can roll over as early as three or four months. Gabe estimates that's her age, so I'm guessing not."

My sister reached over to touch Zuzu's hand, which closed over Holly's finger like a vise. "Of course, you're smart! You've been hanging around with us."

"She ought to sleep well after her gymnastics routine," Mom said as she shifted the baby to her shoulder to burp her. "So you should get a lot of words in tonight."

"Here's hoping," I said, knowing that I needed a computer to be able to type in changes and finish the manuscript. I didn't say anything because I felt a swell of gratitude that my mother and sister were helping me so much. I hadn't found the thumb drive, but I had found an email where I'd once sent my manuscript to myself, so I had an electronic copy of almost everything I'd written so far. No complaints and no excuses. Once I'd gotten the daycare situation sorted out, I could take my longhand notes to the library on Wednesday and use their computers to type in what I had. It would take longer than I liked, but I could do it.

For some reason, I needed to do it. That old compulsion was blessedly back, the one that made my fingers fly over the keys, the one that helped me spin caffeine and imagination into words and those words into stories.

When the doorbell rang, Holly jumped up. "I'll get it."

I took the burped and sated Zuzu from Mom and administered her dose of antibiotics, with a little Tylenol as insurance, then rocked her gently until those beautiful blue eyes disappeared under delicate eyelids with ridiculously long lashes. My Zuzu was going to break hearts just as well as she put them back together.

When I turned around, Gabe stood with his hands in his pockets in the doorway between living room and dining room directly under the mistletoe. Had he forgotten it was there or was he looking for another kiss? There was only one way to find out.

Mom and Holly muttered excuses and made their escape down

the hallway, looking at each other and giggling like middle school girls, so I walked right up to him, looking up. "I didn't expect to see you here tonight."

"I can leave if you—"

"Don't you dare!" I stopped a step closer. "Did you mean to stand right there?"

He chuckled. "Maybe."

We looked at each other, neither one wanting to make the first move. It was nice looking up to someone. Corey had been exactly my height, but Gabe was taller. Corey had—

Corey has no place in this conversation, I thought as Gabe's lips moved toward mine. I wrapped my arms around his neck and surrendered to his kiss even though I knew I shouldn't—not until I had everything straightened out with Zuzu.

But—

When he kissed me, when his hand splayed across my lower back and pulled me to him, I felt alive. It had been so, so long since I'd felt alive. He broke away to kiss my jawline, and I fisted up his sweater. Once his kisses reached my ear, he whispered, "I brought you an early present."

His words and warm breath sent a shiver down my spine, and it took my dazed brain a minute to answer. "What? Why?"

He stepped away, revealing a thin box behind him on the dining room table. "Don't get too excited. I just thought you could use this."

"But Gabe, I don't have—"

"You don't need to get anything for me," he said. "I'm afraid this gift is a little used."

I looked from him to the present, still reeling from his touch but also excited about the gift. At the very least, it didn't look like a game of Jenga. "Should I open it now or wait until Christmas?"

"Oh, I think you need to open it now."

So, I carefully unwrapped the paper at both ends. Holly always ripped with reckless abandon, but I liked to savor the unwrapping because the anticipation was almost as good as the gift itself. Underneath the wrapping lay an oversized shirt box, and I couldn't help but look at Gabe in confusion.

"Go ahead," he said.

When I opened the box, I gasped. There amongst the tissue paper lay a MacBook, not just a laptop but a dream laptop. I ran my finger over a sticker shaped like the Starship Enterprise, then traced the iconic apple.

Gabe winced. "Sorry about that. I was afraid to try to take that off."

He's sorry about a sticker?

"But where? How?"

"I needed a new laptop. You needed a laptop that functioned, so I went to the Apple store today and let them work their magic."

I hadn't heard from him that day because he'd driven all the way to Memphis to find an Apple store and bought a laptop I was pretty sure he didn't need so he could give me this one.

"Gabe, this is too much. I can't take this," I said, shaking my head. A lump climbed up my throat at both the thoughtfulness of his gesture and at how much I really, really wanted that laptop.

"Too bad," he said as he started backing toward the door. "Because you need a laptop, and I'm not going to take that one with me. It's yours now. And aren't you supposed to be writing?"

Ah, a question that used to annoy me but now sounded like the sweetest music.

I backed under the mistletoe, resigned to my new present and giddy about it all at once. "One for the road?"

Gabe smiled. As he took that first step toward me, the world moved in slow motion. I swallowed hard. This was more than a crush. This was—

He stopped just in front of me. "You are beautiful."

In confusion, I looked down at my pajama pants and University of Memphis tank top. A hand traveled to my hair, which I'd thrown up into a bun secured by a pencil.

When he drew me closer for a kiss, I let my arms wind around his neck. He broke off the kiss quickly but gently.

"You're writing, remember?"

My fingers touched my lips. What had just happened here? I'd feel as though I'd fallen into one of my own books except somewhere in the background a baby fussed.

I turned to the bassinet/play yard and my heart squeezed again at the sight of Zuzu's kicking feet. It was almost too much love to handle.

Chapter 42
Gabe

I sat in the truck outside Dad's house for a minute. You couldn't have paid me to quit smiling. From the mystery of how Ivy managed to hold her hair up with a pencil to the way her fingers had reverently traced the Enterprise sticker on my laptop, I had it bad for Ivy Long. For the first time in my life I understood why Dad had walked up to Adelaide and said, "You're the woman I want to marry."

Unlike my dad, I knew better to put those words out into the open. I would never be stupid enough to blurt out such an inelegant proposal. Even so, I wanted to send flowers and serenade her with an Elvis song and to make sure her laptop always, always worked.

Gabe, you're out of your mind.

Maybe, but I'd never felt like this for Brittany. Our engagement had come about because we'd been dating for a couple of years, and she'd been dropping some not-so-subtle hints that she would like an engagement ring for her birthday. I'd proposed. She'd planned the wedding. We'd been roommates with benefits until she found another man.

And I didn't care.

I hoped she and her orthopedist were having an outstanding marriage with gorgeous children and a labradoodle. I hoped Brittany had all of her fancy modern furniture and abstract art and a sleek Escalade to haul those children around because that is what she had always wanted.

I didn't want that.

I wanted a farmhouse full of comfy décor with a garden outside—but no chickens. In my mind's eye, a certain writer who had the shakes from giving up smoking sat at a scarred dining room table, typing on my old laptop. She fit into my fantasy, a fantasy where I wanted very much to pull that yellow pencil out of her hair so it would cascade over her shoulders. Our farmhouse would have room for children, too, at the very least a certain abandoned baby.

My God, that is what I want.

I didn't need my practice. I didn't need my townhouse or the low-slung Jaguar or any of it.

I even wanted to spend more time with my brother, figure out what made him tick.

As if summoned by my realization, Julian pulled into the driveway. We were all going to watch *Rudolph the Red-Nosed Reindeer* together. Dad was so intent on making up for a hundred Christmases missed that I was beginning to fear he had only months to live or something.

He's probably afraid you're running away to Memphis and never coming back.

Well, wasn't he going to be shocked when I divulged my new plans. I smiled at the thought.

"Oh, good. We're just in time," Julian said as I got out of Dad's truck to join them.

"Now, baby," Romy was saying to Portia. "We're watching this old school. With commercials."

"What's a commercial again?" asked the little girl from the on-demand generation.

Once inside, Julian and his family sprawled across the couch. Dad sat in his favorite recliner, and I sat in the other chair, one that didn't have a very good view of the television, but watching the rest of the family watch it was far more fun. Romy muttered under her breath about sexism, the patriarchy, and conformity. Portia thought the Charlie in the Box was scary. Dad and Julian determined that Yukon Cornelius was the true hero of the piece.

"Gabe, why don't you and Julian get some ice cream for us all?" Dad asked.

We'd all had popcorn with the movie, so I'd known this request was coming.

"I think we'd better put little miss to bed," Romy said as Portia yawned.

"I'm not sleepy."

I couldn't help but laugh. "That's what they all say."

Julian scooped up his daughter, and she giggled. "You've got to get your beauty sleep or you'll end up looking more like me than your mama."

"Daddy," she said. "You're pretty."

He gasped in faux surprise. "Did you hear that? I'm pretty."

"Don't let it go to your head," Romy said, as she herded husband and daughter toward the back door.

Once we'd said our goodbyes, I scooped some ice cream for Dad—so he could get the popcorn taste out of his mouth—and was contemplating wrapping presents when my phone rang. "Katherine, why are you calling me on a Sunday night?"

"Because other lawyers can't learn to take the weekend off. I've decided to start saving my pennies and retire at fifty, maybe make pottery for a living then. I can sell it on Etsy."

I wanted to laugh at the idea of the meticulously dressed Katherine in clay-stained clothes in front of a pottery wheel, but I couldn't make the image stick. "Well, until then, do I want to know what these other lawyers are up to? Dare I hope for good news?"

The silence was telling.

"Gabriel, on Tuesday the insurance company is going to settle. I wanted you to know so you could make arrangements to be here. I'll call later tomorrow to let you know where you need to be and when. I thought surely the whole thing could wait until after Christmas, but no rest for the wicked, I suppose. I'll look over anything and everything they want you to sign. I was adamant about the stipulation of no wrongdoing on your part, and it seems the family has decided to focus on the nurse anyway."

"Nettie? That's ridiculous."

"No, good for you. That's what it is."

I didn't feel good about having Nettie shoulder the blame. She, like I, probably shouldn't have come to work that day. Her oldest had been arrested on some trumped-up charge, and she had swiped at her tears all day. I'd been left by Brittany and was wondering what the hell was wrong with me and the life I had provided for her. Even so, Nettie and I had come in and done our job. No negligence on our part had caused the death of Abigail Burton. She had been in the wrong place at the wrong time some point earlier—wherever she'd contracted the bacteria that caused the fatal infection.

"No. I won't sign unless they clear Nettie, too."

"Do I have to tell you what a bad idea this is? She has her own lawyer," Katherine said. I knew she didn't mean to be unfeeling, but she was probably in a hurry to get home or to at least quit working for the day.

"Katherine?"

"Hmmm?"

"I'm serious about this."

"I know you are, and you're stubborn as hell. Let me see what I can do."

"Thank you."

We said our goodbyes, and I left my phone in the kitchen to charge before returning to the living room and plopping down on the sofa.

"Well, well. What took the wind out of your sails?" Dad asked without even looking away from *NCIS* or *CSI* or whichever procedural he was watching. If years of watching detective work on television qualified one to catch murderers, Dad would've made Sherlock Holmes look like Inspector Clouseau.

I surprised myself by telling him the whole story from beginning to end. He harrumphed with a hearty "those asswipes wouldn't know a good doctor if he stared them in the face."

I chuckled at his vehemence, and I think my heart, like the Grinch's, grew three sizes that day.

"Ain't no son of mine mistreating anyone, especially not children or animals. I know that much."

Was this the same man whose approval I'd been coveting for years? "Thanks, Dad."

"You're welcome," he said gruffly. "Did you remember to get the honey buns?"

Chapter 43
Ivy

Mavis called me in to work on Monday, which was usually my day off. She made the excellent point that I'd skipped a day last week. I'd been intending to investigate Little Leaders Daycare anyway, so I called and made Monday Zuzu's first day. There hadn't been that many daycares in the area that met state requirements, but I'd studied all of them, even looking at one closer to Jefferson. When I saw that my former classmate Savannah Snead ran Little Leaders, though, I knew I'd found the one I wanted.

Now, I stood on the front porch of an old Queen Anne house not wanting to actually let Zuzu go. I'd checked her diaper bag three times and made sure that all of my paperwork was ready.

Ivy, you can't ask your mom and sister to watch Zuzu for you. If you're going to make a go of this, then you're going to have to learn to let her be in daycare while you work to find a better job for you both.

I still didn't want to leave Zuzu.

I stepped inside and went over all of the important things with Savannah, but I couldn't make myself relinquish the bucket seat.

"She's going to be just fine. Promise," Savannah said, her blond hair in one pigtail over her shoulder.

I stood frozen. Leaving Zuzu with Mom, Holly, or Gabe was one thing. Leaving her alone in a building that smelled of Clorox wipes was another.

Savannah took my diaper bag and held out a hand.

I had to do this. I had to get used to leaving Zuzu at daycare. At some point I would need to even leave her on my day off because I would be interviewing and looking for a job that paid more so I could better provide for her.

I handed over the seat and immediately regretted it. "Can't I just hug her once more?"

Savannah arched an eyebrow. "No, ma'am. That is a sleeping baby. I'm going to work my magic to keep that baby sleeping as I shift her into a crib. I'm not going to have you wake her up because *you* have separation anxiety like every other new mother."

Mother. Someday this child would call me mother.

"You're not the first mother to leave her baby with me, and you won't be the last," she continued. "You'll miss her a lot more than she'll miss you."

Her words made sense, but that didn't mean I had to like them.

She made a shooing motion with her hand. "Go on now. Shouldn't you be at work already?"

On the wall above a mural of a wolf and a lamb with a little child leading them, a clock informed me that I was running five minutes late. "Shit."

Now both of Savannah's eyebrows were almost up to her hairline.

"Sorry," I whispered as I turned toward the door. "And you promise me you'll call if anything happens?"

"I promise. Go to work. Now."

I gave the wrong change. I dropped some Christmas plates I was shelving. Then I knocked over a container of juice on aisle three and had to get a mop to clean up the mess.

"You okay?" Mavis asked.

"Zuzu's first day at daycare," I said.

I half expected Mavis to say it was about time I'd found a daycare for that child, but instead she patted my shoulder. "First day's always the hardest."

The day had moved at a crawl, but I only had ten more minutes to go. As I rolled back the mop in its bucket wringer contraption, I caught sight of the mysterious redhead over in the bathroom accessories. Gah! Which was better: asking the mystery shopper to wait a minute or leaving the mop in the aisle while I went to help her? I had a vision of Mavis chewing me a new one because I'd left the mop and bucket out, causing a customer to trip. I rolled the mop and bucket back.

"Ma'am, can I help you?" I asked as I rounded the bathroom accessories aisle

She was gone.

We had better not get low scores because this woman refused to let me help her.

I walked the store, straightening one thing after the other, all the while looking for her in other departments. After a complete walkthrough, I clocked out and raced the three blocks to Little Leaders where I was reunited with Zuzu. The little darling grinned at me, and tears streamed down my cheeks. I knew she was probably laughing at me because I'd forgotten to take off my bright yellow smock, but I liked to believe that she recognized me and was happy to see me.

"And we'll see you tomorrow?" Savannah asked.

"Yes to tomorrow but no to Wednesday."

She bent down and shook Zuzu's hand. "I'll see you tomorrow, then, sweet thing."

"Thanks, Savannah," I said.

"It's what I do," she said as she clapped a hand on my shoulder. "You did pretty well, too, Mama."

Mama.

I liked that.

I made my goodbyes and buckled Zuzu in, regaling her with stories about all the things I'd messed up because I'd missed her. Sometimes she answered me back, and halfway home she started her own story full of gibberish. I answered as I should, interjecting with "Oh, really?" or "Is that so?"

As I made the last turn, only a half mile from the house, I noticed someone was following me. I considered driving right past my house and back into town to see how far the person would go but decided I was suffering from a paranoia born of sleep deprivation and a stressful day. Besides, Zuzu's good-natured gurgles had veered into fretting. I'd need to check Savannah's notes, but I'd bet it was time to feed her.

Then the car followed me up the driveway.

I checked all of my gauges. Did I have a taillight out of something?

I stepped out of the car and there was . . . the redhead I'd seen twice now. "Can I help you?"

She sucked in a deep breath. "Yes. I want my baby back now."

Chapter 44
Gabe

When Monday rolled around, I wanted to blow off shadowing Dr. Malcolm, but I knew I had to keep my word. Besides, if I really did want my dream farmhouse, Ellery would be the perfect place to set up shop. I could get a good feel for the place if I observed.

After milking the goats I'd put on dress shirt, tie, and slacks. My loafers were toast, so I had to wear the dress shoes that weren't quite as comfortable. These days most doctors dressed casually, but I had a feeling that Dr. Malcolm went for tradition.

When I arrived at the Ellery Clinic, a line already snaked from the front door under the portico and around the front of the building. I had a feeling the line often looked like this in the winter. Some of the prospective patients were adults, but many were children. I passed the group with a smile. "Good morning, everyone."

No one responded. I didn't have on my white coat yet, and at least one person muttered under his breath about "cutting in line." I didn't correct him. I knocked on the door, but the receptionist motioned for me to wait until seven a.m., so I got my comeuppance. Any other crowd might stampede when she opened the door, but these patients continued forward respectfully, getting either themselves or their children checked in and then having a seat in a waiting room that could've been a throwback to the seventies. No televisions there. Three ancient bubble gum machines were scattered around the room, and the signs above them proclaimed that all proceeds benefited the Lion's club.

I turned from the waiting room and headed toward the examination rooms.

"Well, well, you did decide to come in today," Dr. Malcolm said.

"Of course I did. I told you I would."

"How would you feel about putting in some volunteer hours?"

My first inclination was to decline. Katherine would tell me to think of the liability and say no, but I thought of the long line of people outside, including many children. Yes, I had a lawsuit pending, but I also had my own liability insurance to cover me in situations when I practiced outside of the office for occasions like these. Thinking of the skeptical crowd outside, I asked, "You got a white coat I could borrow?"

Dr. Malcolm grunted and nodded his head in the direction of a small closet, then turned to one of his nurses. "All right, Judy, release the hounds."

My day passed quickly as I went from ear infection to cold to bronchitis to another ear infection. I saw one case of flu, one spider bite, and a case of hand, foot, and mouth. More coughs and ear infections and a couple of stomach bugs. As I treated the children, I noticed something: these parents, for the most part, listened to what I had to say. No one suggested that their precious darling had Fifth Disease when the child had chapped cheeks and needed some Aquaphor. No one lectured me on how harmful vaccines were. No one asked for a higher dosage of antibiotics or demanded that I find something to heal her child that was all natural, organic, and free trade. In short, it was a pretty darn good day.

At lunch, Dr. Malcolm even laughed and cut up. He bought lunch for everyone in my honor.

Once we'd seen the last patient, he clapped a hand on my shoulder. "You lightened my load, Ledbetter. Thank you."

"Consider it an early Christmas present, Dr. Malcolm," I said.

"Well, there will be a place for you here should you ever want one."

One step closer to your farmhouse. "Thank you."

He walked toward the back exit, whistling "Let It Snow" as he went. I went back to the reception area. I'd learned that the receptionist with the friendly voice was Angie.

"Could I possibly get some information on a little girl named Taylor who was brought in earlier in the week with an infected burn?"

"Last name?" she asked without looking up.

"I honestly don't know."

"That's gonna make it hard to find her record."

I tapped my fingers on the counter. Hard to pour on the charm if she refused to look up at me. "I thought you would be the one to remember if anyone did."

She sighed deeply and put down the papers she'd been filing. "Olivia and Taylor Sheffield, I believe."

She typed furiously on her computer and finally turned the screen around to me. "That the one?"

A quick glance told me that Olivia and Taylor lived in the Green Acres Trailer Park, trailer number eight.

"Thanks, Angie," I said.

"Hey!"

I stopped, afraid she was going to tell me I couldn't visit them.

"Leave your white coat here. That is Doc Malcolm's, isn't it?"

That it was. I hung it up and walked through the back door because it occurred to me that the front door was now locked. I rounded the building and squeezed between the building and a few bushes to get to the patient parking lot. If I ever did come back, I needed to remember to park in the back where Dr. Malcolm did.

I'd made it to the only red light in town when I thought, *It might be nice to get the little girl a Christmas present.*

Stopping by the Piggly Wiggly would add another ten minutes to my task and mean I probably wouldn't have time to drive home for a shower before meeting up with Ivy, but it would be worth it. In the end I also bought a little gift card for Olivia. If Taylor's daddy lived with them, he certainly wasn't mentioned in any of her records. Hopefully, I wouldn't end up with any more chickens out of this deal.

Trailer eight lay at the very end of the trailer park. My flashy Jaguar bumped and lurched over the rough gravel road, finally stopping in front of the last mildewed mobile home. As I walked up the steps, one of the boards bowed under my feet.

After the third knock, Olivia peeked over the chain. "Yes?"

"It's me, Dr. Ledbetter. May I check on Taylor and make sure her burns are doing okay?"

She hesitated.

What was going on in there: meth lab? Illegal poker games? Shoe modeling?

When she opened the door, I saw. Clutter sat on every surface. I forced myself not to look around and gape. My nose at least told me nothing was rotting under the stacks of newspapers.

"I'm sorry, it's so messy." Olivia looked ready to cry. "I work two shifts, and I don't feel like cleaning."

"I don't guess you would," I said, stacking some papers so I could sit on the very edge of the couch.

"I'll get Taylor."

When she brought her daughter, the child was rubbing her eyes as though she'd been awakened from a nap. If I'd known, I would've told Olivia not to bother. Still dazed, she didn't mind when I took off the dressing to examine her arm.

Not perfect, but improving.

"Well, keep it up," I said. "Infection's better, but you don't want to stop the antibiotics, cleaning, or Silvadene because it could still come back. And the generic Silvadene is fine, by the way."

Olivia nodded and got Taylor situated on her hip. The little girl clung to her mother, and I had so many questions. How young had Olivia been when she had the baby? Where was the father? Did she need food? Who took care of Taylor while she worked? The poor girl didn't seem to have much of a support system.

"Okay, Taylor, I got something for you," I said as I reached into my satchel and pulled out the stuffed lion that I'd found in the grocery store. It was a little too young for her, but she snatched it closely with her good arm and rewarded me with a precious toddler smile.

"What do you need to say?" Olivia asked.

"Tank you." Taylor threw her good arm around my leg for a hug before wobbling off to inspect her new toy.

"You didn't have to do that," the young mother whispered.

"I didn't have to, but I wanted to," I said. "I also got you a little something."

I handed her the gift card, and she bit back tears.

"I can't take this."

"Of course you can," I said.

"Mama said I've got to earn my own way." She wiped away her tears with the heel of her hand.

"How old are you, Olivia?"

"Seventeen, almost eighteen."

"And you rented this place all yourself and managed to get two jobs?"

She nodded. "Well, Granny signed for it. She said she'd let me live with her, but she's in the nursing home."

"And you have someone trustworthy to look after Taylor while you're at work?"

"Ms. Allen next door does. She lets me pay her a little, but mostly she says Taylor keeps her company."

"And I know you have some chickens. That's a lot for a young woman to bear," I said. "Some adults can't manage what you have, so don't you be ashamed to ask for help if you need it."

"Yessir."

I opened my mouth to tell her I wasn't old enough for the "sir" treatment, but I had to have been in my mid-twenties when she was born, so I could've been her father.

And how would it look for a man old enough to be her father to be seen leaving her trailer after delivering gifts?

I started backing for the door because I realized I'd put myself in a dangerous position even while I was trying to do some good.

I hadn't even thought about how much I might scare Olivia. She was still a kid and living in this trailer all by herself? "I'm going to send someone named Yolanda Gibbons to check on you, okay?"

She nodded, but her eyes looked a little wild.

"Don't be afraid of her because if she can't help you, then she will find someone who can."

She turned the card over and over between her hands.

I paused at the door. "Merry Christmas, Olivia."

"Merry Christmas," she whispered back.

I walked back to my car with a small smile and a full heart.

I could hardly wait to tell Ivy about my day, and I could only hope there wasn't something about the Burger Paradise that caused a man to propose because we were headed to the scene of my father's former crime.

Then again, it worked out for him. . . .

Chapter 45
Ivy

She wants her baby back?

It was only by the grace of God I didn't toss my cookies right there on the driveway. "What do you mean?"

I asked this even though I knew darn well what she meant. She meant she was Zuzu's mother, and she'd changed her mind. She'd even been spying on me at the Dollar General!

What was it the note had said?

Please take care of my little girl.

She hadn't mentioned for how long.

I had told myself I would be okay if this moment came.

Instead, I had the ridiculous, hysterical urge to shout, "No take backsies!" but we were talking about a baby not a toy or a game or an opinion that had been spouted in the heat of the moment. Not only that, but the baby in question had begun to fuss so I needed to get her out of the car and feed her. I unlatched the car seat wondering if I ignored the woman if she would go away.

"I'm Fiona's mother," the woman's voice wobbled. "I think I can take care of her now."

She thinks?

I had rearranged my life to take care of her child, whom she had abandoned, and she *thought* she could take care of her? That she could waltz in and take her back?

Well, of course, she *could*—but not today. Blessedly, some of my foster parent training came back to me.

"How did you even find me?" I blurted.

"You were in the paper!"

Ah, yes. Thanks, Lydia.

"I'm afraid I can't let you. Zuzu's a ward of the state now," I said. "You'll have to speak to her case manager. The police may even press charges since you abandoned her."

Her mouth opened and closed but only a squeak came out. "What are you talking about with the state and the police?"

"When you left her in the manger, that meant we had to call the police."

"No, you didn't!"

"We had to. Then they took her to the hospital to make sure she was okay. Finally, Zu—Fiona entered the system as a Jane Doe. She has a case manager, and I can't just give her back to you because technically she's a ward of the state, like I said."

I studied the woman's face in the diluted winter sun. I couldn't tell her age, but I could feel rage radiating from her. "She's *my* baby."

"But you abandoned her," I said softly.

She let out a primal scream and walked in circles as she pulled at her hair.

Oh, please tell me she's not on drugs.

She took a few deep breaths and turned to face me. "Look, I got in with a bad man and I was afraid he might hurt Fiona, but I'm not with him now. I can take her back. Especially if you're just going to drop her off at some daycare."

My heart sank. The state would give Zuzu back to her mother if they could find any way to do so, and they'd be lenient if she'd felt the baby had been threatened.

I'd known from the very beginning that this scenario was the most likely one.

No, you didn't. Even Yolanda told you that the parent would more than likely never turn up.

"Look, today's the first day she's been in daycare, and that's so

I can make enough money to take care of her. I'm going to look for a better job, but that will take time and—"

"I don't know why you're telling me this because you *will* give me my child back. Now."

"What's your name?"

"My name is Trudy," she said through clenched teeth.

I kept a smile on my face even though the lump in my throat threatened to expand to the point that I wouldn't be able to talk. Tears collected, but I couldn't shed them. Not yet. Zuzu's fussing went up a notch, but I was afraid to take her out of the carrier for fear Trudy would snatch her. As it was, the woman's eyes had darted to the handle I held several times. I shifted the handle of the carrier to the crook of my arm and fished around in the diaper bag with my free hand to find Yolanda's card. "Okay, then. Trudy. Here's Zuzu's—"

"Her name is Fiona," she said as she snatched the card from me.

"Yolanda is Fiona's case manager, and she will be able to explain all of this to you. Right now I have to feed her and change her. I couldn't give her back to you even if I wanted to because it would be illegal. You'll need to call Yolanda."

I backed slowly toward the garage, but she grabbed at the carrier. I hugged it to me tightly. "If you take Fiona, I am legally obligated to call the police and report that you have kidnapped her."

"That's bullshit. She's *my* kid."

Careful to keep my tone low and even in spite of my hammering heart, I said, "But she's legally in my custody."

"You're a real bitch, you know that?"

"I don't make the rules."

If I made the rules, then Trudy wouldn't be able to abandon her sweet baby and then try to take her back. Zuzu was a child, not a yo-yo.

"Fine, who do I have to call?"

"Yolanda. Her number's on the card."

She stalked off, then slammed her car door and peeled out of the driveway with the squeal of tires and the smell of rubber. Zuzu's wails crescendoed.

I walked through the garage and to the back door—my feet now felt as if they were made of lead, but the rest of my body thrummed with unspent adrenalin. I finally changed and fed the baby and calmed her down. Then I handed her to Holly, who, for once, didn't make any smart aleck comments.

I called Yolanda to tell her everything that had happened. She'd already gotten an earful from Trudy.

The whole situation felt like the beginning of the end all over again.

Chapter 46
Gabe

"You sure you don't want something besides that Coke?" the Burger Paradise waitress asked for the fifth time.

"No, thank you."

A glance at my phone told me that it was half-past seven.

I had been stood up.

I'd called at ten after just to make sure I had the time right. The phone was busy, so I figured Ivy had had trouble getting Zuzu settled in. But thirty minutes late without so much as a text or call to say she's sorry? Maybe she wasn't as into me as I'd thought or hoped.

Gabriel, you of all people know that babies can be unpredictable.

But not to call or even text?

I waved for the waitress and put in a to-go order for both me and Dad. If Ivy still hadn't shown up by the time my order was ready, then I would definitely leave. I willed her to show up. I willed her to show up smelling of cigarette smoke and bad excuses, but she didn't.

So I picked up my bag and left.

Disgusted, I threw my phone down on the passenger side seat before setting off for home.

"What are you doing here?"

"So glad that I could have supper with you, too, Dad."

"Naw, I thought you were supposed to be having dinner with

that Long girl," he said as he used his walker to hobble over to the table.

"Operative words being 'supposed to,'" I said. "She didn't show."

"Well, now," he said. "I'm sorry about that."

"It is what it is," I muttered. Maybe I should get that tattooed on my forearm as a reminder. The phrase sure had popped up enough over the past few months.

"I gotta say, that's not like a Long," Dad said before stuffing a fry in his mouth. "Well, I shouldn't say that. Their daddy wasn't no count, but their mama, Genevieve? She was a Parker, and Parkers are good people. Always on time, always hard workers. Every family has a black sheep, but not the Parkers."

"Maybe Ivy's the first black sheep," I said.

"Could be."

But I didn't think so. I texted to see if she was okay, and she finally responded with a **"Can't talk right now."** I offered to come over, but she brushed me off. I could still drive over and make sure everything was okay—check on the baby. Yeah, I definitely needed to check on Zuzu.

"Julian's going to come over to watch *Christmas Vacation*," Dad said. "I do get a kick out of that Cousin Eddie."

This was the happiest my father had been in forever. Were he and I yin and yang? Always destined to be opposites?

"When are y'all going to start the movie?" I forced myself to ask even though I didn't feel like watching anything. I only wanted to know why Ivy was suddenly giving me a very frosty shoulder.

"Just as soon as he gets here."

I opened my mouth to say I would have to pass, but then Julian came through the back door brandishing the Chevy Chase DVD and a six-pack.

Dad said, "Me and my boys are gonna have ourselves a Christmas tradition."

I smiled weakly. "This is turning into a regular old-fashioned Ledbetter Family Christmas."

"We're going to be the jolliest bunch of assholes this side of the nuthouse," said Julian.

Dad cackled. "I can't believe I'm finally going to have Christmas with both of my sons."

And that was the end of that. Ivy could call me if she needed me, but I wasn't going to be the one to break up the father-son bonding experience.

The minute Mavis Staples started singing about Christmas vacation, I jumped up from the couch.

"Where are you going so hot to trot?" Dad asked.

"It's nothing." I sat back down.

"Bullshit, it's nothing," Julian said.

With a sigh I gave them the short version of being jilted and Ivy's less than encouraging texts. "I think I should go over there."

Julian clapped a hand on my shoulder. "She said not to, dude."

"She didn't mean it. She couldn't have."

"Oh, she meant it," Dad said. "You keep your ass here."

"What if something's wrong with the baby?"

My father and brother snorted at the same time. "*That* she would call you for."

"But I gotta go into Memphis tomorrow, and I may spend the night."

Julian looked at Dad and hitched a thumb in my direction. "This one's lovesick. I told him not to mess with Ivy."

I slugged his shoulder.

"Ow, violent, too!"

"Son, she ain't going nowhere. Women, well, women . . ." Dad's grasped for words.

"Women will let you know what they want when they're good and ready," Julian finished.

I only hoped that Ivy wanted what I wanted. Maybe I'd underestimated her love for the baby and overestimated her affection for me.

Chapter 47
Ivy

I didn't sleep. I also didn't take any pleasure from watching the sun rise or the three cigarettes I smoked while I watched it. Unfortunately for my attempts to quit smoking, I remembered I'd stashed part of a pack in the console between the front seats of my car.

"Baby, you're winding yourself up in knots," Mom said once I'd come back inside.

"I can't help it."

"Well, there's nothing you can do to make things move along any faster. You might as well go into work."

I shook my head. No way was I going to go to work and find out that Yolanda or Trudy had come by while I was gone to take my baby.

She's not your baby.

Nor was I going to chance having Trudy come by and either yell at Mom or coax her into handing over Zuzu.

Fiona. You're going to have to call her Fiona.

I'm sure she could spin a pretty enough story to convince Mom even though I'd told her enough about how foster care worked to explain why Trudy couldn't just take Fiona back. I'd been a blubbering mess for most of the morning despite the fact last night's call with Yolanda had gone better than I'd hoped. She'd said she might call or come by today, and that was another reason I couldn't bring myself to go into work.

"You are wearing out my carpet. Can I make you some tea?"

Not gonna help unless you lace it with Valium, Mom.

Someone rapped at the back door. I could tell by the silhouette that it was Yolanda. Mom let her in, and I looked at her expectantly.

"Ivy, you need to sit down."

The world went dark for the tiniest of seconds, so I did as I was told.

"I'm going to put some tea on for us all," Mom said.

"I'd appreciate that," Yolanda said before turning to me. "I want you to remember a certain course you took when you signed up to be a foster parent. Do you remember the one about leaving and loss?"

I nodded, tears streaming down my cheeks. She grabbed my hand and squeezed. Despite the times she'd been stern with me, now here she was concerned.

"Here's what's probably going to happen. Sometime soon the judge is going to grant Trudy visitation. She isn't a prior offender. The baby came to you healthy, and she appears to have acted under duress. Even though she didn't specify a caregiver in her note, she *says* she specifically picked you for the child, which shows some amount of planning."

"But she couldn't have known that Zuzu would come to me. And why would she do that?"

"Her name is Fiona, and no she didn't, but her intent was for the baby to go to a trusted adult."

I couldn't speak.

"Now, here are some things working in your favor."

There was something in my favor?

"Fiona is older than seventy-two hours, which means her case doesn't fall under the Safe Haven laws. She also wasn't left in any kind of designated space. The note that Trudy left doesn't specify a caregiver nor does it indicate she had any intention of returning."

But could I really want to keep a child for myself if I knew that her birth mother wanted her and, from all appearances, could care for her? I looked at the bassinet where Zuzu—no, Fiona—slept, and I knew as much as I wanted to be her new mother, I also didn't want to be the evil woman who kept her from her birth mother.

"That's all coming down the pike," Yolanda said as she took the cup of tea from my mother. "Fiona will be with you for at least the next six months probably, so enjoy your time with her while you can, okay?"

I nodded, but my insides twisted. This was Byron all over again. I would watch another woman visit with the baby I'd grown to love, knowing I would lose her, too.

Yolanda kept talking and I kept nodding even though I only half heard what she was saying about hearings and reunification and visitations and all sorts of other long legal words.

"You haven't heard a word I said, have you?" she finally asked.

"About half of it?"

She cocked her head to one side as if seeing me for the first time. "You were serious about raising this baby, weren't you?"

"Yes."

"Why?"

I shrugged. "I guess it was love at first sight."

"Oh, baby," she said, patting my hand. She took a deep breath. "The deprivation hearing is on the twenty-fourth—"

"But that's Christmas Eve!"

"Yes, and it has to be done before Christmas, legally speaking." Yolanda squeezed my hand. "You knew when you signed up to be a foster parent that the goal would always be to reunite children with their parents if possible."

I nodded while blinking back tears.

She shook her head. "I could wring Chelsea's neck for listening to that doctor friend of yours. You were too fragile for this placement, but I know you love her."

Tears now blurred my vision, my head snapped up as her words registered. "My doctor friend? Gabe?"

"He casually mentioned to Chelsea that you were a foster parent, and she's brand-new. She didn't look at the list or anything. Just saw that you were legit and did her thing."

My throat closed up. Gabe had done this?

I couldn't wrap my mind around that idea, and I wasn't sure if I loved him or hated him for putting me through all of this. I was forgetting something about Gabe, an idea just out of reach.

Yolanda slapped both hands on her thighs before standing, and I walked her to the door.

A few hours later, Mom put on the big band Christmas playlist and tried to convince me to get into the spirit. "Come on, Ivy. If you're going to stay home, the least you can do is make sausage balls."

"I don't want to."

"What else are you going to do?" Mom asked with her hands on her hips.

"Fine," I said with a hiccupping sigh. "I'll do it this afternoon."

"Moping's not going to make it any better."

"I said I'd do it, okay?"

Holly came through the back door in time to hear me. "What are y'all carrying on about?"

I told her about Trudy and Yolanda's visit and the probability that Zuzu/Fiona would be given back to her mother. Holly could only say, "Oh. I'm sorry, Sis."

She walked down the hall to get clothes for a shower, but she returned with my phone. "This was ringing off the hook."

I took my phone and saw I'd missed seven calls from the Dollar General. I took a deep breath and called back.

She didn't even say hello. "Ivy Long, I hate to do this, especially today, but you are fired."

"Mavis, you don't understand. I—"

"No, *you* don't understand. I have put up with your flakiness long enough—"

I held the phone away from my ear, but Mavis kept going.

"You have called in sick twice in less than a week during the holiday season, and you clearly do not have the flu. I run a retail store. Do you know what retail stores do before Christmas? Make enough money to stay afloat during the leaner months, that's what. It's hard for me to make enough sales, though, if I only have one person able to run the register and she can't make change even with the computer telling her what to do. So your final check is in the mail. Don't call unless it's to give me the name of someone who can start tomorrow."

And then she hung up on me.

Now I didn't have a job.

The one thing I had going for me was that I had a job and Trudy didn't. Oh, God. What if I was assuming she didn't have a job? What if she had the job, but I didn't? I might not even last the week.

"Who was that?" asked Mom.

"Mavis. She fired me."

"She did what? Call her back, and hand me the phone." Mom answered and was already raising her voice before she walked outside. That made Zuzu—no, Fiona, no I would call her Zuzu as long as she lived with me—start crying so I went through the mechanical motions of changing her diaper and then putting her down to wash my hands. I made her formula and then picked her up even more gently than usual because I wanted to remember every moment of cradling her next to me, every slurp, every contented sigh, and the heavenly feel and smell of her fuzzy baby head.

Zuzu chose that moment to fart, and I giggled and hugged her to me, planting a kiss on her sweet forehead even as tears still streamed down my cheeks.

Yes, I might even miss that.

When she was done, I burped her and held her favorite plastic keys in front of her. Then we read through the cloth book, looking for that troublemaking hippo a couple of times. Once I thought she'd been in an upright position long enough we went down on the floor and I let her bat at her new baby jungle gym.

I didn't have a job.

Okay, I knew I'd been wrong. I should've trusted mom and gone in to work, but it seemed so unfair. I'd already lost my husband. Now I'd lost my job. Now the universe was going to take my baby.

She isn't your baby. She was never your baby.

At least I had Gabe.

Oh, God. Gabe.

I was supposed to have met up with him at Burger Paradise at seven.

Last night.

That's what I had forgotten.

No wonder he'd sent me those texts.

I thought back to my "can't talk now" and telling him not to come over.

Well, he would just have to understand.

Maybe.

Hopefully.

Chapter 48
Gabe

That morning I drove to Memphis to surprise the staff with an early lunch of Chinese food since I knew my fellow physicians often didn't eat in a timely manner because we had to see a ridiculous amount of patients each day. As a way to get everyone lunch and to reset the clock for afternoon appointments, the whole staff took a break between one and two. Often, work with patients ran over and nurses, doctors, even the receptionists on the front line ran late. I didn't have to meet up with Katherine until four, so the least I could do was feed everyone that day to soften them up.

As I drove through forests, fields, and small towns, I weighed my options. After talking to my financial advisor, it didn't make much sense for me to immediately sell my practice. I was supposed to be back in the office after the New Year, and the logical thing would be to work for a while longer to make sure I really wanted to move. If so, then I could stay in Memphis while I put the condo up for sale and made arrangements.

I didn't know what was happening with Ivy, but I needed to be pragmatic.

While mulling over the situation in spite of myself, I zoned out and got a speeding ticket in Oakville.

At least fuming over the speeding ticket—Oakville had one of the worst speed traps—gave me something new to think about. I was still stewing while I waited for my order to be ready and again while driving over to the pediatric office I'd helped start. When I reached the back door of the building, I was struck by how different my practice was from the clinic in Ellery.

Ellery's clinic had been built in the early sixties and had seen few upgrades or improvements since then. Mid-South Pediatrics, of which I was a part, resided in a building from the new millennium in a well-landscaped area full of other offices and fancy strip malls. I had never once seen a line stretching outside our doors.

Once inside the break room, I laid my treasures out on the table and waited for the others to arrive.

"Gabe!" Clay Richards, one of my fellow doctors, gave me a quick man-hug and rubbed his hands together. "Are you the founder of the feast today?"

"I was in town and thought, *what the heck?*"

"Glad you did. I'm starving, and the wife sent me something with quinoa."

He loaded up a plate, and the others started trickling in. Matt and Tamika came in followed by the last doctor, Priya. Then the nurses entered en masse, but I didn't see Nettie among them. Finally, the receptionists entered, complaining about how no one had left them any sweet and sour chicken. This was quite common because they had to clear out the waiting room before they could join us, so I promised them I would hold back a container for them next time.

"Gabe, sure is good to see you," Clay said. "We've missed you around here."

"Yes, it has been quite busy," Priya added.

"I'm so glad you're coming back soon," Clarice, a receptionist, said. She wasn't supposed to play favorites, but she'd once told me that I had the most requests of any of the pediatricians there. Several people murmured, but no one echoed her sentiment. The little hairs on the back of my neck stood up.

Even so, we ate and laughed, and I fell back into old routines, old jokes, even remembered old patients.

"The littlest Marshall put a tic tac up his nose again?"

"Yeah, you'd think they'd ban the things in that house," Tamika said, watching as the last of the nurses and receptionists made their way back front. She got up and closed the door. That's when I knew social hour was over. "Gabe, I thought we could talk for a minute."

I glanced at the clock. They only had about seven minutes to talk unless they wanted to keep their patients waiting.

"Nothing good ever comes from closing a door because you want to talk," I said. "Are you guys breaking up with me?"

"No," Priya said, hanging on the word in the way only she did. "We've actually decided we would like for you to come back."

They'd decided? I was one of the founding members.

"We're going to take a hit, but I can't imagine the place without you," Clay said.

I suppose you can't, Clay, since we took you in about two years ago.

"What do you mean?" I asked carefully. I thought I knew, but I wanted him to say the words.

He shrugged. "After all of the stories on television and the exposé in the *Commercial Appeal*, we've had a few of our higher-profile patients pull out."

"Geraldine and Clarice get questions every other day from new mothers who are concerned that they might be stuck with you," Priya said.

Stuck with me? I swallowed hard.

I wasn't the favorite anymore. I was the doctor people got "stuck" with.

"This is so ridiculous," I said. "You all know that what happened wasn't my fault or Nettie's. If it had happened to any family other than the Burtons, we wouldn't have even made the news."

"Yeah, but it did happen to the Burtons. And we've been on the news. A lot," Tamika said.

"Priya?" I asked, appealing to my cofounder.

"Well," she said, pausing to weigh her words. "We did have an offer from one of the health care services that wanted to buy us out."

"You know we don't want to do that," I said. The last thing

we needed was some corporation mandating that we only had ten minutes per patient—if that.

"I might have," she admitted. "But they withdrew the offer because they didn't want you to be a part of it."

"Well, then," I said.

Going back to work after the New Year as I'd planned still made the most sense. I didn't want to look for a new job or start another practice from scratch.

But I also didn't want to work with a bunch of people who thought they were doing me a favor by keeping me on in the practice that I'd help build. Dr. Malcolm had treated me like an equal, and the people in Ellery? I'm sure I'd run across an entitled parent like the Burtons eventually, but they'd been so grateful. The nurses had seemed glad to have me there, too. And speaking of nurses. "Where's Nettie?"

No one would meet my eyes. I turned to Priya because I knew she would give it to me straight. "Where. Is. Nettie?"

"We had to let her go."

"You *had* to let her go? You mean you fired her!"

"Well, it was a stipulation of our part of the settlement," Clay said. "We had to think of the good of the practice."

I thought of Nettie with her son in jail. She almost never called in sick. I could count on one hand the number of mistakes she'd made over the years. She was efficient and great with kids, the nurse we called in to administer shots to the most hysterical patients because she was so good at what she did.

"Unbelievable," I said. "Look, I would hate for you to—how did you phrase it? 'Take a hit'? So feel free to pool your resources and buy me out."

One doctor looked to another. They'd already discussed doing so behind my back.

"Come on, Gabe. It could happen to any of us," Tamika said. "We know that."

"It could have, but it didn't, now did it?" They didn't want to take the chance that another high-profile lawsuit might find them. Even though they were physicians with some idea of which illnesses spread and which ones didn't, they secretly feared that being sued was catching.

"Your empathy is overwhelming. Draw up your offer and let me know," I said. "I hope you enjoyed your lunch."

Before anyone could say another word, I walked out of the break room, ignoring the curious stares of a couple of nurses. Once outside I looked at my Jaguar. After I met with Katherine, it would be the next to go.

Chapter 49
Ivy

I'd texted Gabe a million times, but he still hadn't answered. He was probably livid, and I had no one to blame but myself. Even so, I didn't regret a thing. If I were going to adopt Zuzu—even though that was looking more and more unlikely—then he would have to understand she came first for now.

Maybe that was wrong, but her mother had already put a man before her once, and I wasn't going to do that.

Just the thought of it all made me want to attack the last of my pack of cigarettes, but I'd rededicated my life to being a nonsmoker. I would do *whatever* it took to be the better parent, so I'd have to deal even if I had a headache again.

Then there was the matter of finding a new job.

After an hour of fighting to get Internet on the laptop Gabe had given me, I finally managed to tether the device to my phone. It was slow going, and the job sites offered very little.

I banged my head on the table.

"What is it, dear?" Mom asked from the other end of the table where she addressed Christmas cards in a deliberate semi-calligraphy. Holly, meanwhile, banged around the kitchen making supper.

"I can't find a job anywhere," I moaned without even lifting my head. "And now I'm going to have another gap on my resumé."

"You have a resumé?"

"Ha. Ha. Very funny." I finally lifted my head. Despite her barb, my sister exuded melancholy. There was something important that I was forgetting about my sister in the midst of all this. What was it?

"Keep looking," Mom said, snapping me out of my thoughts.

"It's no use. I can't quit smoking. I've gotten fired from my job. I stood up the only man I've been attracted to in the past four years. Zuzu's mother is back. I might as well smoke like a chimney and beg Mavis to take me back."

"You don't mean that," Mom said.

"Oh, but I do. I'd go back to writing, but I screwed the pooch there, too. Just look at this." I waved my hands over the scattered papers from where I'd started entering changes.

"You know what you are good at?" Mom asked as the timer dinged.

"Making sausage balls?"

"Yep."

I couldn't help but sigh. "Let me guess: I make them so much better than you do."

"Also true," she said.

Her request was premeditated, and I knew this because you had to let the sausage sit at room temperature for an hour before you could make the recipe. "Mom, there are only three ingredients: Bisquick, sausage, and cheese. I think you can handle it."

"But mine come out all crumbly, and you promised me."

"Fine, I'm coming."

I mixed Bisquick and shredded cheese, then slit open the tube of sausage, dumping it into the bowl on top of the dry ingredients. Using my hands to mix the three ingredients was my least favorite part of the process. To keep from thinking about the engagement ring and small band I'd taken from my right hand, I said, "Maybe I should try one of these fast-food jobs."

"Ick," said my sister, the nutrition expert.

"Beggars, choosers," I murmured.

Zuzu fussed.

"I'll get her," Mom said before I could even hold up my messy hands and ask. We might not have put up a Christmas tree every year, but we did have sausage balls.

As I worked the three ingredients together, Holly and Mom worked together to change and feed Zuzu. It would figure that I'd have to give her up just as I trained everyone in the house to help.

By the time I had finished creating well over fifty little balls, Holly was peeking into the oven. Something smelled good.

"Don't eat those hands!" Mom was saying to Zuzu. "You're going to need those fingers later. Is that a thumb? Did you catch a thumb?"

The minute I came toward Zuzu, she dropped her thumb and waved her hands while kicking her feet. My heart moved from ache to melt, and I took her from Mom, sitting her up in my lap, her head nestled against my chest while she banged her plastic keys, then crinkled the pages in her new cloth book.

"Soup's on," Holly said, as she placed a steaming lasagna on the table.

"Trivet!" Mom said.

Holly rolled her eyes, but retrieved a trivet and then used pot holders to pick up the glass pan while Mom slid a trivet underneath. I moved Zuzu to a bouncy seat, but she preferred banging her keys to the vibrating sensation.

"Is that meat?" I asked as I pulled Zuzu closer. "Who are you and what have you done with my sister?"

Holly chuckled and studied her plate. "I just felt like something a little hardier."

"Mmm, this is delicious," Mom said five minutes later, but she would've said that about raw Brussels sprouts if that meant she didn't have to cook supper next time.

Zuzu tossed her keys to the floor with authority. I bent to pick them up for her and caught Holly studying the baby with intensity.

That's what I'd forgotten.

Holly had said she was going to the doctor on Monday to see if she were pregnant. I'd forgotten all about it—and everything else—in the whirlwind of meeting Zuzu's mother and losing my job. I started to ask her, but then I remembered Mom wasn't supposed to know.

After supper and dishes, we gathered in the living room to play with Zuzu, who, once again, almost rolled over. I put her on her tummy, seeing that she was getting tired.

"She looks like a little turtle," Holly said.

I couldn't get a read on my sister. She was rather subdued and she was eating meat and carbs. Did this mean that she was pregnant? I wanted to shove Mom off to bed, but she was more awake than usual. Finally I left her in charge of Zuzu and went outside with Holly under the pretense of talking about Mom's Christmas present, which, coincidentally, was something else Holly and I needed to discuss.

"So," I said once we were outside in the dark, sitting on the front porch because I'd hoped I wouldn't associate the front porch with a cigarette. I did anyway. "Are you pregnant?"

Holly stared into the dark for a while. "No."

"But you're eating meat and carbs? I thought carbs were sent straight from the devil to collect on our hips and bellies?"

Holly laughed bitterly. "Yes, well. I apparently need them."

"Really?"

"I, uh, haven't had a period in five months."

"Holly! I thought it was only one."

She sighed and leaned forward on her knees, something far easier for her than me because she didn't have any belly fat unlike the other person sitting on the top step of the front porch. "It's not unusual to skip periods when your body fat percentage is as low as mine is. I definitely don't have a period every month."

I tamped down my jealousy because I had a feeling whatever Holly was about to tell me wasn't worth giving up my monthly hassle. "But is that bad?"

"Yeah, it's bad!"

"Sorry. I didn't know."

Holly sighed. "Because of the bulimia I was already at a risk for osteoporosis and the lack of a period makes it worse. Then there's the low iron, and the possibility of stress fractures. The whole thing adds up to . . . well, to I have exercise less, eat more, and gain weight. And I'm afraid."

A tear slid down her cheek, and she swiped it away furiously. Did that doctor even know what she was doing when she told Holly Long to gain some weight?

I put my arm around her and hugged her close. "I know you won't believe me if I tell you that you're beautiful no matter what, but you are. What can I do to help?"

She shrugged, still silently crying.

I wanted to tell her that it wasn't the end of the world to look into the mirror and see a few extra pounds, but I hadn't had bulimia. When I looked at my body, I didn't see a distorted fun-house mirror reflection the way Holly said she did. So I rocked my sister while she cried because that was all I knew to do.

After I put both Holly and Zuzu to bed, I took out the laptop Gabe had given me. My fingers hesitated over the keys because I felt guilty. I'd never dreamed of having a laptop this nice. He said he wouldn't take it back but maybe he'd changed his mind since I accidentally stood him up. He hadn't called or texted, which didn't seem like a good sign.

I'll tell myself that I'm borrowing it.

Whatever mind game it took to type in the words I needed to add to this story. I'd reached the point of the mistletoe, and I needed everything to come together from there. The denouement, as the French might say.

I took a deep breath and stretched my arms above my head before turning my head one way, then another. I couldn't make Gabe call me back. I couldn't help my sister with her body image. I couldn't make Mavis hire me or make Trudy leave Zuzu with me. I couldn't even control whether or not my publisher bought this story. I could only control one thing: whether or not I finished it.

Chapter 50
Gabe

"Katherine, I told you that I would not sign anything unless I knew Nettie would be in the clear."

"I was afraid you were going to say that," she muttered as she picked up her phone. In a tailored suit with pumps and with her blond hair swept up, she looked more like a television drama lawyer, but I knew better. She negotiated on the phone while simultaneously checking her email. At one point she sent me to the snack shop on the bottom floor of the shiny building where she had her office.

At the time I'd thought she was hungry, but when I returned I'd realized she wanted me out of the room so she could talk openly. I put her skinny latte on the desk, and she looked up with a small smile of victory. "Courier will be over in thirty minutes."

"And Nettie's in the clear."

"She is in the clear."

Once I'd signed all of the paperwork, I turned to my lawyer. "What do you know about small-town practices?"

Getting the Jaguar traded in and a new pickup purchased took another three hours of my time. By the time I reached my condo, I collapsed on the bed too tired to sleep.

Two more texts from Ivy. I responded "Can't talk right now" because what was good for the goose also had to be good for the gander, right? Besides, I wanted to be able to look into her eyes when she made any explanations. If they were good ones, I'd know.

The next morning I drove straight to Ivy's house. Once I arrived, there were two unfamiliar cars in the drive, which should've been a hint that my presence wouldn't be welcome. Instead I walked right up to the back door and rang the doorbell with all of the righteous indignation of a besotted man who'd been stood up.

Holly answered the door. "Gabe. You might—"

"Where's Ivy?"

Rather than answer she stepped to the side, and I walked through the kitchen into the dining room until I caught sight of strangers in the living room. I stopped in my tracks underneath the mistletoe, glad to have spindles to grab because a somewhat familiar stranger held Zuzu and was babbling about missing mommy.

One look at Ivy's stricken face, and I knew Zuzu's mother, like a bad penny, had turned up.

Gibbons, Yolanda Gibbons sat on the end of the couch, giving me some serious side-eye.

I knew the woman on the couch, but I couldn't remember when or where.

"I, uh, just wanted to make sure you're okay," I said to Ivy, my mind still searching its memory banks for the woman on the couch.

Ivy plastered a benign smile on her face. "I'm fine."

"Well, after you didn't show on Monday night—"

"Oh, is this a boyfriend? You couldn't even dedicate a week to my child before you got a boyfriend?" asked the redhead. She turned to Yolanda. "I bet *he* isn't on the approved list."

"Actually, he is," Yolanda said drily.

"Trudy Wright!"

She stiffened, then turned to study me. Her green eyes widened in surprise. "Gabriel Ledbetter."

"How are you, Trudy? I haven't seen you in forever."

"Are you sure you can't have this conversation later," Ivy said through a smile that looked more like a grimace of pain.

"Yes, please," Trudy said loftily. "I only have two hours for this visit."

"Okay, then," I said, having been dismissed by two women. "I'll be going."

In the process I backed into Holly. After apologizing to her, I walked back to my truck as quickly as my legs could take me. When the door slammed, I looked behind me to see Ivy flying through the garage and out to the driveway, shooting daggers from her eyes. "What were you thinking?"

"I was thinking there had to be a good reason why you didn't show up the other night."

"There was, and you would've known what it was if you'd answered your phone."

"Well, you could've used yours to give me a head's-up on Monday night, now couldn't you?"

She pinched the bridge of her nose. "I don't want to fight with you."

"Then don't fight with me." I reached for her, hoping for a hug or a kiss, but she took a step backward.

"I can't do this right now, Gabe."

"You can't or you won't?"

"Both."

"Do you mean to tell me you're going to let what Trudy said get to you?"

"Yes. I mean, no. Not exactly. It's complicated."

I laughed, but nothing about this conversation was funny. "It's complicated?"

"I can't do anything to jeopardize what little chance I have of adopting her."

"But you're not going to be adopting her. If Trudy is her mother, then the whole thing is over."

The minute the words left my mouth I knew I'd made a mistake. Her already red eyes filled with tears.

"Come on, Ivy. Don't you think it would be better for Zuzu to be with her birth mother?"

She wiped at her running nose with the back of her sleeve. "Yes. No. I don't know."

"You can't be selfish," I said in the gentlest voice I could. "You have to do what's best for the child."

"Oh, now I'm selfish?"

I ran a hand through my hair. I needed to cut my losses before this argument passed the moment of no return. "That's not what I said."

"Oh, it's what you said."

I took in a couple of deep breaths. "Look, this isn't the time to be having this conversation. I can see where you might be upset and—"

"Where do you know Trudy from?"

"What?"

"Where do you know Trudy from? Why did you give her such a warm greeting?"

Bloodshot eyes indicated Ivy hadn't slept well. She smelled of a recently smoked cigarette. I knew she wasn't in the right frame of mind for a talk, but I couldn't stop myself. "Trudy was in the class that graduated behind me. Quiet girl, though."

Ivy crossed her arms. "And?"

"And, well, Trudy smelled."

"Ha!"

Her malicious glee caught me off guard. "No, not ha. The other kids made fun of her. No one would sit with her in the cafeteria for lunch—at least not until I invited her to sit with me."

"Aren't you the white knight?"

"Ivy, what is your problem? You knew this might happen."

"And you did, too, but you took it upon yourself to throw out my name, and you had no right. You didn't know me. You didn't know that I'd already lost one foster child to his mother, and it almost broke me. Now here I am again, and this time I don't even have Corey."

No, but she did have me. Or at least she could have.

You will not be jealous of a dead man. You will not.

Tears welled in her eyes, and I pulled her close. "I'm sorry. I didn't know."

She pushed me away. "Then why did you do it?"

I thought of her that evening with the setting sun casting a heavenly glow on her. "When I saw you the night you found Zuzu, you took my breath away. You were beautiful. You were beautiful because you were happy. I think that's why I said something to Chelsea. I just wanted you to be happy."

"Sometimes I feel like I will never be happy again."

Her words sliced through me. "I thought I meant more to you than that."

She waved her hands. "You do, but then there's Zuzu. Now I don't know what to do."

"But Ivy, you're the woman I want to marry."

Even as the words spilled out of my mouth I knew I shouldn't be saying them but was powerless to stop them. So much for not being an idiot like my father.

Her eyes widened, and she took a step backward. "Are you seriously asking me to marry you at a time like this? We haven't even known each other a month."

"I know that, but—"

"No buts. I can't handle this right now on top of everything else."

"But I want to be there for you. Let me be the one you lean on this time."

"This time? I'm still trying to keep the baby, and you're already talking as though losing her is a foregone conclusion."

Why had I driven here first? Why hadn't I driven away once I saw the two cars?

"Okay, okay. I'm leaving," I said as I backed toward the truck. "We can talk about this later."

"No," she said. "No, we are not going to talk about this later."

"Ivy," I warned.

"What kind of man proposes after less than two weeks? What do you want from me? You know I have nothing." She paused and then repeated her own words as if hearing them for the first time. "I have . . . nothing."

"Ivy," I said again.

"You go," she said, shaking her head as though trying to shake me away with her thoughts. "You, you just go. I'll get your laptop."

"For heaven's sake, keep the damn laptop," I said, jumping into my truck before she could bring it back to me. I peeled out of the driveway on two wheels, leaving a spray of gravel in my wake.

Chapter 51
Ivy

What in the hell had I done?

You dumped the man who gave you a laptop and asked you to marry him.

But who proposes like that? And he didn't even ask. Was he trying to make this all about him? While I was in the middle of a crisis?

I walked back inside, hoping no one inside had heard our argument. Before I made it to the living room, I heard Zuzu's laughter, and I froze. Jealousy curled inside. She wasn't supposed to laugh for anyone but me.

As I rounded the fridge and stopped in the doorway between the spindles, Trudy bent over and blew raspberries on her daughter's stomach. Zuzu cackled, and Trudy's smile erased all of her worry lines. She looked tired, but beautiful nonetheless.

You are *being selfish.*

Just because I didn't like what Gabe said didn't mean he wasn't right. Zuzu—no, Fiona—deserved to be with her mother if at all possible. I swiped at my tears. I couldn't go back in time and be nicer to Trudy when she ambushed me or undo the slammed doors, but I could control my demeanor from this point forward. When Trudy stood at the end of her visit, I nodded for Mom and Holly to keep Zuzu and followed both her and Yolanda out to the driveway.

"Trudy, I owe you an apology," I said. "I wasn't as nice as I should've been."

She kept blinking at me.

"I got too attached to Zu—Fiona. She is adorable as you well know. I think I thought she might—" I stopped there because both she and Yolanda would think I'd lost my marbles if I told them that I thought Zuzu had been sent by my dead husband. "It doesn't matter what I thought. My job was to take care of her while you couldn't, and I will be as cooperative as I can until we get everything straightened out in court."

"Court?"

Trudy's eyes bugged out in a way reminiscent of an animal mesmerized by headlights.

"The deprivation hearing," Yolanda said patiently. Her tone indicated she had already been through all of this with Trudy once before.

"We still have to do that?"

Yolanda fixed her with a stare I knew a little too well. "Yes, we do. And you need to be there. You're lucky no one pressed charges against you for abandoning Fiona."

Trudy's eyes narrowed. She didn't trust me. "Take care of my baby girl."

"Of course," I said, holding it together until she'd backed out of the driveway and disappeared over the rise.

"You did well," Yolanda said. "Well, other than your little spat with Dr. Ledbetter, you did well."

"I don't think you have to worry about any more spats with Gabe," I said.

"Oh, no. Don't tell me that you kicked him to the curb just as I was beginning to like him."

I nodded, and opened my mouth to speak, but instead I started to cry.

"Oh, baby," Yolanda said. "It'll be okay. No matter what happens it's all going to be okay."

Chapter 52
Gabe

I rolled into the driveway behind dad's house and banged on the steering well while using a few choice words to make myself feel a little better

What had I been thinking?

I'd never intended to blurt out those words, dammit.

Face it, Gabe, for a man raised by two aunts, you have the worst luck with women.

A small part of me said not to give up just yet. The rest of me said I wasn't going to go bowing and scraping after being so summarily dismissed. Crazier things had happened than proposing nine days after meeting, and I hadn't done anything to merit her anger.

You could go back.

No, I'd burned all of my Memphis bridges, and I didn't want to live there anyway. So what if I ran into Ivy in the grocery store or Burger Paradise? Who's to say she ever felt about me the way I thought I felt about her?

Maybe you got caught up in the Christmas spirit or the peace of finally knowing what happened to Mom and meeting Julian. Maybe watching him with Romy and Portia got into your head.

Yeah, I was pretty jealous of what my brother had. I'd have to get over that, too.

Looking beyond the hood of the truck and into the pasture, I saw goats grazing.

In my haste to get to Ivy, I'd forgotten to milk the goats. Lucky me. I'd get to hear more about full udders. Might as well change into my loafers, though, and not ruin these tennis shoes, too. I slammed the truck door shut, which wasn't fair to the truck, and made my way to the back door to get my loafers.

"Surprise!"

I paused with the screen door still open. "Huh?"

"What took you so long?" Portia asked, her little fists on her hips.

"I guess I just drive slow," I said, not wanting to tell anyone about my detour.

"Happy birthday, Gabe!" Romy said as she put a cardboard cone hat on my head and gave me a kiss on the cheek.

Well, I guess it is my birthday.

If I dated all of yesterday's papers with the eighteenth, then it would stand to reason that today would be the nineteenth.

I got dumped on my birthday.

Nope. Wasn't going to think about that now. Ivy was probably right. And I should've known better than to use the word *never* because my father's genes had shown themselves today.

"Happy birthday, brother," Julian said, coming in for an awkward half hug.

"Took you long enough," Dad said as he slowly moved forward with the help of his cane. "I was afraid I was destined to spend another one of your birthdays alone."

"But—" I started to say he hadn't attended one yet when I remembered he'd been there on my original birthday. I hugged the old man tight. "I'm glad to have a birthday with you."

"My turn!" cried Portia, who was over her snit already and wanted to sit in my lap. I think she thought buttering me up would get her a bigger piece of cake, but she didn't count on her mother doing the cutting. She led everyone in a rousing chorus of "Happy Birthday," and then we had cake and ice cream for lunch.

"Presents!" Portia cried. She scooted off my lap and ran to the living room.

"You already got my present," Dad reminded me.

"Yes, I did. Thank you."

Portia tugged on a heavy bag and dragged it to my feet. "This one is from Mommy and Daddy."

"Is it?"

"Well, that and I milked the goats for you again," Julian said.

"I appreciate it. Yesterday was rough, and I forgot to text you," I said as I removed tissue paper, then reached inside the gift bag and pulled out . . . a boot? Two boots. "You bought me boots?"

"Rubber with a steel toe. Now you don't have to keep wearing those sad loafers," he said.

"Thank you," I said, surprised at my own gratitude.

"Size twelve, right?"

"Yeah." I looked at Romy and said, "He got me boots."

She grinned. "He does that. I would call him the Boot Fairy, but he doesn't like it."

"I want boots," Portia said.

"Baby, just as soon as your little foot is big enough to fit into a pair of work boots, then I will get you a pair. Promise," Julian said as he hoisted the girl up into his lap.

"I want cowboy boots," she said.

Julian started to promise her those, too, but Romy shook her head and Julian decided it was time to distract Portia with her favorite program, the one about the handyman with the talking tools.

I had tried on my boots and found them surprisingly comfortable when I turned to Romy and said in a low voice, "No cowboy boots?"

"No way am I paying that much for a pair of boots that she'll probably outgrow in sixth months. She can wait until she's a little older."

I nodded.

And decided to buy my niece a pair of cowboy boots.

As Romy teased Dad, and Julian and Portia's laughter wafted in from the living room, I couldn't help but smile. Sure I had an empty spot in my heart that I had reserved for Ivy, but I would survive. I had a family, and Dr. Malcolm had already offered me a job—I hoped he wouldn't renege on that.

But even if he did, apparently one could make a living from dairy goats.

For supper that night we all decided to go to El Nopalito for my birthday. I had informed all family members that they were not to mention my birthday, but Portia was cute and she knew it. As we were finishing our supper, she announced, "It's my uncle Gabe's birthday!"

Of course, that meant wearing a sombrero and hearing "Las Mañanitas." At least I got sopapillas out of the deal. Once Julian and Romy had taken their little troublemaker to put her to bed, Dad and I were left alone. He drummed his fingers on the table, and I knew what he wanted before he asked. "Mind if I go outside for a smoke?"

"Go on, Dad," I said.

Then to the right of the door I saw Trudy. She sat alone just as she had in high school. I got up—they needed to bus the table anyway—and approached the booth where she sat. "Mind if I sit down?"

She shrugged.

"So, you left us a baby," I said.

"Gabe, you wouldn't even begin to understand," she said, studying the print on the wall, one of a woman with an armful of calla lilies.

"Try me."

"Look, I've made a few bad choices, but the worst of them was marrying Vince," she said.

"Is he the father?"

She gave me a withering look. "No. Thank goodness. But now he won't grant me a divorce."

We sat in silence. She traced the ring of water from where her glass had sweated. "He wants to keep me around as his punching bag."

My fists tightened under the table. I had no use for men like this Vince. "Are you safe?"

"For now," she said. "I found a women's shelter in Jefferson, and I own my car. That's about all I have going for me."

"And Zuzu?"

"Her name is Fiona," Trudy said through gritted teeth. "She is Fiona Susan, named for each of my grandmothers. I don't know why your little girlfriend insisted on giving her that stupid name."

"We were watching *It's a Wonderful Life*. I think Zuzu is a nickname for Susan, though," I said. "Kinda amazing she stumbled on that since you didn't leave a name on the diaper bag."

"I'm not leaving my baby with that woman. She took her to a daycare. If I wanted my baby to go to daycare, then I could've managed that myself."

Based on the price of daycare, I doubted her. I also knew better than to argue.

Dad waved at me through the plate glass window, and I held up one finger. "Ivy's not so bad, you know. She loves your daughter."

"Well, she can't have her."

"I didn't say she could, but this isn't easy for her, either. I give you my word, as a doctor, that she's been taking good care of Zu—Fiona."

"Whatever." Trudy leaned her head back against the wall, and I wondered if she were waiting for someone or merely killing time she didn't want to spend at the women's shelter. "I need to get Fiona back and get out of Dodge before Vince comes back from Florida."

"If you need a place to go, call me. You don't deserve to be anyone's punching bag."

She handed over her phone, and I typed in my number. I hoped she would agree with me or at least promise to call, but she said nothing. "Well, it was good to see you, Trudy. Do take care."

I slid out of the booth, but she grabbed my hand. "Gabe, thank you. You really were the only person nice to me in high school."

"That's a damn shame, Trudy."

She squeezed my hand. "And what are the odds we would meet in this one traffic light town after going to school together in Germantown?"

About as good as Ivy giving your daughter the nickname Zuzu without knowing her middle name was Susan. "I'd say the odds weren't very high."

She squeezed my hand, and I took the opportunity to swipe her check.

"Gabe!" she protested.

"No, this one is on me," I said. "Save your money for more important things."

"Thank you," she whispered.

By this time Dad had to have winded himself from all of the gesticulating. I mouthed once more for him to wait before paying Trudy's check.

Chapter 53
Ivy

Folks say to sleep while the baby sleeps, but I wrote while the baby slept. I wrote in spurts both night and day for the greater part of a week because, why not? I had no job. I had no boyfriend. Soon I wouldn't have a baby, but writing allowed me to escape into a different world and not think about that prospect. I'd agreed to more visitations than I would like, but Trudy came by almost every day. At this point, Yolanda didn't always come with her. After all, I'd said I wouldn't stand in the way of reunification. As soon as Trudy left and Zuzu was asleep, I retreated back to my keyboard.

Also, if I was awake and writing, then Holly couldn't sneak off to use the elliptical without my seeing it. So far she'd been strong, but as much as I wanted a cigarette, I knew she had to want to exercise. I couldn't control what she did at work, but I could keep an eye on her at home.

Finally, at three o'clock in the morning on December twenty-third, I typed, "The End." I knew my copy editor would delete it, but I liked to type it in anyway. Not only did I have this glorious rush of accomplishment, but it also reminded me of all of the old black-and-white movies that ended with a dramatic swell of the music and "The End" in large script.

When it came time to attach the file to an email, though, I hesitated. My first thought was always that something else could be corrected. Every sentence could be finessed once more. Typos popped out of the woodwork like roaches and were almost as difficult to eliminate.

Ivy, you have to send it. Your goal is to fulfill your contract. That's it.
Once again I went to attach the file, and I stopped short.

I had promised Gabe that I would change the name of the hero to his. I couldn't change the heroine's name because she had made an appearance in the first book. Also, it would be weird to write about a character with my name.

But my hero? He'd only been referred to as Lancashire or the duke thereof, so I had had to create his first name and surname for this book anyway. Well, a promise was a promise. I did a find and replace. One by one, all of the Johns became Gabriels. Then I did the same with the possessive forms.

Finally, I saved the file and prayed I could get the Internet to work long enough to accomplish the task at hand.

Once the email had been sent, I sat in my chair and stared at the laptop that wasn't really mine. My joy had melted into sorrow because the manuscript, while an accomplishment, was a project completed and thus another thing lost. Funny how the endings to most books—whether reading them or writing them—always felt bittersweet, the satisfaction of completion mingling with the sadness of there being no more story to tell.

Yawning and stretching as I went, I crept into the living room and looked over the side of the play yard where sweet Zuzu slept on her back, her hands in little fists on either side of her head. Soon, she would be able to roll over. I wondered if she would sleep with her little booty in the air as Byron used to do. Maybe she would stay with me long enough for me to find out.

Probably a washed-up writer with no day job wasn't the right person to care for her—and that was before anyone considered the sister with an eating disorder, the mother with debilitating plantar fasciitis and a fondness for whiskey, or the fact that the aforementioned writer couldn't seem to quit smoking.

But I still loved that baby girl, and that had to count for something.

Collapsing in the recliner beside the play yard, I squeezed my eyes together, trying to will myself into thinking of another story to write, something to begin even as I was looking at so many endings. Nothing came. I'd exhausted my gray matter in completing this book. I had nothing.

Except Corey's letter. It was the only thing I had left—or at least it soon would be. I'd seen to that.

I reached over the little table where I'd put my purse and fished around inside for the letter. The only writing on the front of the stained and creased envelope was my name, written in the spiky handwriting of a man on morphine. The seal had started coming undone at the triangular bottom of the flap and on one of the corners as if begging me to go ahead and open it.

I could picture Corey now, up in heaven. For once he wasn't hanging out with another famous dead person, but he was wearing his holey jeans and his favorite T-shirt, the one that said, "Secretly hoping chemo will give me superpowers."

Did I want to do this?

When I tried to picture his smile, his image faded for me. I couldn't quite see him, and I panicked for a minute, grabbing my phone and looking at my background picture. Crooked smile, one dimple, and I knew what he would say: "Ivy, open the damn letter. I appreciate your stubbornness, but this has gone on long enough."

When I opened this letter, there would be nothing left of Corey, no more surprises.

But maybe I had to lose everything to start over again.

I ripped open the envelope and took out the letter. I hesitated before unfolding it. Wasn't morphine an opiate? Isn't that how Coleridge came up with "The Rime of the Ancient Mariner"? If this was an albatross haiku complete with skunk balls, I was going to be so upset with Corey and wish for him to run into Melville in the great beyond and have to listen to all of *Moby Dick* read aloud. With a deep breath I opened the letter:

Dearest Ivy,

I only regret one thing: dragging you on this journey with me. Sometimes I think you would've been better off if I'd pretended I wasn't home that evening you came looking for me. Selfishly, I'm glad I didn't.

I wish you wouldn't worry so much. Pretty sure I've seen the other side, and it's all going to be okay. Promise. Don't worry about me and don't wallow around for five years doing nothing. I know you.

Write books. Travel the world. Meet a more handsome man than me. (I know, I know. It's going to be hard, but I have faith in you.) Have babies if you want them, and keep your family close. They took good care of me, and I bet they'll take even better care of you.

Corey

P.S. Cancer really does suck skunk balls. Negative two stars. Do not recommend.
P.P.S. I love you. I never told you enough.

I cried, but I also laughed. Then I looked up to the sky and whispered, "I only wallowed four years, thank you very much."

Chapter 54
Gabe

I came in from milking the goats to see Holly's car in my driveway.

I couldn't picture Holly, paragon of health, chatting with Dad while he chain-smoked, but there she was at the kitchen table, playing dominoes with him and Portia, who'd been left with Grandpa so her parents could do some special shopping. When I walked in, Holly stood. "Where have you been?"

I kicked off my boots. "Milking goats."

"You do know that the hearing about Zuzu is happening today, right?"

"And?"

"And? Don't you think you need to be there for Ivy when the judge makes his decision?" Holly gestured too widely and disrupted the train of dominoes in front of her.

"Why aren't you there?" I asked.

She sighed as though I were the stupidest human being on the planet. "Because I asked and she told me no. Mom asked and she told her no."

I turned my back on her to get a drink of water from the sink. "Then she obviously doesn't want anyone with her."

"You're an idiot for thinking that, and I'm an idiot for asking instead of just doing. She needs someone with her. Forgiveness is easier than permission. It's in two hours."

I didn't move.

"Did you hear me?"

I turned around and met Holly's gaze. "Your sister made it very clear that she wanted nothing to do with me. I believe her words were 'you just go.'"

Holly rolled her eyes. "If she's so over you, then why did she rename the hero of her manuscript after you?" .

My resolve began to crumble. "Because I teased her about it?"

"Dude. You would've never known whether she did or she didn't, now would you?"

I didn't have an argument for that.

She stood and took her coat from the back of the chair.

"But we're not done," Portia said.

Holly smiled at her. "I'm sorry, baby, but I have to go into work. Thanks for letting me play dominoes, though."

She patted Portia's springy curls and left.

"You take her place, Uncle Gabe."

From the angle of Portia's dominoes, Grandpa had been helping my niece a great deal. It didn't seem much like a game.

"I'd love to, but I smell like goat," I said.

"You can play while you smell like goat," Portia said. "I can't smell anything for the cigarettes anyway."

Dad had been taking a puff, but took in too much and went into a hacking fit. In the process, he accidentally swiped another portion of the train away.

"Those aren't good for you, Grandpa," she said gravely before turning to me. "You take your shower. We gotta start another game, and you gotta go to the thing."

"What thing?"

"The thing Miss Holly told us about."

Oh, this little pitcher did indeed have big ears.

"You don't worry about that, Portia. Santa's coming tonight."

She crossed her arms and stuck out her lip. "But Miss Holly said you needed to go to court."

"Miss Holly needs to mind her own business," I said as I left the kitchen and headed for the stairs. Bad enough to have embarrassed myself in front of Ivy. Even worse that she'd practically laughed me out of the driveway.

"No," Portia said. I turned around in time to see her stomp her foot. "You two love each other. Miss Holly said so. Fix it."

A headache bloomed behind my left eye. "Baby, I'm afraid adult things aren't that simple. Miss Holly doesn't know what her sister wants."

"She said you have to go."

"Portia. Darlin' . . ."

"That's what I want for Christmas. I want you to go fix it."

What in the world?

"But what about your 'really nice present'?"

She shrugged. "Mommy says Christmas is about people, not presents."

I'm being schooled by a kid.

Dad appeared behind her, leaning heavily on his cane. "Go on, son. What can it hurt?"

It could hurt in all sorts of ways I didn't want to discuss with him. Sure, I was attracted to Ivy. Sure, I admired her for taking in Zuzu, and I'd even admitted I wanted to marry her only to be shot down. What happened if she lost the baby, though? I'd seen her bitterness at the mere idea, and she'd lashed out at me. She obviously didn't think of me in the same way I thought of her. She was still thinking about her husband, for heaven's sake. "Dad. She told me to leave."

He waved away my words. "Was she upset?"

"You know she was."

He paused. "We take it out on the people closest to us because we trust they can take it."

"That's ridiculous! I told her I wanted to marry her, and she told me to go away. This isn't going to be another perfect love story like you had with Adelaide!"

As soon as the words left my mouth, I regretted them. Actually, it sounded a lot like Dad's love story only I hadn't brought any flowers or sang any songs. Portia's eyes had gone wide, and Dad's bottom lip trembled.

"Son, ask yourself one question. If you stay away, will you ask yourself what-if?"

Dammit, I was getting hammered from both the young and the old.

"Adelaide didn't tell you the whole story."

"What?"

He chuckled. "She always left out the part where she told me I was wasting my time."

"She said she laughed at you."

"Oh, she did, but sometimes you just know. I knew with your mother. I knew with her. No sense in wasting time if you know what you want."

My socked feet had gone cold, and I could smell myself even if Portia couldn't smell me. "You're missing the point, Dad. She doesn't *want* me, so it doesn't matter."

I started up the stairs, but Dad banged his cane on the floor. "Don't you walk away from me, boy. It doesn't matter if she told you to go. What matters is if she told you not to come back."

I stood frozen on the last step.

"Did she, Uncle Gabe?"

"No," I admitted, though it pained me to say so.

"Then I'd say you better go," Dad said.

Chapter 55
Ivy

I sat outside the courtroom waiting for the deprivation hearing. Zuzu slept in the baby carrier to my side, and I tucked her blanket around her because it was drafty in the hallway.

Someone sat down beside me, and it took me a minute to recognize Trudy. She took a shaky breath. "Yolanda told me that I would have to work it out with you if I wanted to see Fiona on Christmas because I've used up my mandated visitation hours for this week already."

She had come by yesterday, but she couldn't possibly think I would keep the baby from her, could she? She'd been dropping by almost every day, and I hadn't said a word.

"Of course, I'm not going to keep you from seeing her on Christmas Day," I said.

Her shoulders sagged with relief, and she turned to face me. Her left eye had been blackened. I hadn't noticed as long as she was sitting with her right side to me.

"Trudy!"

"I'm fine," she snapped.

"We'll probably be at home all day, but I'll call you if something changes," I said.

"Thank you," she said. She marched toward the courtroom

doors, but did an about-face. "Why are you suddenly being nice to me? Are you playing me?"

My eyes widened. "No! I wouldn't do that to you."

"You seemed ready to keep my baby before."

Taking a deep breath, I told her a little bit about Byron. About how I'd done this once before, about how Yolanda had told me that in many cases such as this the mother never returned. "I allowed myself to get too attached, but I want what's best for Zu—Fiona."

She nodded, then headed back for the courtroom.

I stood, too, grabbing Zuzu's bucket seat and pushing past some people leaving to find a place. Technically, I didn't even have to be there, but I needed to know. My heart beat so quickly, and, once I'd taken a seat, I wiped my sweaty palms on the pants of my last good suit. Blessedly, no one could see that the waist was held closed by a safety pin because I'd worn a long burgundy shirt that covered the fly. Obviously, I would need a new wardrobe for any potential job interviews.

Zuzu slept on. I'd tried to keep her awake for as long as I could after her last feeding in the hopes that she would fall asleep in the car and then sleep through this case. Goodness knows she slept through Mom's vacuuming earlier. Yolanda came forward as well as a couple of lawyers, one for each side.

The hearing was called to order, and I drew up my legs as someone approached, but the person sat down beside me rather than trying to brush past me.

Gabe.

He didn't smile. He looked as though he half expected me to chew him out in the middle of court, but I wouldn't, not when relief washed over me at the sight of him. He offered a hand, and I took it.

When I looked back, Trudy's lawyers were asking for a continuance of some sort.

"And where is the mother?" the judge asked.

"I'm here, Your Honor."

Lawyers, the judge, even Yolanda and Trudy—they all spoke, but my ears only registered buzzing.

I ran out of air, the courtroom started to spin. Gabe leaned over and whispered in my ear, "Breathe, Ivy, breathe."

While I was trying to make up for the oxygen I hadn't been sucking in, the judge went back and forth with Trudy's lawyer about reunification or non-reunification. The judge, as Yolanda had said, didn't care much for Trudy's actions.

In the end, custody remained with the state and placement remained with the foster parent, otherwise known as me.

Gabe squeezed my hand.

Once the hearing was adjourned, I continued to sit there as people milled around me, most of them entering the courtroom for the next case. A shadow fell over me, and I looked up to see Yolanda.

"How are you holding up?" she asked.

"I'm fine. I'll have to enjoy raising her while I can."

She sighed. "I'm afraid you're going to get more attached, and it will be that much worse."

I acknowledged her fears because they were my fears, too. "Yes, but I have time to study and learn and prepare."

"All right, but you'd best get that baby into her own bedroom instead of the living room this week, or you and I will be having words. Also? Get a job."

"Yes, ma'am."

I held my breath waiting for her to say something about Gabe, but instead she nodded in his direction.

Trudy came down the aisle next, but she walked quickly and wouldn't look at me. She swiped at her eyes, and I felt a stab of compassion. It was no secret she'd hoped the judge would award her custody of her daughter again. Based on her black eye, the judge probably made the right decision.

"You ready to go?" Gabe asked.

I nodded and got to my feet and put the car seat over my arm as I navigated both Zuzu and me through the crowd and out of the courthouse into the brisk December afternoon. The gray skies threatened snow, but a white Christmas in West Tennessee was a rarity.

"Thank you for coming," I said to Gabe.

"You're welcome. Since I was there at the beginning, I felt I should be with you today, too."

We stood there. He shifted from one foot to the other. I moved the carrier from right arm to left, shivering because my heavy coat couldn't keep up with the chill.

"Well, Merry Christmas, Ivy Long. I guess I should be going."

"Not until I apologize," I said.

He crammed his hands in his pockets. He wasn't going to make this easy for me, and I supposed that was only fair.

"I'm very sorry for the way I acted the other day. I shouldn't have yelled at you like that."

He looked at the ground but smiled as he did. "Maybe it wasn't the best time and place for a proposal."

"Did you mean it?" I blurted.

His smiled faded, but his eyes locked with mine. "Of course I meant it! I wouldn't have said it, if I didn't mean it."

"But I'm a mess, a hot mess." Before he could answer, fat flakes fell from the sky, making me laugh as I looked up. "And heaven agrees with me!"

"I don't think that's what heaven's saying."

His eyes met mine, and I felt that same pull I'd felt on the back stoop.

He's the one.

Hopefully, I hadn't messed everything up.

I started to tell him Corey was sending the snow, but I knew he didn't want to hear about Corey. My mouth clamped shut. I'd once told my late husband I thought snow was romantic. Today it felt more like his blessing.

As the snow caught in Gabe's red hair and then melted, my heart caught. I had been right about snow. "Then what is heaven saying?"

"It's saying that—well, it's saying we should get the baby out of the snow." He took the baby carrier, which, truth be told, had been weighing heavy on my arm, and we skipped across the street to stand under the awning of a coffee shop set to open in the New Year.

"As you were saying?"

"If I were to promise not to propose for at least, say, a year, do you think we could start over?"

"I would love to," I said. "Well, I don't want to do the drive-through Nativity part again. My legs are cramping just thinking about it."

He laughed out loud. "I have hung up my robe for good."

"I sent in my book," I said.

"Did you?" he murmured.

"I did."

"I'd say that's cause for celebration."

"Usually is," I said, my heart speeding up again because I hoped his idea of celebration was similar to mine.

"Come spend Christmas with my family tomorrow," he said.

"But—"

"Oh, invite your mom and sister. I heard you talking with Trudy. Invite her, too."

"Really?"

"Of course," he said as he pulled me close.

I turned up my face hopefully, and he obliged me with a kiss. I sighed into the familiarity of him. He tasted of peppermint, and when our kiss ended, I noticed he had a candy cane hanging over the corner of his shirt pocket.

"For now, though, you need to take that baby home before she gets cold or the snow starts sticking. Doctor's orders."

Chapter 56
Gabe

Thanks to Portia's poignant speech about people being more important than presents, Romy and Julian managed to talk Dad into going over to the Satterfield place for Christmas Day. At my request, Ivy talked her mother and sister into going, too. We didn't know if Trudy would show up, but we had at least extended the invitation. Dad and I pulled up to the old green farmhouse that belonged to the Satterfields, and our truck was the last of several cars parked on the gravel driveway. Dad said, "I still don't see why we all had to come over here."

"Portia wanted to spend Christmas with *both* of her grandfathers."

"It's weird."

"Maybe." But should it be? It wasn't like any of us had other parents or siblings. Since we were lucky enough to be in one postage stamp of the universe, why shouldn't we all break bread together?

"Little heifer's too big for her britches," Dad muttered, but he couldn't hide his smile. He loved that little girl most of all, so he opened the door and wrestled with his cane, getting out of the truck with a grunt.

"Nah," I said as I opened the truck door. "Portia is my only niece and perfect in every way. She gets what she wants."

Dad muttered something about how kids today were spoiled rotten as we walked up to the front door, but he had sent me to the Tractor Supply to get his granddaughter a model tractor that cost almost as much as my first junker car. He didn't have any room to talk about spoiling anyone.

"Merry Christmas!" Romy met us at the door and hugged us, then excused herself to head back into the kitchen. My eyes went immediately to Ivy, and she glowed there with Zuzu sitting on her lap. Holly lay on the floor playing Candyland with Portia. Through the doorway to the kitchen, I saw Mrs. Long setting the table. I could hear Julian in the kitchen trying to convince Romy to get off her feet. Then another voice—it had to be Romy's dad—told her she ought to listen to her husband.

The next thing I knew Julian had been exiled to the living room where we all sat. He plopped down on the corner of the couch dramatically and asked, "Is it too early for a beer?"

I sat between my brother and Ivy, turning to kiss her before asking him, "Why'd you get kicked out?"

"Something about how Hank was needed because he was frying the country ham but I was not. Otherwise she would've sent us both out here."

When was the last time I'd eaten country ham? It would wreak havoc on my blood pressure, but my mouth watered at the thought of it.

"Dad, sit down," I said when I realized my father still stood just inside the door, looking lost.

"Sit right there," Julian said, pointing to the recliner across from us.

"That's Hank's chair. I can't sit there."

"*Hank* is in the kitchen," Romy said as she breezed through the living room and opened a closet on the other side of the room to get a stack of cloth napkins. "So you go ahead and sit in his seat."

"Mommy, when can we open presents?" Portia asked before turning her gaze longingly to a small tree with a ton of presents underneath it. The box containing the tractor sat to the side overshadowing the tree.

"After dinner," Romy said. "You've already got all your presents from Santa Claus this morning. Play with those."

Portia pointed at Holly and stuck out her bottom lip. "She keeps winning!"

Mrs. Long stopped in the doorway and mouthed to Holly, *Let her win.*

Holly rolled her eyes but managed to coax Portia into another game. I noticed she didn't *let* the little girl win, but she did explain how the cards determined whether or not a player had to move back or go forward. A few minutes later, we heard an excited shriek. "I won!"

The shriek was so loud we almost didn't hear the hesitant knock. Romy rushed through the living room and wrestled with the old wooden door, her face quizzical. Ivy stood slowly, her eyes darting to the little bedroom off the living room where I could see Zuzu napping in the play yard. She forced a smile on her face and stepped forward. "That's Trudy."

"Oh, hey! Come on in, Trudy," Romy said.

Trudy had dyed her hair black, and the new color only made her complexion look paler. "I . . . I don't want to intrude."

"Nonsense," said Ivy. "We invited you here, and we meant it. I think you're just in time for dinner."

"Oh, the biscuits!" cried Romy. She ran back to the kitchen while Ivy made introductions to those who didn't know Trudy. Then she led her to the bassinet so she could see Zuzu.

Mr. Satterfield found another chair, and we all crowded around a table laden with chicken and dressing, fried country ham, biscuits, green beans, mashed potatoes, sweet potato casserole, and fruit salad. I'd never sat at a Christmas table so full of people, but everyone only laughed as elbows jostled and knees bumped into each other.

"Julian, say grace," said Hank.

Julian bowed his head, and we followed suit. He thanked God for all the usual stuff, but then he thanked the Big Guy for bringing us all together, and I couldn't help but think we wouldn't all be together like this if it hadn't been for a baby left in a manger, found by a lost woman who latched on to a lost man who found a niece and then a brother and finally a father. Now that lonely mother had also joined our fold—even if only temporarily. Ivy squeezed my hand under the table for the Amen.

Just as Romy said, "Dig in!" Zuzu cried. Ivy put down her napkin, all set to back away from the table. Trudy had done the same. I put a hand on Ivy's forearm and nodded to Trudy. "I'll get her."

After lunch, we lolled around the living room like a bunch of bears on the cusp of hibernation. To be quite honest, hibernation sounded like heaven, especially since I had my arm around Ivy.

The lone exception was Portia, who'd recovered her energy within fifteen minutes of eating and was jumping up and down hollering, "Presents! Presents! Presents!"

Romy sighed, running her hand over her flat belly, a belly that would give me another niece or nephew one day. "I'll read the tag. You take it to the person."

The little girl ran from person to person like an elf who'd had a double espresso. Soon we each had at least one present in front of us. Portia, of course, had about five. The room came alive with the rips of wrapping paper and squeals of delight. Dad opened up the jumbo box of honey buns I'd got him. "Very funny, son."

"I thought so. Don't lose the note on top."

He squinted as he read the piece of paper that promised I'd plant him some pear trees in the spring. "Well, now. I like that idea. Thank you."

Holly got workout clothes and a beginner's knitting set. "Knitting?"

Ivy shrugged. "You need a new hobby."

Holly wadded up a ball of wrapping paper and threw it at her, but I easily deflected it.

Mrs. Long had a stack of little things: word search puzzles, chocolate-covered cherries, and a new caftan. Then she turned to a larger box. "Is this mine, too?"

"Go on, open it, Mom," Ivy said. Holly's grin took up most of her face.

Mrs. Long sucked in a breath and I waited for another "Oh my stars!" but instead I got an "Well, I'll be. That sure is a pretty new vacuum. And it's a Hoover, too!"

"We thought you might need another one," Ivy said.

"Just in case," Holly added.

"Well, thank you, girls!" Mrs. Long looked like she was on the verge of tears. I had never seen a woman that happy over getting something domestic as a gift.

Dad and Hank opened up identical blue plaid shirts. Julian and I looked at each other and shrugged—apparently, great minds thought alike.

Romy had opened all of her presents—almost all of them books—and was sitting on the floor in the corner already reading one of them.

"You going to open your other presents?" Ivy asked.

I'd already opened my present from Julian: a goat that pooped jelly beans. "I don't think anything tops the goat."

"Something might," she said.

I ripped into a present and found an album with pictures of my mother and a young Dad. "Thank you," I said.

Dad nodded his acknowledgement.

Then I turned to my other present. Inside the box was a copy of Ivy's manuscript along with a trucker's hat on which she'd used fabric paint to write, *Her Mad Vicar.* I put it on, and she reached behind the sofa cushions to get a matching one that said, *His Wanton Widow.* "I'm sorry it's not more. I'm awful at getting gifts."

I leaned over to kiss her. "I think this is a pretty darn good gift. At least you didn't get me something like Jenga."

For a second, her face froze in surprise and then she grinned widely. "Right?"

"Just as long as you remember that the laptop was your present."

"I do, and I put it to good use as you can see."

I ran my fingers up the manuscript. "I see that."

"Where's Julian's present?"

"I got him a new tractor," Romy said without even looking up from her book. "That's his Christmas-Birthday-Anniversary-Next Christmas-Next—"

"I think they get the idea, dear."

Portia meanwhile had lain waste to her corner of the room near the tree. She opened the present from Dad first and then sat on the miniature John Deere tractor as if it were a throne. She oohed and aahed over a marker set—Romy was going to kill Holly for that one. She set the clothing aside gently, and opened another game, and some dolls. Now she had her hands on the corner of my present.

"Is it really nice?" she asked.

"Really nice," I said.

She ripped off the paper and opened the box to find a pair of red cowboy boots. She clasped her hands underneath her chin, her mouth making the cutest "O" before saying, "For me?"

I ignored the glare coming from Romy and resisted the urge to look at my partner-in-crime, my brother. No need to incriminate him for helping me figure out the size.

"Oh, thank you, Uncle Gabe!" She hopped off the tractor and kicked off the shoes she was wearing, stepping into the boots before running across the room to give me a hug, kicking my shin with her new boots in the process. I tried not to wince. It'd be the cutest bruise ever, now wouldn't it?

"Oh, there's one more," Romy said, reaching underneath a swath of wrapping paper for a little box. "I almost didn't see it."

"Take this to Trudy," she instructed her daughter.

All eyes moved to Trudy who sat in a chair from the kitchen in the doorway that led to the bedroom where Zuzu lay. She blushed. "For me?"

Her fingers shook as she tore the wrapping to reveal a velvet jewelry box. She snapped it open, then turned it around so we could see a gold locket.

"It's a heart," Ivy said. "Because when, well, when Zuzu—I mean Fiona—goes to live with you again, you'll always have a part of mine."

I squeezed Ivy's hand, so proud that she could find it in herself to be generous to this woman who'd called her names and who'd put her through the emotional wringer.

Trudy, for her part, swiped at tears and stood. "I don't have anything to give you, but a hug."

Ivy stood. "And that's enough."

The two women embraced. Ivy said something about going to the kitchen to check on dessert even though not a one of us could eat another bite if we tried.

Portia hopped into my lap with a book that she insisted I read to her. I did as she requested but looked back frequently for Ivy, sometimes chancing a glance at Trudy, who opened her jewelry box to smile at the necklace, then gazed at a sleeping Zuzu. Before long Dad was snoring, then Hank followed suit. Soon everyone including Portia had heavy lids. My tongue felt heavy after eating so much, but I made my way through *Fox in Socks*. I laid Portia down beside Julian, who'd told us over lunch that the child had been up at three, five, and seven that morning. He put an arm around his girl, and I went to find Ivy.

She slumped against the sink, jumping up and wiping away tears as I entered the kitchen. I wrapped my arms around her, and she quietly cried. I wanted to tell her it would be okay, but having Zuzu go back to her mother would be bittersweet at best, so I simply held her.

"I'll get over this eventually, right?" she finally whispered.

I kissed her forehead. "Of course, you will. For what it's worth, I think you're doing the right thing."

She nodded and burrowed back into my arms, laying her cheek against my chest.

"Ivy, can I talk to you?" Trudy asked from the doorway.

I let her go, but I didn't want to.

Chapter 57
Ivy

I agreed to talk with Trudy even though it was the last thing I wanted to do.

"Can we go outside?" she asked, tentatively. She'd already put her locket on, and my heart clenched at the sight of it.

"I'll get your coats," Gabe said. He tiptoed into the room where Zuzu still slept and grabbed our coats from the pile on the bed. We tiptoed out the back door so we wouldn't disturb the nappers and started walking down the dirt road that led deeper into the Satterfields' farm.

"What is it?" I asked, painting a smile on my face and hoping that my tone was cheerfully brisk despite my clogged nose and raw throat.

"I was just thinking . . ."

I longed to rush her, but I knew it would do me no good. We walked past a barn on our right and toward a sweet gum tree to the left. Trudy stopped to kick at the sweet gum seed on the ground. "Remember yesterday when you said you wanted what was best for Fiona?"

I nodded.

"I think it might be best for her to stay with you," she said with a small voice. "If you were to adopt Fiona, would you still let me be a part of her life?"

For a second I thought I might faint. The earth spun for a minute. "Of course."

"I need to think about it," she said softly. "But you have something that I can't give her: a large family. I wasn't worried about material things because those aren't important when it comes down to it, but I don't have any family left now that Dad's gone. I also have to get rid of Vince. He threatened Fiona, and that's why I left her in the manger in the first place. I knew he would never think to look for her there, and I was afraid he might hurt her to get back at me. Now he's back from Florida."

She gently touched her black eye, and I swallowed hard. "You know I'll keep her safe. But what about you?"

"I'm going to get a divorce and get him out of my life, but it's taking time. And I'm going to need help."

"I don't know anything about—"

"No. You'll help me by keeping her safe. But I can't just abandon her. I thought I could, but I can't . . ."

Her voice had trailed off, and my heart hammered. I wanted to yell for her to finish, but I pressed my lips together. Finally, she spoke: "I guess I never thought I could have it both ways, that she could get a better home and I could still see her."

"We could have lawyers draw up papers to that effect," I said even as I knew my lawyer and Yolanda would both be less than thrilled. Leaving a door open to Trudy would mean taking the risk that she would take Zuzu away from me in the future, but it was a risk I would have to take because we needed to do what was best for the baby, not what was best for me. "You know I love her."

"I do, but I had no idea you had a whole family like that." She waved her arm out to indicate the farmhouse that held the people I loved best.

I drew my scarf tighter and smiled. "I didn't known I had a family like that, either."

"They're really something," Trudy said.

"That they are."

She started walking back in the direction of the house. No doubt her feet were as cold as mine. About two inches of snow lay on the ground out here even though it hadn't stuck to any of the paved roads.

"Oh, and Ivy?"

"Yeah?"

"You can call her Zuzu as a nickname if you want to. It's kinda grown on me."

Epilogue
Ivy

By the time the next Christmas rolled around, several things had changed. I had a new job working in the library and was writing a new book. Finally. Gabe had begun his own practice in Ellery and had shaven his beard. I told him he might have to grow it back because I couldn't stand for him to be any more handsome. Holly had managed to gain fifteen pounds. I'd quit smoking: three-hundred and fifty-eight days without a cigarette—not that I was counting. We'd almost talked Mom into surgery for her feet, too—and *that* was the very definition of a Christmas Miracle.

When we gathered at Hank Satterfield's house, I marveled at how many of the things were the same. Same tree, same meal, same people stuffing themselves silly. Portia was a year older and reading *Fox in Socks* to Gabe instead of the other way around. Zuzu toddled around the living room with me hot on her heels because the Satterfields hadn't babyproofed—after all, Portia's baby brother was only a few months old and Portia was beyond basic babyproofing.

"How'd the hearing go?" asked Mr. Ledbetter.

I was surprised Gabe hadn't told him. "We're sticking with the same arrangement for now. Trudy said she might stop by later if she can get off work on time. I made her a plate."

"Well, now," Mr. Ledbetter said. "Ain't that something."

"Yes, it is," I said.

"Hey, Ivy, come here," Gabe said. "I forgot I had another present for you."

"Another one?" I asked. He'd found out about my wish for a Princess Leia somehow, and, being Gabe, had bought an expensive one that Portia had commandeered. Wrapping paper lay knee-deep in the living room, and I picked up my feet and watched where I stepped because I didn't dare step on one of Portia's toys with its tiny, delicate accessories.

"Come on," he said.

"Where are we going?" I asked when I reached the doorway.

"We're not going anywhere. Yet," he said as he took out a sprig of mistletoe and hung it on a hook above the doorway that led to the kitchen.

"What are you up to, Gabriel Ledbetter?" I asked, my arms crossing instinctively.

"First, to soften you up I'm going to kiss you," he said, which he did. Then he took a little box from the pocket where he usually stored his candy canes. He had waited that year and not a moment longer.

My hands traveled to my mouth.

"Ivy Long, will you do me the honor of being my wife?" He flipped open the box to show me a ridiculously large diamond.

"Oh. My. Stars."

Where had that come from? Was that my mother's voice? Had I turned into my mother?

"Yes!" Holly cried from the corner of the room. "You owe me fifty dollars."

No, I had said those words.

"Is that a yes?" Gabe asked, his smile fading a little and his eyes hopeful.

"Yes, yes, a million times, yes!"

He spun me into the kitchen, and the entire living room cheered. I'd hardly slipped the ring on my finger before Holly stood beside me with her hand out. Gabe reached into his back pocket for his wallet and took out a crisp fifty to hand to her.

"How did you know I would say that?" I asked.

"Honey, you said you never would. It was bound to happen sometime."

Then he kissed me again, and I looked around the room, my heart bursting with gratitude. The material things were nice, sure, but the people were the most important part. I stretched out my hand, the huge diamond casting a galaxy on the opposite wall. The diamond was pretty, but the man, now, *he* was the best of all.

"Girl, put that thing away before you blind someone," Mr. Ledbetter said, so I put my hand in Gabe's and took in the scene. Romy and the baby, Julian and Holly putting a dollhouse together for Portia. Zuzu in Mr. Ledbetter's lap and Portia in Mr. Satterfield's. This year it was Mom's turn to nap, and she had well earned the right. Looking around the room, I took mental snapshots, putting each one into a figurative scrapbook and finally looking up at my fiancé, who stole another kiss.

And I felt all of those things and pondered them in my heart.

OH MY STARS

Sally Kilpatrick

ABOUT THIS GUIDE

The suggested questions are included to enhance
your group's reading of Sally Kilpatrick's
Oh My Stars.

Discussion Questions

1. What would you do if you found a baby in a manger? Would you want to keep it?

2. The toughest question in this book is what would be best for Zuzu. As the author, I struggled with which scenario would be best for not only the baby but also for Ivy and Trudy. What do you think? Should Zuzu have gone back to live with her mother? Should Ivy have cut Trudy off? Do you think their arrangement will work?

3. Each of the Long women has a weakness: exercise, booze, or cigarettes. Did you find their addictions believable? Do you think they will learn to manage or overcome them? Why or why not?

4. Ivy's manner of grieving is often unconventionally flippant. Do you know anyone else who approaches grief in a similar way?

5. Would you read Ivy's books? Why or why not?

6. Which character did you empathize with most and why? Do you have a favorite?

7. Most of the characters in this story have a hard time with the holiday season. What are some things we can do to help others who are sad at this time of year? How does this season make you feel?

8. As I wrote, I tried to leave lots of snippets of Christmas cheer. What are some of the references you found to Christmas movies, music, and television shows?

9. What are some of your favorite holiday traditions?

10. Icicles: delightful, tacky, or Satan's torture devices?

11. What is your favorite holiday movie and why?

Sausage Balls

This recipe was passed down to me from my mother, who got the recipe from Harvette Croom. At this point, it ain't Christmas in La Casa Kilpatrick until I make a batch of sausage balls.

3 cups of Bisquick*
1 pound(ish) of shredded cheddar
1 pound of sausage (I prefer Jimmy Dean Hot**)

Lay sausage out for an hour and *only* an hour. Mix the Bisquick and the cheese. Then fold the sausage into the mixture, which requires using your hands to break up the sausage and squish everything around. I'd suggest taking off your rings and making sure your nails aren't too long. Ask me how I know.

Once you've worked the ingredients together into one huge hunk of dough, start molding balls of approximately an inch and a half in diameter—although size, for once, doesn't really matter. You may need a bowl of water to dip your fingers in from time to time.

The original recipe calls for putting the balls on a cookie sheet and freezing them before storing. Personally, I put those bad boys straight into a gallon freezer bag as I go. As long as you don't squish them, you should be able to come back later and break off what you need. I generally have 40-50 balls from one batch.

If you're cooking them immediately, I hope you've been preheating the oven to 350°F. You'll need to cook them approximately 15-20 minutes or until done. If, like me, you put them in the freezer and then cook them for breakfast, preheat the oven to 350, then cook for 30 minutes or until done. It's hard to burn sausage balls, but it can be done.***

*You can use gluten-free Bisquick, but you'll need slightly less of it, and the mixture will be super crumbly, so you'll definitely need that water to help you shape the balls.

**I know, I know. The jingle about how I need to pick up a pound or so of Tennessee Pride is still etched into my gray matter, but Jimmy Dean works better with this recipe for some reason, although I have a feeling it's all a matter of personal preference, ya know?

***I think there's a reason why I write novels instead of cookbooks.